DEADLY SINS

MARK EL-AYAT

Mark El-Ayat Publishing

Book Cover by Mark El-Ayat

First edition 2024

ISBN: 979-8-9889467-2-4 (eBook)

ISBN: 979-8-9889467-1-7 (Print)

To my parents and brothers who never stopped believing in me. Your love and support are the magic behind every page I've written.
To my dogs, Antar, (also known as Hercules) and Lucy, whose energy and love were the daily dose of motivation I needed.
Without you all, my world, and this book, would be incomplete.

ABOUT THE AUTHOR

Mark El-Ayat is a writer with roots deeply planted in the Bay Ridge area of Brooklyn, New York. His journey into the world of storytelling and writing was kindled during his high school years, thanks to an insightful English teacher who transformed his perception of literature. This newfound appreciation for reading and writing soon blossomed into a passion for crafting engaging short stories and screenplays.

Mark's academic path reflects his diverse interests. He graduated from John Jay College of Criminal Justice with a BA in Forensic Psychology in 2017 and later earned a BA in English in 2022. This unique combination of forensic psychology and English literature infuses his writing with a deep understanding of the human psyche, adding layers of complexity to his narratives.

Outside of writing, Mark is a passionate cinephile, immersing himself in everything from psychological thrillers like Alan Parker's *Angel Heart* to Denis Villeneuve's *Prisoners* and to comedies such as Robert Zemeckis *Who Framed Roger Rabbit* and Shane Black's *The Nice Guys*. These films have not only entertained him but also inspired aspects of his own writing.

Mark's hobbies also extends to the realm of video games, where he enjoys a spectrum of experiences from retro classics like Nintendo's *Super Metroid* to modern RPGs like FromSoftware's *Bloodborne* and *Elden Ring*.

When Mark isn't writing or gaming, he's always at the gym trying to surpass his personal records in weightlifting.

At home, Mark finds balance and inspiration in the company of his two beloved dogs: Antar AKA Hercules, a chill and patient pit-bull mix and Lucy, a tiny chihuahua with a feisty and energetic personality. Their unconditional love is a constant source of motivation.

Mark's literary tastes are as wide as his interests. He holds a special place for dystopian narratives, with George Orwell's *1984* and *Animal Farm* ranking high on his list. The horror genre captivates him as well, with Stephen King and Edgar Allan Poe being his go-to authors for a blend of horror and humanity.

With *DEADLY SINS*, Mark El-Ayat invites readers into a world shaped by his diverse influences and rich experiences, promising a journey that's as intriguing as it is thought-provoking.

INTRODUCTION

Welcome to *DEADLY SINS*, a series very close to my heart. When I initially started writing this book, my objective was to create narratives that go beyond mere entertainment.

Each story in this series is a labor of love and empathy, reflecting the various shades of human emotion and struggle. I often get asked, "Are the sins in your stories the actual mental illnesses?" And I always respond with a resounding NO. Instead, these sins are like markers, pointing toward the less visible, often misunderstood paths of mental suffering.

By reading the stories, you will uncover the reason behind the characters' struggles.

In creating these narratives, I consciously chose not to name the illnesses or bring in a psychiatrist character to diagnose them.

Why?

Because my aim is not to label or define these characters by their struggles, but to paint a picture of their experiences, one that resonates with respect and understanding. As someone who has always been fascinated by the human mind and its intricacies, I believe that stories have the power to open our eyes and hearts to the realities of others.

This series is an exploration of how our actions, choices, and, yes, our sins intertwine with our mental well-being. Each story explores the connection between the overwhelming feeling of pride and the silent suffering caused by envy, shedding light on how these timeless sins can affect the internal struggles we face.

Through *DEADLY SINS*, I invite you into a world where mental struggles are as real as any physical ailment, though often invisible. These stories are my way of fostering a deeper understanding and empathy for mental health issues, aiming to chip away at the walls of judgment and stigma.

So, I welcome you to join me on this journey. Let's turn the pages together and see the world through the eyes of characters who might be more like us than we realize. *DEADLY SINS* is not just a series of stories, it's a journey towards understanding the silent battles many of us face.

CONTENTS

PRIDE
NATTY OR NOT

I

It's another day at Atlas Athletic Club in Brooklyn, a temple where the dedicated and the driven worship strength. The air is thick with determination – and ego. Muscle heads, some undoubtedly aided by more than just protein shakes, flex and lift, striving to outdo each other. Among them is Tyler Masterson, commanding the bench press with a focus that borders on obsession. With each lift of the 315lbs barbell, his presence demands attention, his effort echoing through the chorus of "Indestructible" by Disturbed in his headphones. Yet, as he racks the weight after his eighth rep, a fleeting shadow of dissatisfaction crosses his face. Another two or three reps wouldn't hurt, he said to himself.

The men's locker room is humid, full of sweat and body odor swarming the sauna and showers. Men of all shapes, sizes, and ages are changing in and out of gym outfits. Some, leaving, bid farewell to their fellow fitness friends. A tall, muscular bodybuilder mixes pink powdered pre-workout in a bottle of water and shakes it up before sipping it. Stepping out of the steaming showers, a power lifter with a stocky physique and a jiggling belly quickly dons his briefs after tossing aside his towel. Freshman college students, with C4 Energy in hand, enter babbling about a frat party they attended last weekend. They pass Tyler staring at himself in the mirror, observing his chiseled body. One would think he's a Greek God. A body that people would compare to the naked statues at the museums. He flexes with both arms out, trap muscles popping out. He relaxes, then turns to his side and strikes a pose, curling his arm up, biceps turning into a ball with a vein bulging. A young, scrawny gym member watches from the corner of his eye, admired by Tyler's shape. "I'll be like you one day," he says.

Tyler changes poses, turning to his other side. "Maybe," Tyler says, flexing his shoulders. "Just make sure to eat a shit ton." He barely glances at his admirer. Instead, he focuses on his abs. More body fat needs to be shredded, he says to himself. That means an extra half an hour on the StairMaster every day. Frustrated, he grabs a towel and heads to the sauna.

Tyler observes an older man sitting across from him, engaged in conversation with another older man, as he contemplates his own self-value. He sits there staring blankly at the wooden seats, observing the steam flowing. Sweat spills out of his skin, splashing against the tiled floor. He focuses on food. Thinking about what he's going to eat. Will it be eight ounces of chicken breast and broccoli or six ounces of salmon with asparagus? As he dwells on his hunger, someone snaps their fingers to him, grabbing his attention. Felix, a long-time friend from the gym, fist bumps Tyler happily. Proud of what Tyler has achieved so far.

"Looking great!" Felix says as he sits next to Tyler.

"Wish I could say that I feel the same." Tyler says.

Felix looks at him, baffled, thinking this must be a joke. "You kiddin' right, my guy?"

"Bro, I feel small."

"Nah, nah, we're not having this again. Last year, you were fat. Remember that?"

"And now I'm skinny. I feel light as fuck, but I don't have a full six-pack." Tyler stands flexing his abs as hard as he can.

Felix is in awe, not about the abs, but about Tyler's clear delusion. He shows off his barely noticeable abs for comparison. "Your abs are showing more than mine. Chill out." Felix says, sits back down with Tyler. "Are you competing?"

No answer. Just a blank stare. Tyler is unsure of how to answer the question. Then he notices an abnormally large bodybuilder. The two always pass each other, greeting with a nod, and nothing more. Just a sign of respect for both lifting heavier than the majority. This time, their glances last the longest. A wave of Felix's hand hovers over Tyler's face. He turns to Felix, taps him over the shoulder. "I'm not." He turns back and notices the bodybuilder is not there.

"Then what are you buggin' out for?"

After a moment, Tyler says, "I don't know." He leans back against the wall. "I honestly don't know."

"You need to focus more on other stuff, Tyler. Focus on improving in other parts of your life. You nailed the fitness part. Now, what? Your YouTube channel? Personal training gigs?" Felix says.

A nod from Tyler. Something he's been doing the past few years ever since he was shamed for being fat. Losing his girlfriend that he still thinks about from time to time, even though he vows to never get back with her. The relationship they had, he thought, would last forever. High school sweethearts. But no. He notices now how things went wrong, and blames his obesity at the time. It was much more than that. During their third year in the relationship, Tyler caught Ashley with her much older personal trainer walking into a Days Inn. A little birdie, his neighbor, Old Man Jasper from down the block, gave Ashley's whereabouts through text. Old Man Jasper was always a fan of Tyler. Liked him better as a person and thought he deserved better. Not a fun way of hearing about his girlfriend, who claimed it was just a client-trainer relationship. Ashley has been fucking the trainer every weekend except on one occasion when she reluctantly went on a getaway trip with Tyler to the Poconos. During that time, she tried her best to avoid having sex with him. Barely gave him any attention and mostly spent time on her phone, which made Tyler wonder what was going on. The truth was, Ashley didn't want to make it obvious that she cheated with a well-endowed man.

There are still pics of Ashley in Tyler's phone gallery that he scrolls through from time to time to remind himself about his purpose. To be a better man than he was yesterday. He says that to himself in front of the mirror, sometimes in his room, before bed or after breakfast, when he's about to get ready for a five-mile run, or whenever he loses motivation in general. The pictures of Ashley and the perverted personal trainer add more fuel to the fire. He continues to scroll through them as he waits for an Uber outside of the gym in his oversized hoodie and Under Armour duffle bag around his shoulder. Then a voice from around the corner by the parking lot. "Yo," a deep voice calls out.

"Yeah?" Tyler says to the wind, wondering if it's to him.

"Down here." The bodybuilder from the sauna emerges from the parking lot. He gestures for Tyler to come down. Seems sketchy at first, but they see each other all the time. What could go wrong? Tyler says to himself.

Late at night, the parking lot is quiet, barely any cars left. The bodybuilder leans over the latest Audi, tinted from the top down. Blacked out. He watches Tyler make his way to him and greets him with a nod, like he usually does. "It's good to meet you." The bodybuilder says. "They call me Wade." He says, hand out for a proper greeting. "And you are?"

Tyler, almost reluctant, shakes Wade's hand. "I'm Tyler." Now there is a little more comfort between the two.

"Nice to finally talk, no?"

"Yeah, I guess," Tyler says, looking around the parking lot. "What's up?"

"Saw you struggling," Wade says, shoulder shrugging. "Thought I might offer some services."

Tyler's body tenses up, breathes slightly faster as he continues looking for a way to escape. "W-what kind of service?" He says, voice stuttering.

Wade gestures with his head to the car, letting Tyler observe it. Almost mesmerized by how beautiful the car is. Must be a lease, he says to himself.

"Honestly, man, I appreciate your help, but I'm straight."

"What?" Wade says, voice sounds confused.

"Look, I get it. We see each other here and there, but it's just not my thing."

"What are you talking about?"

"You know…" Tyler gestures back to the car with exaggeration.

Wade gives a stare, pondering, then comes to a realization, eyes wide up. "Oh, no. Hell no. Wait a minute. You thought…" Wade chuckles to himself, slaps his knee. "Wait, wait, you think I'm trying to…" Wade can't even finish his sentence without laughing. He then wipes sweat off his face, relieved.

"You're not gay?"

"Well, I'm actually bi, but that's not the point."

"Then what were you trying to offer? I'm confused now."

Enough of the games. Wade pops open the trunk, which reveals a wooden container. He cracks it open, revealing vials labeled **TESTOSTERONE**. "It's time to take your bodybuilding game to the next level." Wade pulls out one vial and holds it up to Tyler, who observes it with his heart beating faster. "It's new in the market. Lesser side effects. This isn't even out in this country yet."

"It's steroids. Anyone can get steroids."

"No, no, no. This is a different kind of anabolic steroids. This, my friend, can help you feel much better about yourself and help you accept your body. Keeps you less insecure. You'll feel much happier." Wade says, voice confident. He even passes it to Tyler for him to hold.

Never in his life would think he needed steroids. Nor was he encouraged. Never cared since he already had a lean body. This time, he can actually be stronger, passing his lifting plateau, which has been bothering him for some time already. A year straight thinking about how to beat his personal records without struggling, yet here he is, standing in front of the man who is willing to change it all for him.

"Tell you what. I'll give you a discount."

II

Tyler comes out of the shower and grabs a robe from his bedroom to dry up. The thoughts of Ashley swarmed his mind in the shower that he needed to get out quick. He realizes the lighting in his bathroom and the lack thereof in his bedroom created this design of shadow over his body. He disrobes and observes his chiseled body in front of the mirror in his bathroom. His abs are not showing as much. He flexes his core muscle much harder, trying to get them to pop out. He lifts his iPhone up, and snaps a photo of himself. The picture doesn't do him justice. There is not enough lighting. He adjusts the lightbulb to face his side and now it only shows the top half of his abs. A slight four pack. The flexing becomes a chore after snapping his twenty-fifth picture. Something needs to be done. He notices the bottom of his stomach bloating from the protein shake he had earlier. Something he regrets doing. Cursing under his tongue.

The computer desktop sits on his desk with a camera pointing at him. He grabs a shirt with the logo of a yellow muscled bull with a mean look, sporting a nose ring holding an energy drink. Under the logo, the label says "Mean Bull Juice." He turns on the camera, adjusts the lighting to make it look more presentable. He makes sure the shirt shows the logo properly. Then adjusts the angle of the energy drink itself, showing the label. He faces the camera and speaks. "Hey everyone! Today, I've got something really special to share with you all. Say goodbye to mid-session fatigue and hello to explosive energy with Mean Bull Juice!"

Later, as his video sponsoring the energy drink plays, Tyler observes the vial he bought from Wade. He contemplates hard. Just imagine all of those muscles that couldn't come out. Now they can in six to twelve weeks. He'll have the best looking physique than anyone else out there. There is an opportunity to not only look bigger, but to lift heavier as well. He goes through a piece of poorly written document on "Cycling." These are basic instructions on how to apply what's in the vial to the body. Then he turns to his YouTube page, noticing already four hundred thousand views in just under two hours. Views he got because of his natural way of achieving his looks. His honesty and raw personality trying to help others achieve their goals in the gym. Then stares at the vial again, gripping it. He stands in front of the mirror flexing his muscles, trying to see every piece of muscle.

***

The morning news shows chilly temperatures in the low fifties and upper forties. This weather doesn't bother Tyler as chows down four egg whites with three strips of turkey bacon. As he sips water alongside his meal, he can feel the refreshing coolness quenching his thirst and bringing a sense of contentment. However, he can't help but feel uneasy as he tightly grips the vial. He daydreams of standing on stage with his masterful physique and everyone praising him. Taking first prize while greeting everyone on stage who are also happy for him. The love from others would be like being part of the popular crowd in high school. A scenario that never once occurred, no matter how hard he tried to get people to like him.

The fridge opens up. Tyler jumps and quickly pockets the vial as he turns to his father, Mike Masterson, grabbing the almond milk. His physique was definitely that of an athlete. He plays soccer here and there with some friends even though he has a slight herniated disk in his lower back after picking up a bag of groceries that was heavier than usual. Age is always to blame, even if you're only fifty-eight. As he gazes at his son, a feeling of pride fills him, realizing how much he has nurtured himself. Tyler, the Greek God his father always says. Then brings up something Tyler completely forgot about. "When are we going fishing?" Mike says.

"Oh shoot, pops." Tyler says. "We definitely have to go when the weather gets better. I mean, look at the forecast."

"So what? We'll layer up. Grab that hoodie that you keep showing to your viewers. It's thick."

"I'd really like to, but only when it gets warmer."

"Okay, okay. I'll hold you to it." Mike pours the almond milk and drinks. "How's the YouTube thing going?"

"Off to a good start. Just hit above five hundred thousand views and counting," Tyler said.

"Congrats, Tyler!" Mike says, taps his shoulder with a bright smile. "When are we celebrating?"

"Once I hit the million subs."

"By fishing, right?" Mike says, giggling.

"Fishing isn't really my thing, though."

"I know I'm only teasing." Mike's voice dropped as he spoke, lacking enthusiasm. "I just want to spend time with you."

"I understand." Tyler said, feeling guilty. "Let me focus on this first."

"No problem." Mike says, then kisses his son's forehead. "Gonna step out for a bit."

***

Monday, or what gym bros call it, International Chest Day. The benches were crowded with people, particularly young ones who came in groups. Each of them are trying to out-lift one another while the barbell until it nearly crushes a high schooler's neck. Quickly, a bodybuilder comes to the rescue and reracks the barbell. The gentle giant makes sure the young member is fine and gives brief advice about why one can't do that. He lets him be after that.

Today, though, is not chest day for Tyler. It's back and biceps day since he did chest and triceps the day before. He sets up a camera stand by the pull-down machine. He attaches his phone and angles it in a way to get good lighting. Then takes a seat, knees under the pads, grips the stainless steel bar on the edges, then pulls down as the name states. Tyler pulls the bar down to his chest, lifting a total of 220 pounds, and then raises it back up. He repeats this set ten more times. After slamming the weights, he checks on the video on his phone. Unsatisfied as it shows acne on his shoulder blades. Fuck. He curses under his tongue and grabs the Mean Bull Juice hoodie. He sets up the camera again and repeats his set. Satisfied with the video, he moves on to the next workout.

The seated row machine wore a laminated sign, 'Out of Order', glaring at Tyler. As his eyes caught the disheveled cables, a surge of frustration welled up inside him. With a sudden, jerky movement, he swung his duffle bag down with a thud that echoed off the gym walls, its contents jostling audibly. He stood there for a moment, staring at the machine, his chest heaving with quick, agitated breaths. The plan had been to feature the seated row in his next video – now what?

Grumbling under his breath, Tyler scooped up his bag, his movements sharp and erratic. He strode over to the T-bar, setting down his equipment with more force than necessary. He fiddled with the camera stand, his hands moving briskly, almost angrily. Every adjustment seemed to be a battle, his brow furrowing with each slight movement. Once the camera was set, he gestured pointedly at the two forty-five pound plates he had loaded, his motions stiff and exaggerated. Positioning himself, his posture rigid with barely contained irritation, Tyler prepared to begin, trying to channel his frustration into the exercise.

A slight bend to the knee, butt out, and leaning forward, making his body almost a ninety-degree angle. He grips the handles and starts pulling up to his lats. As he does so, a young gym member with broccoli hair passes in front of the camera and keeps it going. Tyler slams the weights pissed off. "Hey!" Tyler yells out to the young gym member. "Can't you see I'm fucking filming a set?!"

The young member turns around, confused. "S-sorry bro." He says, voice quivering. Confused. "I didn't see it."

"Open your eyes then!" Tyler says, shakes his head. Then he notices, as he sets up the camera again, other gym members glancing at him. "The fuck are you all staring at?" He says. After a moment, the gym members return to their workout routine. Tyler sees himself in the mirror with his hands above his hips. He then flexes his muscles because, of course, he does. What bodybuilder doesn't get the chance to see what he has achieved?

"Looks like you're enjoying it." Wade says, approaching Tyler, fist bumps him. "You just started, no?"

"Yeah, but I'm getting these pimples on my back." Tyler says, pointing at the acne while facing the mirror.

"Ah, I see. I'm surprised it happened right away."

"Is that normal?" Tyler asks.

"Yeah, yeah, of course it is. How do you feel in general, though?"

"I feel great, actually. I'm happier — well, I mean, was happier. Kid came in front of my camera."

"Ah, it's okay. You'll have plenty of content to add."

"I'm more worried about how my body is going to look. My skin was smooth. Now it has lots of red flares and pimples."

"Finish this cycle and you'll see how much different and better you'll be."

"Twelve weeks you said, right?"

"Twelve weeks."

Tyler then adds another forty-five pound plate on top of the others. "Could you make sure no one steps in front of the camera, please?"

"Of course!" Wade takes guard of the stand, observes Tyler through the phone camera.

Tyler performs a clean set without hesitation. Wade gives a nod of approval.

***

It's been a month, and Tyler's body significantly changes... for better and for worse. He has seen so much more acne. His hair is thinning up and notices some hair follicles all over his pillow. Even while showering, after scrubbing shampoo over his head, he lathers down some more hair off the top of his head. Now he's more worried as he sees himself in the mirror. He throws in a couple of flexes and noticing his body getting bulkier. He poses as if he's in a competition.

Through the video content on the desktop, people are making comments that are as what Tyler expects.

Amazing routine! I've been using this lately, thank you!

Tyler Masterson at it again with the perfect form and workouts. I don't go to anyone else for advice but yours.

I used your diet plan and wow, I lost so much weight and got much leaner. You're the man!

These comments are inspiring, leaving Tyler filled with joy. Inspiring others boosts his ego more than any weight could. Especially when scrolling through his Instagram @TherealTylerMasterson with a blue checkmark next to it. Aside from the many direct messages he receives from fans and women trying to get his attention, he reads the comments many people made on his professional shot of him flexing at the gym. This time, the comments are more ruthless. Many of the comments show syringe emojis. Then he reads comments like:

A body like that is impossible to achieve natural.

Bruh he says anyone can achieve their goals. He also forgot to add lots and lots of tren that comes with it.

Was part of your diet trenbolonie sandwich?

Then there were GIFs of a nurse squirting out a syringe, another GIF of someone taking the flu shot, and another GIF of a dancing syringe. These comments are only the few out of the many positives. But Tyler immerses himself into the negative. He types out a response but realizes this is not something he wants to engage in and backspaces the text. He faces the mirror once again, his eyes fixated on his abs, appreciating the results of his relentless training and discipline. Fuck the haters, he says to himself.

III

The gym has now become like a video production studio for Tyler's workout routine. Felix assists with the camera, making sure no one steps in front. Members are now more intimidated by Tyler whenever he approaches a machine. Some much weaker members give up their bench for him without him having to ask how many sets are left. The level of grandiosity has worsened as he increases his muscle mass every week by acquiring new cycles from Wade.

Despite the negative press, his videos are still attracting a massive audience, with view counts exceeding two million. The subscriber count is now one and a half million, with people wanting more. This all started when Tyler updated progress videos and how one would achieve them in a matter of time while continuing to sponsor Mean Bull Juice heavily.

The capital gains increased immensely. But Tyler barely looks at his bank account. He continues to stare intently at his reflection in the mirror, examining his muscles. The frustration arises in his eyes as he squeezes his stomach to see more abs. He counts four and wonders where the others are. He stretches out his skin from his stomach and wonders if there is still fat.

A phone call from an unknown number. Something Tyler hasn't seen in a while. Suspects its spam and rejects it. Only for the voicemail to say it's from Power Podcast, a fitness podcast that interviews the influencers in the fitness industry. Quickly, with hesitant hands, he drops the phone as he attempts to call back. "Hey, hey," Tyler says, voice excited. "Sorry I missed your call. I was editing."

"Hey, Mr. Masterson!" Kevin from Power Podcast says, also with excitement. "We were worried you'd not take our call." This was followed by a laugh.

"With you guys? Not in a million years." Tyler sits down, smiling.

"How are you doing today?"

"Just... well. I'm, uh, you know, came back from the gym."

"I can imagine how much work that has been going for ya."

"It definitely feels like work, that's for sure."

They expressed each other's love for their influence involving the fitness industry. Starting from building confidence in people to younger generations looking up to them.

"I'd like you to come to our show. Speak about your upbringing and experience and inspirations. I'm sure many, including your followers, would like an in-depth analysis of who Tyler Masterson is outside of the gym."

"Kevin, it would be an honor."

"Awesome!"

They wish each other well before hanging up. The joy in Tyler's face could light up the darkness in his room. He can see all of his detailed muscle physique as he continues to flex his muscles. He relaxes and takes a deep breath and throws on a shirt so he doesn't have to see his body. In fact, he even covers the mirror with a beach towel to prevent from even looking at himself.

Early morning gets busy in Midtown. Most people are rushing to get to work. Though the environment may be stressful as one bumps into another, Tyler seems to get all the space he wants as he walks through in his tight clothing and sunshades. As people pass him, some glance at him, either he looks familiar, or it's because he's the oddest looking one compared to most people walking around. Tyler is greeted by a doorman as he enters the tall glass building through the revolving door.

Looking through his phone, he sees the directions of where to go. **Floor 32.** Tyler rides the elevator among others who are dressed in suits. It stops at some floors while some exit. Tyler can't help but glance to the side at the mirror, showing his buff arms. He slightly flexes his triceps, watching the muscles squeeze itself out of the shirt.

DING!

The elevator doors open on the thirty-second floor. After a deep breath, Tyler steps out and turns to the right direction where the wall mount shows Power Podcast with the logo of a microphone flexing as if it has the anatomy of a buff human. He walks in through the glass double doors, where he is greeted by the front desk secretary. "Hi," Tyler says, voice gentle. "I'm here to see Kevin Power."

"Yes, Tyler." The secretary says with a smile. "He stepped out for a minute and will be back."

"Awesome. Should I wait outside or?"

"You can sit across. It's fine." She directs Tyler to the cushion chairs by the window where the view of the city skyline is shown along with other neighboring glass skyscrapers. Tyler, basking in the tranquility brought by the breathtaking sight of the morning sun, momentarily experiences a rare sense of calm and contentment. His gaze then drifts to a fish tank, sparking a sudden realization. Pulling out his phone, he begins scrolling through an array of fishing rods on Amazon. Confronted with an overwhelming variety, his brief serenity gives way to frustration, creasing his forehead as he browses. After a moment's hesitation, he adds a few rods to his cart. Shifting gears, he then composes a text to his dad, infused with warmth and affection, 'Happy birthday, Pops!' and adorns it with a string of festive emojis. "Tyler?" Kevin's voice comes from the entrance.

"Mr. Power!" Tyler says, standing, shoves his phone in his pocket as the bodybuilder that Kevin is approaching. They dab it up and throw their arms around each other. Kevin squeezes Tyler's arm with surprise and eyes widen. "Woah, my guy. Those guns look lethal! Are you juicing or something?" Kevin says with a laugh.

Tyler forces a smile as his voice clamors. But right before he's about to answer, Kevin leads the way to the podcast room, where two more hosts join.

"I'd like to introduce you to the team, Tyler," Kevin says, motioning towards his two co-hosts, who are also bodybuilders. As Tyler walks in, Kevin points to a blonde-haired, blue-eyed surfer dude with a fake tan, saying, "That's Scott." Scott waves with a smile. Kevin then gestures to a bald Latino with a full beard, stating, "And that's Ramon. He's our editor." Ramon salutes and greets Tyler with a "Sup." Kevin directs Tyler to an empty cushion chair by the desk, while Scott hands him a Beats headset.

"I don't need to tell you what to do, right?" Scott asks.

"No, I think I know how to put headsets on." Tyler says, getting a few chuckles from the podcast crew. He adjusts the mic that's hanging above the stand closer to his face.

Kevin claps his hands together, rubs them with excitement. "Okay, folks, we are ready." Kevin says, as Ramon hits the record button. The conversation starts with a greeting, introducing Tyler as a YouTube fitness influencer who has inspired many young generations to look up to him. Tyler speaks about his journey from when he was young and obese, losing his high school sweetheart to a personal trainer. The crew let out groans in response to this.

"She was for the streets to begin with." Scott says. Though he means no harm by stating this fact and feels that he was making Tyler feel better. It's the opposite effect.

"No, no. I can't say that."

"My man, if she cheated on you with her personal trainer, then I'm sorry. There was a chance she might have slept with others before you. I'm just sayin," Scott says, shoulders shrug.

"Look, we were in love. We dated for almost four years."

"Okay, look, maybe the first year she was loyal to you. But after that, nah. I don't accept that, dude."

Kevin jumps in. "When did you start gaining weight?"

"I'd say about Junior year in high school. This was after my mom passed."

"Oh, sorry to hear," Kevin says, voice genuine.

Scott then jumps in. "Dude, I get it. But girls see fat people as lazy, none providing or even lack security."

"Bro, I was in high school. What could I provide or secure as a sixteen-year-old?" Tyler says, voice getting angrier.

"It's okay, man. Not all of us are blessed."

Tyler turns to Kevin, confused. "What the fuck is going on? Am I being pranked or something?"

Kevin waves off to Scott with the statements, then turns back to Tyler. "When did you decide that bodybuilding was your thing?"

Tyler, calmer, sits back as he switches glances between Scott and Kevin. "It wasn't until a year after we broke up. Right before my third year at Hunter College."

"How long have you been working out for?"

"Almost five years now."

"Well, you look amazing. I think you deserve all the credit."

"Thank you."

"However, I'd like to bring something up and Scott and Ramon can back me up here. We went to a bodybuilding convention. I believe it was two years back, you'd say?" Kevin seeks confirmation from his co-hosts, who both nod in approval. "And we asked notable bodybuilders about the use of steroids in the industry. We'd like to know your thoughts."

"As in, should people take steroids?"

"More or less. But let me clarify, it's more about the honesty of steroids. Basically, the question is, are you natty or not?"

Tyler looks around the studio, wondering if the question was rhetorical or an actual question. Just to confirm, "Are you asking me personally?"

"Yes." Kevin says.

Tyler didn't expect this as he remembers the dinner he had. Not once was the idea of steroid use going to be part of the questions. Though, this is something he should've expected since this is a bodybuilding podcast. Why not ask such a question, but why not be prepared for it? His eyes still dart around them. It has been almost thirty seconds of awkward silence.

"Tyler?" Kevin says.

After a deep breath, Tyler nods. "I'm not natural."

"I fucking knew it." Scott says. "I fucking told you, guys. There was no way in hell that his body could be achieved naturally."

Tyler continues, "I never said I was, though."

"But you are influencing younger generations that this body is achievable."

"If you paid attention to my videos, it's what workouts to perform and why it works. I also show my body progress. But I never once said I was a natural athlete."

Kevin, Scott and Ramon look at each other. Ramon nods to Tyler. "It's true. He didn't really say in any of his videos, he was natural."

"But don't you think kids will see you and have this belief that your body is achievable naturally?"

"Yes, but everyone's bodies are different. There are people out there that can achieve size more naturally than others. Like Scott, for example, he may be bigger up here, but down there not so much."

Scott rises from his seat, but Kevin and Ramon hold him back. "Woah, woah, woah! Scott! This is not the way to treat our guests. You should know better!" Kevin says.

Scott relaxes and walks towards the exit door of the studio. "I bet you he kissed his ex after she blew the personal trainer."

Tyler sets the headsets down, swings his fist to Scott's face. Ramon grabs Tyler, pins him against the wall. "Chill the fuck out!" Ramon says, voice demanding. But Tyler remains calm. He doesn't even look into Ramon's eyes. Instead, looks passed him, staring blankly.

"Let me go so I can go home." Tyler says, voice calm.

After a moment, Ramon gently lets Tyler go as Kevin escorts Scott, who holds his bleeding nose. Tyler gives a nod to Ramon and walks out.

IV

The shirt is off once again. Tyler's expression grew somber as he examined his body in the mirror, noticing every flaw and imperfection. He flexes his chest and abs, trying to get every piece of muscle fiber to pop out. Then a phone call from Wade. "What's up, stranger?" Wade says, voice ominous. "Still got a few more cycles to go."

As Wade's voice fills the room through speaker phone, Tyler flexes in front of the mirror, hoping that this time his muscles will reveal the desired definition. He relaxes his body and picks up his phone. "Same spot like last time."

"You already know."

The needle penetrates Tyler's butt-cheeks while in the showers of the locker room. After he lets the water rain down on him for a cleanse, he grabs a towel and stands by his locker, where he scrolls through his phone. He flips through several images, featuring a cute redhead girl with a smile. Her Instagram handle is @GingerGhostAshley. Tyler scrolls as far down as five years ago. Almost five hundred posts deep. A younger Ashley, hair dark red, giving a cheesy smile dressed in all black at a pumpkin patch. A familiar comment Tyler himself posted five years ago. "One of the best days ever. Love you beautiful." Following a kissing emoji. Her reply, "Love you too, my booger." Following seven hearts and kissing emojis.

Tyler can't help but smile at her photo. It brings back good old memories when they spent time at the pumpkin patch on Staten Island. He remembers picking her short little body up and carrying her around while she would laugh and tickle his then fat body. As he reaches the top page of her profile again, he notices the follow button awaiting his decision. He clicks on her first pic, a shot that looks professionally done of her standing by a graffiti wall, in her all black signature outfit and a wool beret. The comment section is all of her girlfriends complimenting her, with some giving multiple heart emojis. Then the occasional thirsty men with rose emojis. One stands out to Tyler. A profile handle @Freddy_ManeIfbb who gave muscle arm emoji. This makes him click the profile revealing to be the personal trainer Ashley trained with in the past, Freddy. His profile picture is of an oiled up man posing his muscles on a stage with medallions around his neck. Tyler stalks through the profile, revealing nothing but bodybuilding pictures. As he observes Freddy's body, Tyler looks at his own in front of the mirror. He compares his chest and abs with his. Tyler flexes his chest and arms, then compares it to Freddy's. It gets frustrating the more he switches from one pic to the next as he continues to compare his body.

For the first time in a while, Tyler is able to hold down the flat bench. He pushes 135lbs for twenty reps as a warmup. Adds another plate each side, making it 225lbs and pushes it for fifteen. He sips BCAAs in a container and then adds a quarter plate on each side of the barbell, making it 275lbs for a count of twelve reps. Another sip from the BCAA and replaces the quarter plates with 45lb plates, making it 315lbs. This goes for a clean ten reps. Almost a struggle, but he made it. He continues to add more weight, a quarter plate, making the barbell 365lbs. He drinks more from the BCAA as it's been almost a month since he's exerted this level of effort. After a deep breath, he lifts and pushes the barbell for a good clean six reps.

What a rush! The energy is exploding in Tyler.

Next, he swaps out the quarter plates for 45-pound plates, increasing the total weight to 405 pounds. Tyler never pushed that amount of weight in his life. Something he's dreamed of doing for a long time. He looks around for a possible spotter, then looks at himself in the mirror and sees how pumped he is. He takes off his shirt and flexes his pecks and snaps a photo. A thought comes to mind, putting the weights back and trying again later. But the demon inside keeps pushing him to push that weight and show the world how strong he really is. Prove himself is what he keeps repeating. Continue to inspire the younger gym members and push what the body is capable of doing.

Fuck it.

"Through the Fire and Flames" by DragonForce blares into Tyler's ears, pumping him up. He smacks himself across his face, lays down on the bench and grips on the barbell. After a deep breath, he exhales and lifts the weight off the platform. His arms shake as he slowly brings this massive weight down to his chest, then pushes up. It stays in place. Tyler is stuck and can't push it any further than his chest. SLAM!

The barbell slams into his collarbone, cracking it, then tilts to the side, dropping all the 45lb plates on the floor. Loud metal thuds and clanging echoes around the gym for all members to hear. Several people rush to help him and observe that Tyler is in extreme agony, desperately clutching his shoulder.

V

In the sterile brightness of the emergency room, Tyler sat gingerly on the examination table, his shoulder immobilized and throbbing painfully. He winced as a nurse adjusted the sling supporting his injured arm. Beside him, his father sat with a worried frown, his eyes reflecting the fluorescent lights overhead. Tyler sat uncomfortably on the hospital examination table, a sling immobilizing his injured shoulder. His father, seated beside him, wore an expression of worry mixed with relief. "Hey," his father said softly, reaching out Tyler's hand, gently grasping, "how are you holding up?"

Tyler blinked, his memories of the gym incident fragmented. He recalled the sharp, engulfing pain, the concerned faces of fellow gym-goers, and the urgent ride in the ambulance. His voice was raspy as he answered, "I'm managing, I guess."

His father, without a word, handed him a plastic cup of water. Tyler sipped the water, the cool liquid soothing his parched throat, a comforting reminder of his father's care during past illnesses. A brief chuckle escaped his father's lips, tinged with nostalgia.

Pulling back, Tyler winced, feeling the acute pain from his injury. "I was stupid, Dad."

The concern in his father's face deepened. "Why push yourself so hard with those weights?"

Tyler's breath quivered. "Ego," he whispered.

"Ego can be dangerous, son. The weights aren't going anywhere."

Before Tyler could respond, a doctor entered, clipboard in hand. "Tyler Masterson?" he asked, looking over his notes. "How are you feeling?"

With a wry smirk, Tyler responded, "Like I've been hit by a truck."

The doctor nodded empathetically. "You'll need to avoid lifting anything heavy for at least six to twelve weeks. Take it easy and start slow."

A heavy feeling of disappointment settled on Tyler, his dreams of maintaining his muscular build slipping further out of reach. He instinctively flexed his abs, seeking some reassurance. Noticing this, the doctor added, "Your condition isn't permanent. Focus on healing for now."

"But my body, my training…" Tyler's voice shook.

"Eat well, stick to your nutrition, and you'll recover," the doctor reassured.

As the doctor left, Tyler's frustration surged. He clenched his fist, but the sharp pain from his injury reminded him of his current vulnerability.

It wasn't long after Tyler faces himself in the mirror, only in his boxer briefs and shoulder sling covering the bandages. The same old routine in his room when facing the mirror. Flexes most of his muscles with his free hand. He relaxes his arms and slouches as he looks at his own eyes with the thought that his muscles won't be as defined or bulky while healing.

The desktop turns on and adjusts the camera. A script shows up at the desktop with Tyler going over it line by line. After a deep breath, he hits the record. "Hey, everyone. Tyler Masterson here with an update of what's going on. As you can tell, I'm pretty banged up." He points to his sleeve. "Yesterday, I was benching like everyone else at the gym. It was a very good day, actually. My energy levels were through the roof. I'm telling you, the greatest feeling is when you know you can out-lift the world. Unfortunately, the world fell on me when I attempted a P.R. by benching four plates." Tyler looks down in silence for a moment, then looks back at the camera. "I swear I thought I had it. When the barbell came down, my body knew this wasn't going to happen. But the stupid thing was not me lifting the weight... well, actually, it definitely was part of it. But it's the fact that I didn't get a spotter. Because of this, the doctors said I have to take a break from the gym for at least six to eight weeks. Sorry folks, won't be putting out gym content until I'm healed." Tyler stares at himself on the screen then turns to his father, who is sitting in the kitchen alone drinking tea. He returns to the camera, feels more determined. "And I will come back, better, stronger. But more careful. Until then, I will be posting workout routines, diet plans, and progress with my injury. Stay safe!"

After the post, an overwhelming amount of positive comments flood his channel. This was unexpected since being exposed to steroids use. Though there are very few negative commenters still posting about it, they were easily outshined by comments wishing him well and to take care of himself first. Health first, work later. Then they are followed by flexing arm emojis. Tyler gives a nod of acceptance and sits with his father, having tea.

Invited back to the studio, Tyler accepted and joined Kevin and Ramon. Kevin made sure to discuss Scott's departure from the podcast due to unprofessional antics. The last thing the podcast needed was to have hate and controversy when all they try to do was inspire others and share a journey that people can learn from. Tyler, in his sling, seems to be in good spirits. He's laughing more with Kevin and Ramon. His voice is relaxed, bringing out nothing but positive vibes.

"It's good to see you happier," Kevin says, voice genuine.

"Well, I'm trying, Kev." Tyler says, voice still shy. "I guess I needed a break from the gym."

"How long has it been already?"

"Already two weeks."

"And that's two weeks without working out?"

"Yeah, man. Two weeks without touching a weight."

"I don't think I can go a few days without at least one exercise. What about you, Ramon?"

"Not even two days." Ramon says.

This really has been quite the ride. Tyler contemplates his workout routine and his body image. There is a stillness in his thoughts as if there is no bother. Like an acceptance. "You just have to live with the fact that we're still vulnerable pieces of flesh, no matter how strong we are. It's safe to say I got lucky that I wasn't injured worse in other parts of my body where it would leave me immobile. I'm happy that my back is not injured at all."

Kevin and Ramon give a nod, agreeing with the statement. "So, what will you do in the meantime?"

VI

The golden hues of the setting sun danced on the water, casting long shadows of the tall trees lining the riverbank. A lone boat bobbed gently in the rippling waters, where Tyler and Mike sat, their fishing lines thrown into the vast expanse, waiting for the thrill of a catch. Mike's gaze frequently shifted to the sling, cradling Tyler's arm, a quiet concern etched on his weathered face. "You sure about this, Ty? We could've waited."

Tyler flexed his uninjured arm, a half-smile playing on his lips. "If we waited, we'd miss this." He gestured to the serene surroundings.

Mike chuckled, the sound blending seamlessly with the distant calls of birds and the rhythmic hum of cicadas. "Always in a hurry, just like when you were a kid."

A gentle tug on Tyler's rod interrupted their conversation. He pulled, hopeful, but the line came back empty. "Almost had it," he murmured, more to himself than to Mike.

Mike, with a sly grin, teased, "Remember when you used to think any tug was a giant fish? Always aiming high."

Tyler smirked. "Some things never change."

The two sat in companionable silence, absorbing the surrounding tranquility. The weight of past struggles seemed distant, replaced by the present's calm reassurance. "You still doing those videos?" Mike's voice was soft, cautious.

Tyler hesitated, his fingers brushing the phone in his pocket. "Sometimes. But after the injury, I've been rethinking things."

Mike nodded, understanding shining in his eyes. "Maybe it's time to show them the real you. The journey, not just the destination."

With a newfound determination, Tyler took out his phone. "How about now?" He started a live video, the camera capturing Mike's surprised expression. "Everyone, meet my dad, the legendary fisherman."

Mike's laughter echoed over the water as he waved. "Hey there!" The moment was interrupted by a forceful tug on Mike's rod. "Hold on, Ty! This is a big one!" As Mike wrestled with the line, Tyler's camera captured every moment. The determination in Mike's eyes, the sweat on his brow, and finally, the triumphant hoisting of a magnificent sea bass.

GLUTTONY
YEAR OF THE PIG

I

The Blue Goose Sports Bar is a cacophony of cheers and chatter, the air heavy with the scent of spicy wings. It's the venue for the lively tenth annual chicken wing eating competition, an event that's transformed into a celebrated local tradition. The competitors bask in the otherworldly radiance of the neon lights, embodying the essence of seasoned warriors. Among these mighty titans, Vincent Porcher, an enigma, stood among the burly figures. His thin-framed build was a stark contrast that was hard to ignore. His clothes drape loosely over his thin body, making him seem almost ethereal. Sunken eyes, encircled by dark shadows, only intensified the weariness etched into his expression.

Vincent's gaze sweeps the room, his expression unreadable. A patron, leaning on the bar, nudges his buddy, "Take a look at that guy." The patron says. "He's like a walking stick figure!"

As the competition is about to kick off, one can almost taste the buzz of excitement in the air. The event organizer, Bob, a man with a booming voice and a larger-than-life personality, grabs the microphone. "Ladies and gentlemen, welcome to the ultimate showdown of guts and glory!" He introduces the contestants amidst a thunderous applause. "And now, give it up for the reigning king of the wing, the devourer of all, Big Pete Henderson!" Bob's loud voice carries throughout the bar. The crowd erupts into a frenzy of cheers as a confident, burly man and a cheeky grin steps up. He waves at the crowd, basking in their adoration, his championship belt glinting under the lights.

"And now, brace yourselves for the beloved beast of Blue Goose, the unbreakable, the unstoppable, Iron Jack!" Bob's voice resonates with enthusiasm. Stepping into view is a man whose presence is a force of nature. With a stocky build and warm smile, Jack wins over the crowd. He raises his arms in a triumphant gesture, and the bar erupts into a roaring cheer. Unlike the sleek muscle of the reigning champion, Jack's strength lies in his rugged, everyman appeal, making him a relatable and much-loved figure among some patrons.

When it's Vincent's turn, there's a ripple of murmurs. "And here's the dark horse, Vincent Porcher!" Bob says, voice filled with amusement.

Vincent steps forward, his movements deliberate, almost mechanical. He receives a friendly slap on the back from Tyrone, a hefty competitor known for his hearty laughter. "Better watch out, twig, I might just eat you by mistake!" The crowd erupts in laughter. Vincent offers a thin smile, but his eyes remain cold and distant.

The whistle blows, and the competition erupts into a frenzy of flying wings and dripping sauce. Vincent, a whirlwind, devours wing after wing with his fast-moving, efficient fingers moving in a blur. The crowd is stunned into silence, then explodes into cheers. As Vincent continues his implausible feat, a woman in the crowd leans in, whispering to her friend, "There's something off about that guy." She says, voice concerned. "He looks sick or something."

With the blast of the final whistle, the contestants take a step back, their breaths ragged and their faces covered in sauce. Vincent stands still, his breathing even, his expression unchanged. Bob announces the results, and it's a close call. Tyrone emerges as the victor, having impressively consumed 237 wings, while Vincent, the enigmatic newcomer, trails a mere three wings behind at 234. His unexpected and remarkable performance leaves an indelible impression on everyone.

After the event, the bar buzzes with talk about the "ghost" who almost devoured his way to victory. Vincent, on the other hand, is already at the door, his exit as puzzling as his entrance.

Outside of the bar, the cool night air does little to alleviate the weight pressing down on Vincent's chest. Leaning against the wall, he closes his eyes briefly, his stomach churning with sickness. "What am I doing?" he mutters, his words dissolving into the noise of the dispersing crowd. He glances down at his sauce-stained clothes, feeling a deep-seated humiliation clinging to him. In a moment of reflection, he reaches into his pocket and retrieves twenty chicken bones – the difference between victory and second place. With a swift motion, he discards them into the dumpster. He catches a glimpse of the animated bar, buzzing with conversation after the competition. "Fuck the prize," he whispers to himself. With each step he takes into the night, he can feel the judgmental stares from the patrons settles on his shoulders, planting seeds of insecurity.

II

The Kansas farm, with its fields of emerald green and tilled earth, sprawled out beneath the vast, unending sky like a picturesque patchwork quilt. High above, the sun beamed down as a radiant ball, casting playful shadows that swayed and twirled across the land. The idyllic landscape was adorned by the old farmhouse, its weathered wooden exterior telling stories of generations gone by. The gentle breeze caused the nearby corn stalks to sway and dance in harmony.

In this enchanting setting, there was one discordant note. A young boy, thin as the reeds by the creek, with eyes that held a depth beyond his years. Vincent, with his tall and skinny body and messy hair with a slight curl at the tips, glided through this world like a ghost. The farm's vibrant setting overshadowed his existence.

His mother, Anne, was the soul of this pastoral domain. Her hands, though calloused from labor, were gentle as they tended to both crops and kin. Her voice, when she called Vincent in from the fields, was a melody that seemed to harmonize with the rustling leaves and chirping birds. Yet, these tender notes carried a hint of unease, her eyes betraying an unspoken concern.

Vincent's father, Thomas, was the embodiment of quiet strength, standing as a sentry for the land. As rough and weathered as the oak trees on their land, the man's features told the story of years spent farming. His words, though rare, were often overshadowed by the sigh of the wind or the creaking of the barn doors. To Vincent, his father was a mystery, a figure as unmovable and incomprehensible as the ancient hills that lined their land.

Thomas was already out in the fields, his attention devoted to their most cherished cow, Molly. He tended to her with a gentle touch, brushing her coat and speaking to her in low, affectionate tones. Vincent watched from a distance, a pang of longing in his chest. The care and attention his father lavished on Molly stood in stark contrast to the stern, sparing affection he offered his son. It was in these quiet moments, observing the bond between man and animal, that Vincent felt an acute sense of alienation – a yearning for a connection with his father that seemed as distant as the horizon.

In the farm's tranquility, Vincent's behavior began to change, his hushed whispers revealing a hidden struggle. Each mealtime turned into a tense battlefield, with his fork and knife reluctantly engaged in the silent warfare. He devoured his food with haste, his fork practically flying from plate to mouth, while his parents dined at a leisurely pace. His meals were no longer about satisfying hunger but devouring everything in sight, leaving no leftovers in what used to be a household where food was savored and shared.

His mother's eyes filled with questions that never quite reached her lips. Often lingered on the empty dishes, her unease growing.

His father, a man of few words, finally broke his silence one evening with a stern, disapproving remark about Vincent's excessive eating.

As Vincent reached for what would have been his fourth helping, his father's hand shot out, covering the serving dish. "Enough, Vincent!" he said, his voice firm, echoing in the quiet kitchen. "This isn't a pigsty!" His words hung heavily in the air, a stark reprimand in their otherwise reserved household. With his fork suspended in the air, Vincent's face turned red with shame. His mother, her expression of worry, remained silent, her eyes shifting between her husband and son.

As days rolled into weeks, Vincent's struggle grew more pronounced. His stomach would audibly growl at odd hours, even shortly after meals, a growling beast that refused to be tamed. Sometimes, in the dead of night, Anne would hear faint noises from the kitchen – the creak of the cupboard, the rustle of wrappers – and she'd know Vincent was there, feeding his insatiable hunger in the shadows.

Anne quietly joined Vincent in the kitchen, her heart heavy with maternal concern. She watched him for a moment before wordlessly preparing a sandwich, adding extra slices of ham she had reserved just for him. As she handed it to him, their eyes met – a silent exchange of understanding and gratitude.

But their quiet moment was shattered by the sharp voice of Thomas, Vincent's father. "What the hell are you doing, Anne?" he demanded, his silhouette looming in the doorway. "He needs to learn control, not be babied."

Anne's expression hardened, a rare flash of defiance lighting her eyes. "He's hungry, Thomas. I can't just watch our son suffer like this."

The argument between Anne and Thomas escalated, not just in volume, but in intensity. Thomas, a man of rigid principles, believed firmly in strict discipline, a belief that sometimes manifested physically. As their voices rose, Thomas's hand, which had been slamming the table in emphasis, suddenly reached out and grabbed Anne's arm with a firmness that was too familiar. "I'm in charge here!" he barked, his grip tightening.

Anne winced but held his gaze, her voice trembling, "Let go of me, Thomas!"

Vincent, witnessing this, felt a surge of anger and helplessness. His father's old-school methods, which often extended to harsh physical reprimands directed at both him and his mother, cast a long shadow over their household. The sight of his father's hand on his mother was a painful reminder of the many times discipline had crossed the line into something darker.

During their confrontation, Vincent's gut feeling urged him to protect his mother. But years under his father's strict rule had instilled a deep-seated fear that rooted him to the spot, his fists clenched in silent frustration.

The conflict ended as abruptly as it began, leaving the kitchen charged with unsaid words. In the corner, Vincent stood as a silent shadow, feeling the familiar agony of hunger consuming him. As his parents' attention turned away from each other, Vincent quietly slipped out, seeking solace in the only way he knew.

As the sun arched high above the fields, casting a blanket of heat upon the earth, a restless unease took hold of Vincent. Something within him stirred, a silent whisper that grew louder with each passing hour. As he worked in the fields, uprooting weeds from the fields, his mind wandering to a dark place.

With each passing moment, the air grew cooler, and the sky painted with hues of orange and pink. Vincent couldn't help but be drawn to the barn, where Molly, their oldest and most beloved cow, awaited his attention. Grazing serenely, she remained oblivious to the storm brewing inside the boy who observed her. Vincent's thoughts raced with a scheme that appeared both fearsome and obligatory, a pathway to pacify the unrelenting hunger that consumed him. With the stealth of a shadow, Vincent waited until the farmhouse lights dimmed, and the world around him slipped into slumber. He slipped into the barn, the familiar smell of hay and livestock enveloping him. The peacefulness of the surroundings made the impending act even more jarring.

Bathed in muted lighting, Molly's eyes sparkled with a gentle curiosity as Vincent came closer. His heart pounded in his chest, a drumbeat of both fear and need. He reached out, his fingers trembling.

***

The night was unusually quiet, the familiar chorus of crickets and night birds conspicuously absent. Earlier, Anne had noticed Vincent's increasing restlessness and his odd eating habits, which had grown more pronounced lately. His chair at the dinner table was empty, his absence at this hour unusual and unsettling.

Anne, feeling increasingly anxious, took the LED lantern from the living room and started scouring the house. She checked his room first, half-expecting to find him hunched over a late-night snack, but the room was empty, his computer still humming softly in the corner. She glanced through the bathroom, even peeked into the garage – all the usual places he might be. Each empty room added to her sense of unease.

Finally, with nowhere else left to look, Anne made her way to the barn. As she neared, a strange, metallic scent filled the air, unfamiliar and alarming. Her hand shook slightly as she reached for the barn door, the sturdy, modern structure contrasting with its age-old purpose. Flicking on the high-powered lantern, she pushed the door open.

The harsh white light revealed a scene far removed from the barn's usual orderliness. From the neatly stacked hay bales and the clean, organized tools, a chaos unfolded before her eyes, one that her mind struggled to comprehend. The sight was horrific.

Vincent, her son, was present in a bewildering scene that was hard to make sense of. Molly lay still, her form distorted in the low light. The deafening sound of Anne's scream pierced through the stillness of the night, a raw and gut-wrenching cry that mirrored the anguish of a mother's shattered dreams. Vincent turned, his eyes wide and wild, his face smeared with blood.

Anne recoiled, her grip on the lantern loosening as it trembled violently in her grasp. The sight before her was a stark, brutal contrast to anything she could have ever imagined about her son. The dim glow of the barn barely illuminated Vincent, who stood there, almost blending into the encroaching shadows, a figure teetering on the edge of an unfathomable darkness.

Awakened by Anne's piercing screams, Thomas stormed into the barn, his face set in a hard line, anger pulsing through his veins. The sight that met him – Molly's motionless body and Vincent, covered in blood – ignited a fierce rage within him. His usual stoic demeanor gave way to a harsh, commanding presence. "Vincent!" he bellowed, his voice roaring through the barn. "What in God's name have you done?" His eyes, usually impassive, now burned with a fire of paternal wrath and a deep, unsettling shock at the carnage before him. "I ask you again, boy! What the hell have you done?!"

***

In the days that followed, the Porcher household sank into a somber routine. The dining room was filled with an eerie silence during meals, the empty spot where Vincent used to sit casting a haunting shadow over the family. Anne did her chores of scattering feed to the clucking chickens, who pecked around her boots eagerly, collecting the morning's eggs from beneath the hens, placing them carefully in her basket and weeding around the young tomato plants in the garden. Her once warm eyes now pools of sorrow. She would often pause, a hand lingering on Vincent's bedroom door, torn between a mother's love and the fear of what her son had become. The son who was once gentle had transformed into a voracious being, compelled by an unquenchable and horrifying appetite.

Thomas became a figure of silent deliberation, his interactions with Vincent brief and fraught with unspoken disappointment. He continued his routine of general maintenance around the farm, fixing the fence broken by a manic pig. Still, the burden of a decision clouded his mind while he tended to the fields.

Finally, on a cool evening as the sun dipped below the horizon, casting long shadows over the farm, Thomas called a family meeting. Tension filled the air in the living room. "We can't go on like this," Thomas began, his voice heavy. "We need to send Vincent away."

Anne's eyes filled with tears. "No, no, no. We can't do that, Thomas?"

"It's too dangerous to have him here. Not just for us, but for the rest of the animals."

"He's our son!" Anne yelled out.

"Not anymore! He has gone way too far by kill... eating... Did you not fucking see what he has done?!"

Anne began to let out a cry. She nods, understanding her husband's decision.

Sitting in silence, Vincent's head hung low, exuding an undeniable air of acceptance.

The words hung in the air, a sentence that shattered the last pretense of normalcy. Vincent lifted his head, his eyes meeting those of his parents. There was no anger in his gaze, only a deep, resounding sadness, an acknowledgment of a truth he had known since that fateful night in the barn.

Anne reached across the table, her fingers brushing Vincent's. "I still love you, Vincent," she whispered, her voice laced with a mother's heartache. She kisses his forehead.

Vincent nods to his mother. "I love you too."

Thomas's voice was firm. "You'll be going to a friend's in New York," he said, not meeting Vincent's eyes. "Brian is a property manager for a large apartment building in West Harlem and has agreed to give you an apartment. You'll get yourself sorted out there."

Vincent's heart sank at the words. New York was a world away, a place of unknowns. The idea of leaving the only home he'd ever known for the streets of a city he'd only seen in movies felt like a sentence to exile. His father's decision was final, a cold severing of ties under the guise of tough love. There was no room for protest, no space for pleading. The decision had been made, and Vincent was to be sent away, out of sight, his presence too much of a reminder of a family tragedy they all wished to forget.

Leading up to the days of his departure, a somber stillness settled over the Porcher farm, casting a shadow over each and every task. As Anne moved through Vincent's room, she carefully packed his belongings, each item a stark reminder of the son she once knew. There was his well-worn Kansas City Royals baseball cap, faded from countless days under the sun. Placed beside it was a group of CDs, featuring a blend of early 2000s rock bands and country artists such as Garth Brooks, Metallica, Tim McGraw, and Nirvana, reflecting his eclectic music taste. Anne folded his clothes, a few flannel shirts that had seen better days, a pair of jeans with frayed hems, and his favorite t-shirt emblazoned with the logo of a local tractor company. Tucked away in the corner of the closet was his old Game Boy Color, still loaded with a Pokémon cartridge, a relic of a simpler time in his childhood. Every object represented a memory they had together, now carefully being packed into a tired little suitcase.

Thomas busied himself with repairs around the farm, the rhythmic clank of his tools punctuated by the distant sound of the refrigerator door opening and closing, a reminder of Vincent's ceaseless need to eat. He avoided the barn, haunted by memories of Vincent's act, and instead focused on tasks that kept his hands busy and his mind away from the painful reality of his son's condition.

In the shrinking world of his bedroom, Vincent alternated between resentment and worry. Using his CD player he got as a gift a few Christmases ago, he listened to the once comforting song, *Boulevard of Broken Dreams* by Green Day, now seemed to amplify his own inner struggles. The guitar riffs and pounding drums mirrored his growing bitterness towards his father, whose decision to send him away felt like an abandonment, a rejection of his own son. Then, he grew concern for his mother. He saw her tired eyes, heard the strain in her voice, and felt a nagging guilt. She was his anchor, the one who had always shown him kindness and understanding. Now, as he prepared to leave, he couldn't help but worry about her. Would she be okay without him? Could she handle the farm and his father's stern ways on her own?

As the day of his departure neared, Vincent felt increasingly isolated. Emotions swirled around him like a whirlwind, anger, concern, and a deep sense of loss, all contending for his attention. He worried about the future, about what lay ahead of him in a city as vast and unknown as New York.

On the morning of his departure, Vincent awoke to an emptiness that felt more acute than ever. His first act was to visit the kitchen, hastily eating whatever he could find, leftovers from the previous nights almost leaving nothing behind except an empty fridge. He carries his bag on his shoulder, the meager contents rattling with each step.

The walk to the train station was a blur, his mind consumed by the gnawing sensation in his stomach, each step a reminder of the endless appetite that had driven him to this point. The station, with its smells of diesel and distant food vendors, only aggravated his hunger, making him acutely aware of the emptiness inside. Vincent sits on the bench, waiting for the train. His stomach twists and churns. Despite his attempt to pay attention to the surrounding noises, thoughts of his next meal dominated his mind. The hunger clung to him like a constant companion, its persistent whispers drowning out the approaching train.

The moment Vincent stepped onto the train, he was enveloped in the irresistible scents of snacks and coffee, intensifying his longing. He settled into his seat, his stomach growling audibly, a stark reminder of the journey ahead, not just in miles, but in the endless quest to satisfy an appetite that seemed to have no end.

III

As the evening settles in West Harlem, the neighborhood's worn edges became more pronounced under the sparse glow of flickering streetlights. Harlem was always filled with sounds. There were conversations murmuring in the distance, occasional laughter from late-night wanderers, and the constant rhythmic hum of the sleepless city. The streets, quieter now, were lined with tired buildings whose shuttered windows and graffiti-stained walls spoke of hard times. Among those buildings, there was low-income housing with a dimly lit facade, symbolizing the challenges faced by its residents. Vincent found solace in a building that has become his current refuge. This building was where his father told him to meet Brian, a short, pudgy old man who Vincent had never heard of.

The apartment was a small, cramped space with thin walls they seemed to breathe along with the building's other occupants. Despite its sparse furnishings and peeling paint, it served as both sanctuary and prison, offering a place to hide yet no escape from oneself. The view from his lone window was a collage of fire escapes and brick facades, interspersed with the occasional flicker of a television screen from across the way.

Vincent wrestled with the aftermath of his latest binge. The competition had left him drained, yet his insatiable hunger, a relentless demon, clawed at him with renewed fervor. He sat hunched over on his bed, surrounded by the outcome of his frantic eating – a mess of empty wrappers and scattered takeout boxes. He was a silhouette against the dim light from the window, his body a map of bones barely covered by skin, his eyes hollow pools reflecting a life consumed by an endless hunger. As he sat there, the room seemed to close in on him. The walls whispering echoes of his despair. He thought of the competition, of the fleeting moments of fulfillment as he ate, only to be replaced by a deep, gnawing emptiness that no amount of food could satiate.

He lay back, his gaze fixed on a crack in the ceiling. His mind wandered to his mother, her face a fading memory tinged with sadness and longing. He needed to see her, to bridge the chasm that had grown between them, but the journey felt as insurmountable as the hunger that gripped him. After leaving the farm, he lacked the confidence to return to Kansas, even after all these years.

An unexpected knock at the door sent a jolt through Vincent. Hesitating, he finally opened the door and was surprised to see Lisa, a caseworker, whose presence in his solitary world causing him to feel uneasy.

"Hi, Vincent? I'm Lisa, from the Community Support Center downtown," she introduced herself, her voice tinged with a warmth that felt foreign in the starkness of his room. "Do you have a moment?"

Vincent, taken aback, managed a nod, stepping aside to let her in. A feeling of impending doom consumed him as his heart raced. "What's this about?" he asked, his voice unsteady.

Lisa walked in, her eyes briefly scanning the messy room. "I wanted to talk to you in person," she began, her tone shifting to one of gentle seriousness. "We received some news at the center. It's about your mother, Anne."

Vincent's face tightened, a flicker of fear passing through his eyes. "What about her?" he asked, the words barely escaping his lips.

"I'm sorry to tell you this, but your mother is very ill."

"How ill are we talking?"

"Her medical team informed us she has been diagnosed with stomach cancer. It's quite serious," Lisa revealed, her words deliberate, yet filled with empathy.

Cancer. The word hung heavily in the air. Vincent stiffened, his voice a mere whisper. "How... how bad is it?"

"Bad, Vincent. It's advanced. She's in the Via Christi Hospital St. Francis in Wichita, Kansas. They're doing everything they can for her," Lisa explained, her eyes meeting his with a compassionate steadiness.

A wave of emotions crashed over Vincent. He looked away, his eyes watery, disbelief clouding his face. He murmured incomprehensible words to himself, the walls of his room seeming to close in on him.

Lisa reached out, then hesitated, respecting his space. "I know this is hard to hear. If there's anything you need, any way we can help you see her."

Vincent, overwhelmed, sat on the edge of his bed. "I haven't seen her in years. I don't even know if she'd want to see me now," he admitted, the burden of years of separation pressing down on him.

"Actually, Vincent, that's why I'm here. She's been asking about you. I think she'd very much want to see you," Lisa said, her voice a gentle reassurance in the thick air of despair.

As he took a deep breath, his mind was overwhelmed by a flurry of thoughts and emotions. "Really?" Vincent said, seeking reassurance.

"Yes." Lisa said, offering him her business card.

Vincent takes the card with trembling hands.

"Please call me if you decide you want to go. Our support center can try to assist you in getting some funds from our Emergency Family Reunion Program."

Vincent gives a light chuckle, knowing that this program will barely give the right amount of funds. "How much am I going to have in my pocket? For basic shit." Vincent asked anyway.

"We'll provide for transportation, meals–"

"Yeah, yeah, yeah, how much?"

Lisa, almost hesitant, spits it out. "Around $300."

Vincent shakes his head, then lowers it. He knew the answer would be low for him. He needed to make sure, just in case. But the money is still too low and would have to figure out to make much more.

Lisa gives an offering hand. "Please, call us, Vincent. We're here for you."

Vincent nods a thank you as he gripped Lisa's business card. He watches Lisa make her way out.

Then came the irritable growl of his stomach.

IV

The lights on the building are still as blinding as the morning sun in Times Square. Advertisements of many various brands, from fashion like Gucci and Balenciaga to the upcoming *Joker* film. Tourists from all parts of the world come collectively to Times Square, taking pictures of anything they set their eyes on. Whatever it is they think is amazing is definitely something a New Yorker can care less about. Most tourists then turn to watch street performers by the red stairs in the middle of the bowtie section. A group of street dancers doing all kinds of aerobic dance moves stunning the crowd. A man dressed as Spider-Man snaps photos with a little Asian boy who flicks his wrist, pretending to shoot a web. But one performer stands out from the rest.

As Vincent steps onto his makeshift platform, his enthusiasm masks an undercurrent of discomfort. "Step right up, step right up!" he calls out, his voice steady despite the internal battle within. "I can show you all the magic of the world, but first I need a volunteer." He points to an Italian man, almost unsure, until his excited wife nudges him on. Vincent shows him a deck of cards, trying to focus on the trick while fighting the distraction of his growling stomach. "Pick a card and show everyone, except me."

The Italian man pulls out an Eight of Clubs and shows it to the crowd.

"Now, put it in the middle of the deck." Vincent says, looking away as he cuts the deck in half.

The Italian man places the Eight of Clubs face down, but without noticing, Vincent scratches the edge of the card, then closes the deck. Vincent's skilled hands move almost automatically, but his mind occasionally drifts to the relentless pangs of hunger. He tries to focus, to maintain the facade of the confident performer, but his body betrays him with its hungry needs.

"Time to witness a miracle." Vincent shuffles the deck, then passes the deck to the Italian man. "Now you do the same and cut."

The Italian man takes the deck and shuffles it poorly, then cuts it in half. He hands it back to Vincent, who eyes three Hedge Fund Hotshots watching intently. The approach of them, clad in their sharp suits, came with an air of mocking condescension that intensified Vincent's discomfort. Their dismissive smirks and patronizing laughter echoed through Vincent's ears, each chuckle a sharp jab to his confidence. They clapped with over-exaggerated enthusiasm, their sarcastic cheers thinly veiling their scorn. "Bravo, truly mesmerizing!" one of them exclaimed.

As Vincent's stomach growls painfully, cringing, he thinks, *Not now, please*. But the hunger refuses to be ignored, leaving him breaking a sweat. Then glistening in his eyes, a sparkling watch on one of the bros. Vincent quickly shifts focus on the magic act.

"Okay, now tell us your card," Vincent says.

"Um, you want me to say it out loud?" The Italian man says.

"Yes, yes, go on."

"Okay, eight of clubs."

"Couldn't have picked a better card." Vincent says, takes the deck and spreads them slowly, revealing one card face down out of the face-up cards. "Take that card and show it to the crowd."

The Italian man takes the card, and to his surprise it's the eight of clubs. The surrounding people applaud.

"Thank you, thank you. Please don't forget to donate." Vincent says, but some people ignore and walk away, including the Italian man who pats Vincent's shoulder and walks away with his wife. It was not an unfamiliar experience for him. A few coins tossed here and there in the black duffle bag. A few singles, too. As Vincent counts the little change he has, the Hedge Fund Trio approach with laughter.

The bigger one and leader of the sharp suited knuckleheads standing in between his minions approaches condescendingly. "Do magic for us." He said, his tone laced with mockery.

"You know, I would, but –" Vincent's stomach growls, cringes in pain.

"Aw, what's the matter? Someone is a little hungry?"

As Vincent glanced at the big bro's wrists, he couldn't help but be captivated by the mesmerizing sparkle of the diamond watch. "You know what? I'll do a trick for you."

"That's a good monkey." The big bro laughs along with his minions. The one finance minion wearing a red striped tie offers peanuts from a bag he's eating from.

"You work for peanuts?" The red striped bro says, laughing.

This isn't the first time Vincent has been ridiculed by shitty men like them. However, there's something about these assholes that intensified the feeling of humiliation, particularly when it's delivered by the big one with his fat face that practically invites a punch. So, he takes the deck of cards, pulls out two kings, hearts and diamonds. "I want you to take these two kings." Vincent says as he hands over the kings.

"And do what with them?" the leader of the hotshots asked.

"You want magic or no?"

"Fine," the leader said sarcastically. He takes the two kings. "Now what?"

"Hold them up in front of you." Vincent gestures with his hands to bring them up.

The hedge fund minions watch their leader do so.

Vincent takes his wrists, gently crosses his arms back and forth. "Did they change?"

A laughter from the trio. "No."

"No?" Vincent, once again, swings the man's wrists, crossing the cards. "How about now?"

"What are you trying to pull?"

Vincent lets go of the man, and gestures to the cards revealing the red kings are now black, spades and clubs.

The trio are amazed at the trick. "Holy shit." As they look up, Vincent vanishes. "Where'd he go?"

Then the quiet minion notices their leader's watch is gone. "Dude, your watch."

In a panic, the big bro looks down at his naked wrist.

"Over there!" The red striped tie minion points to Vincent running through a crowd of people. They ran after him.

Vincent ran past vendor after vendor, dodging people as they walked towards his way. He turns the block and ran up to Eighth Avenue, found an alleyway and jumped in the dumpster. He heard the trio pass. After a few moments, Vincent hopped out of the dumpster, took one step... WHAM! The big leader of the trio gave a hook to Vincent's face, dropping him. The trio then stripped Vincent and searched for the watch, but can't find it. They ask and ask, but he claimed to not have it. They fling the clothes towards him and kick Vincent's ribs, face, and chest while stomping on his back. After a moment, leaving Vincent bleeding, the leader calls it off. "I'll buy a new watch." They walk over him, and the quiet bro spits on Vincent's head. The confrontation leaves Vincent hurt and humiliated, but more so, it's a stark reminder of the lengths to which he must go to feed his unyielding hunger.

Behind the dumpster, Vincent hunched over, driven by necessity. He forced two fingers down his throat, targeting his uvula. The first few attempts only brought dry gags, but then, with a convulsive effort, he induced vomiting. It's a violent, wrenching experience, sending waves of pain through his body. As he retches, the Rolex watch he had swallowed earlier forcefully ejects from his mouth and lands on a piece of discarded cardboard.

Exhausted, Vincent slumps against the dumpster, gasping for air. His hands, trembling and slick, comb through the mess to retrieve the watch. It's coated in vomit, but even in its soiled state, the luxury of the Rolex is unmistakable. For a fleeting moment, despite his suffering, Vincent feels a twinge of triumph.

But then his stomach growls again, louder and more insistent.

With a determined mindset, Vincent approaches the task of cleaning the Rolex, aiming to restore its shine. He first finds an old, discarded water bottle nearby and fills it with a leaky faucet at the back of a building. With the bottle in hand, he carefully rinses the watch under a steady stream of water, washing away the layers of grime and vomit.

Next, he tears a piece of cloth from an already tattered part of his clothing, using it, and gently wipes down the watch. He rubs carefully, mindful not to damage the delicate craftsmanship. As he polishes, the watch gleams once again, reflecting the light. The diamonds sparkling even under the dim streetlight. Finally, Vincent uses his breath to fog the face of the watch, polishing it with another clean section of cloth, bringing back its shine. The Rolex now looks almost as good as new.

As the sun sets, the sky undergoes a transformation, turning into a breathtaking display of vibrant oranges and pinks that instantly transports Vincent back to the peaceful evenings on the farm. Vincent's journey through the neon-lit labyrinth of New York City was a sensory overload, with the stolen Rolex weighing heavily in his pocket, intensifying his feelings of urgency and unease. He maneuvered through the vibrant streets of Times Square, the scent of sizzling street food lingering in the air, as he made his way towards the less crowded area of Midtown West.

He found himself standing before a small, nondescript jeweler's shop nestled between a closed-down laundromat and a fancy Chinese restaurant. The enticing smell of Chinese food reached his nostrils, making his mouth water and stomach violently growl.

Vincent's eyes were immediately drawn to the sign hanging above the jeweler's shop with a bold proclamation that read "WE BUY JEWELRY." Hesitating for a moment, Vincent felt the pang of hunger gnawing at him, a cruel reminder of his pressing need. Swallowing his apprehension, he pushed open the door of the jeweler shop, a bell tinkling softly above him, announcing his entrance into a world far removed from the chaos of the streets.

Inside, the shop was a quiet haven, its walls lined with glass cases filled with an array of jewelry that gleamed under the soft lighting. At the counter, the elderly Turkish man's weathered hands held a loupe to his eye as he examined a piece of jewelry with meticulous care. He looked up as Vincent approached, his gaze sharp and assessing. Vincent, feeling the intensity of the jeweler's scrutiny, tightened his grip on the Rolex, acutely aware of how out of place he must seem in his disheveled appearance. Clearing his throat, Vincent laid the Rolex on the counter.

"I have something you might be interested in," he said, trying to keep his voice steady.

The jeweler put aside his current work and reached for the watch. His fingers were deft and experienced as they turned the Rolex over, examining its face and diamond band. Vincent observed, experiencing the overwhelming heaviness of each ticking second. His stomach growled, a humiliating reminder of his dire state, but he tried to focus on the jeweler's reaction.

"Hmm, a Rolex," the jeweler murmured, his eyes scrutinizing the piece. "Where did you get this, if I may ask?"

Vincent shifted uncomfortably. "It was a lucky find," he said, avoiding the jeweler's gaze. "Just stumbled upon it."

The jeweler eyed him skeptically. "A 'lucky find'? You do realize items like this don't just get 'stumbled upon' every day."

Vincent felt a rush of anxiety. "I understand, but it's mine now, and I need to sell it. I need the money."

"Did you steal it?" The jeweler said in a firm tone.

Vincent doesn't answer. His body was shaking, not wanting to respond.

The jeweler leaned back, assessing Vincent with a keen eye. "Doesn't matter. Even if you didn't, buying items with unclear history comes with its risks. You know that, right?"

Vincent nodded, the urgency in his voice rising. "Yes, I know, but I'm not here to cause trouble. I just need a fair price."

After a tense moment, "I'll give you three grand."

"Come on, you know it's worth much more than that."

The jeweler hands back the Rolex. "I already told you. I don't know where it came from. This is my price."

Vincent's stomach growls, reminding him he was in no position to argue. He accepted the offer, relief washing over him as the cash was handed over. As Vincent pocketed the money, the jeweler's gaze softened.

"You look like you're carrying more than just the weight of this watch," the jeweler said, voice gentle. "If you don't mind me saying."

Vincent pocketed the cash quickly, eager to leave. "It's nothing. Thanks for the deal." He turned to go, but the jeweler's next words stopped him.

"Hold on a moment. I've seen many faces in this shop, and yours seems troubling. Talk to me. Are you in debt?"

Vincent hesitated, a part of him yearning to share his burdens. "It's... my mother," he finally admitted, his voice barely above a whisper. "She's sick. I need to get back to Kansas to see her."

"Kansas, huh?" The jeweler's voice was soft, inviting. "That's a long way from here. It must be important for you to go back."

Vincent felt the walls he had built around himself begin to crumble. "Yeah, she's not doing well. Cancer." His voice trailed off as his stomach growled audibly, an embarrassing reminder of his constant battle. "I haven't seen her in years. I just... I need to be there, you know?"

"Oh, I'm so sorry to hear, my friend." The jeweler said, voice sympathetic. Then heard the growl and gave Vincent a knowing look. "How will you get there?"

Vincent shrugs his shoulders. "I'll figure it out."

The jeweler continued, "I think you should talk to someone who can help you plan this properly. Do you have a caseworker or anyone who helps you with, you know, life stuff?"

Vincent hesitated before mentioning Lisa from the Community Support Center. "Yeah, there's Lisa. She offered her help."

"That's perfect," the jeweler said with encouragement. "Give her a call. Tell her about your plans. She can help you sort out the details, maybe even find you some financial assistance or a program that can help with the travel expenses."

Vincent hesitated slightly when considering asking for help, but he also recognized the wisdom of the jeweler's advice. He nodded slowly. "Okay."

"Good," the jeweler said, patting Vincent on the shoulder. "It's a smart decision."

A feeling of guidance washed over Vincent for the first time. A call to Lisa, he thought, might just be the first real step towards seeing his mother again.

After leaving the shop, Vincent was overwhelmed with various emotions. There was fear for what awaited him in Kansas, but also relief at having shared a piece of his burden. The jeweler's kindness, unexpected and sincere, was a small beacon of hope in his troubled life. Vincent felt a connection to someone, marking a significant moment in his life that reminded him of the value of human compassion. The waft of food lingered in the air, causing his stomach to growl louder. He turns to the Chinese Restaurant next door. One meal before leaving won't hurt.

IV

The Golden Dragon teemed with the lively sights and sounds of the Year of the Pig celebrations. Red lanterns hung from the ceiling, gently swaying and casting a cozy, warm glow that enveloped the families and friends seated around tables adorned with mouthwatering, steaming dishes. Laughter and chatter filled the air, mingling with the tantalizing aromas of sizzling meats and rich spices.

Vincent stepped into the restaurant, the dim lighting casting a cozy ambiance over the otherwise lively space. The noise and color seemed to amplify his sense of isolation. He moved through the crowd, his movements hesitant, his clothes, a worn out hoodie and stained jeans marked the difference from the well-dressed patrons. He chose a table against the wall, turning away from the restaurant's lively heart. Around him, children giggled as they chased each other between tables, their parents indulging in animated conversations. Couples shared intimate glances while enjoying meals together. It was a scene of communal joy and belonging, something Vincent longed for.

Vincent's eyes scanned over the menu, each page revealing a variety of mouthwatering dishes. Hunan beef with its promise of spicy warmth, succulent Shanghai soup dumplings waiting to burst with flavor, crispy Peking duck glistening with a caramelized glaze, Szechuan eggplant in a garlicky, tangy sauce. There were delicate steamed fish dishes infused with ginger and scallions, and hearty Mongolian lamb, redolent with the aroma of cumin and chili. He noted the vibrant greens of bok choy in oyster sauce and the comforting simplicity of congee, a rice porridge that spoke of home cooking. The list goes on and on from the fiery kick of mapo tofu to the subtler, anise-infused braises of red-cooked pork. There were Cantonese dim sum selections, an array of delicate parcels like shrimp har gow and pork siu mai, alongside northern Chinese staples like hand-pulled noodles drenched in rich bone broth.

When the waitress came, Vincent pointed to these and more, a mix of rich and simple, spicy and mild, his choices a random selection driven by his insatiable hunger rather than culinary preference. His voice was low, almost hesitant, as he ordered.

The waitress, raising her eyebrows in surprise at the quantity, jotted down his order. As for Vincent, he made an effort to fade into the background, wanting to dissolve into the joyful ambiance of the restaurant. He slouched in his seat, tugging his worn hoodie tighter as a shield from others' gazes. His eyes, once sharp and alert, now darted around, avoiding any direct contact, searching for shadows and corners to hide in. The nearby laughter of a birthday group and the soft murmur of an elderly couple's conversation stressed his solitude. In the vibrant and welcoming ambiance of the Golden Dragon, Vincent strived to be a solitary presence, constantly observing his surroundings and withdrawing into himself.

When the first of his dishes arrived, Vincent's facade of calm disintegrated. The sight and smell of the food unleashed something primal within him. A steaming platter of Peking duck, its skin roasted to a perfect crisp, glistening under the restaurant lights, was set before him. Beside it, a dish of Hunan beef emitted wafts of chili and garlic, the meat tender and richly coated in a spicy sauce.

The waitress laid down a bamboo steamer and lifted the lid to reveal delicate Shanghai soup dumplings, their thin skins holding a fragrant broth and a morsel of savory pork. Next came the Szechuan eggplant, its deep purple hues striking against the bright red of the chili oil, the aroma hinting at a complex blend of spices.

Vincent's eyes widened, and he felt a surge of saliva in his mouth. With his eyes fixed on the plate of food, he reached for the chopsticks, his mouth watering. He started with the duck, tearing into the crispy skin and succulent meat with an intensity that was almost ferocious. He moved quickly to the beef, the heat of the chilies stoking the fire in his belly.

Around him, the restaurant's patrons took notice. Conversations faltered as people turned to look at the man attacking his meal with such desperate voracity. A child's voice piped up, loud in the sudden hush, "Mommy, why is that man eating like that?" The mother hushed her child, but her own eyes were wide with curiosity, yet concerned.

Vincent was barely aware of their stares. He devoured the dumplings, not even pausing to let the steam escape, the hot broth scalding his tongue. Then he reached for the eggplant, relishing the hit of garlic and the numbing tingle of Szechuan peppercorns. As he devoured each dish, his hunger momentarily abated, but he couldn't escape the nagging realization that it was just a temporary fix.

His presence caused a disturbance, spreading discomfort throughout the room. The sounds of laughter and merriment in the restaurant faded as Vincent's solitary struggle cast a shadow over the festive atmosphere.

The restaurant manager, Mr. Chen, had been observing Vincent with growing concern. As Vincent's eating became increasingly frantic, Mr. Chen made his way over to his table, his expression professional. "Sir, I'm sorry, but your... your way of eating is causing some distress among our guests," he said carefully, trying not to offend.

Vincent, his mouth full, looked up in shock, his chopsticks frozen mid-air. "What do you mean?" he demanded, his voice rising. "I'm a paying customer, just like everyone else!"

Mr. Chen hesitated, aware of the growing number of eyes on them. "I understand, sir, but we have families here, children... your behavior is... it's a bit disruptive."

Vincent slammed his chopsticks down, anger flaring up. "So what? I'm eating, not doing anything wrong!" His voice echoed in the now quiet restaurant, drawing gasps from the nearby tables.

A father with young children interjected, "Listen, you need to calm down."

Vincent turned to the man, his frustration boiling over. "Go fuck yourself and mind your business!" He stood up, towering over the table, his face flushed with anger.

The situation escalated quickly, patrons standing up, some trying to intervene, others pulling out their phones.

During the chaos, Vincent caught a glimpse of a young child clinging to her mother, eyes wide with fright. The sight pierced through his anger, hitting a nerve. He looked around at the scared faces, the concerned staff, and the disrupted joy of the evening.

A rush of shame flooded Vincent's senses as he fully grasped the impact of what he had done. Without another word, he reached into his pocket, pulled out a couple of hundred-dollar bills he got from selling the Rolex, and threw them on the table. Then, with his head down, he pushed his way through the crowd and hurried out of the restaurant.

***

The chill of the night air barely registered against his heated skin as Vincent stood alone in the dimly lit alley beside the Golden Dragon. With the door closed, he was immediately struck by the absence of noise, surrounded only by a suffocating silence. He leaned heavily against the rough brick wall. He could feel the coarse surface scratching against his skin, his gasps for air mirroring the heaviness in his heart.

His mind replayed the scene over and over; the frightened faces of the patrons, the worried look of the manager, the sharp cries of the child that had cut through his anger. It was as if he had been watching someone else, a stranger driven by primal urges, far removed from the person he once was or hoped to be. The realization struck him hard, a jarring wake-up call to the chaos his life had become.

Vincent closed his eyes, trying to steady the tumultuous emotions swirling inside him. The sound of his mother's voice echoed in his mind, a distant but constant reminder of the love he still held onto, the connection that remained unbroken despite the years and miles that separated them. It was this connection, this faint glimmer of hope, that he clung to now in his darkest hour.

With a shaky exhale, Vincent pushed himself off the wall. The few hundred dollars he had left from the Rolex sale felt like a small fortune in his pocket, a lifeline thrown to him in a sea of turmoil. Determination began to seep through the cracks of his despair. He decided it would be best to see his mother, despite the relentless hunger. This will give him some semblance of peace, some sense of normalcy in the chaos that was his existence.

Stepping out of the alley and into the night, Vincent looked towards the distant lights, waving his hands. "Taxi!" He called out. For the first time in what felt like an eternity, Vincent felt a flicker of hope ignite within him. A guiding light in the darkness, leading him towards a reunion that held the promise of redemption and the chance for a new beginning.

V

Vincent stepped out of the cab at JFK International Airport, his heart racing. He had his boarding pass ready thanks to the kind Turkish jeweler. However, he felt a gnawing hunger that clawed at him with little relief. Clutching the remaining money from the Rolex sale, he entered the terminal, overwhelmed by the sights and sounds.

The terminal seemed to stretch on endlessly, shops and cafes just opening up for the day's business. The smell of fresh coffee and pastries wafted through the air, taunting him. He knew he should eat something before the flight, but the thought of parting with even a small amount of his precious funds made him hesitate.

Vincent found a seat in a less crowded section and sat down, his eyes focused on the boarding pass. It wasn't just a piece of paper; it was the gateway to his past, to a mother he hadn't seen in years, and to answers he wasn't sure he was ready to face.

As the time for boarding approached, Vincent found himself caught in a slow, heavy march towards Gate 15. Each step echoed the tumultuous mix of emotions churning within him. He was not just leaving a city; he was leaving behind a life that had been both his refuge and his prison, stepping into a realm of uncertainties and long-buried memories.

The airport's intercom system crackled to life, its voice a monotone contrast to the internal chaos Vincent was experiencing. "Attention passengers, Flight 527 to Wichita, ICT, is now boarding at Gate 15. Please have your boarding passes and identification ready."

Vincent shuffled forward, his fingers tightening around the worn edges of his boarding pass. The surrounding sounds – the click of suitcases, the murmur of conversations, the distant laughter of children – all seemed to blend into a distant, indistinct hum. His focus was singular: the gate, the plane, the journey ahead.

"Sir, can I see your boarding pass and ID?" the gate agent asked as Vincent reached the front of the line. Her smile was routine, her eyes briefly meeting his before scanning the documents.

Vincent handed them over, his throat tight as he tried to muster a response. "Here you go," he managed, his voice a hoarse whisper.

"Thank you, Mr. Porcher. Enjoy your flight," she said, handing back his documents.

Vincent nodded, his response lost in the sudden announcement that echoed through the terminal. "Final boarding call for Flight 527 to Wichita. All passengers should now be at Gate 15."

Stepping onto the jet bridge, Vincent felt a strange sense of detachment. The narrow passageway felt like a tunnel between worlds, a bridge from his past to an uncertain future. He boarded the plane, the air heavy with the scent of recycled oxygen and faint traces of perfume and cologne.

Finding his seat by the window, Vincent sank into it, his gaze locked on the tarmac outside. He watched as luggage was loaded, as the ground crew signaled to each other with practiced efficiency. The world outside seemed both incredibly close and impossibly far away at the same time.

As the plane taxied to the runway, Vincent's thoughts were a whirlwind. New York, with all its chaos and struggle, was receding into the distance, becoming a part of his past. Ahead lay Kansas, the land of his childhood, and the mother he hadn't seen in years.

Deep within him, the familiar pangs of hunger continued clawing at his stomach, a constant reminder of his battle. Yet, in this moment, they seemed distant, muffled by the pounding of his heart and the rush of emotions flooding his mind. His usual urge to seek out food was there, but it was subdued, overshadowed by the magnitude of his journey.

Vincent pressed his forehead against the cool window, watching as the city became a patchwork of lights, then disappeared into the darkness. He was airborne, bound for Wichita, bound for a confrontation with his past and, perhaps, a chance at reconciliation. The engines roared, lifting the plane higher into the sky. Vincent experienced a brief moment of freedom, as if the high altitude could separate him from the clutches of his disorder. But the gnawing hunger persisted, a reminder that no matter how far he traveled, it would always be a part of him.

VI

As Vincent gazed at the airplane window, his focus was on the rolling clouds, yet a gnawing hunger that plagued him on multiple levels consumed his thoughts. The steady hum of the aircraft offered a little distraction from the turmoil within. The elderly woman next to him, noticing his distant gaze, ventured a conversation. "It's beautiful, isn't it? The clouds, I mean," she said, her voice soft and tinged with warmth.

Vincent turned towards her, offering a faint smile. "Yes, it's... peaceful," he replied, his voice barely above a whisper.

"I always find flights to be a good time for reflection. A pause from the life on the ground," she continued, her eyes gentle and understanding. "Are you visiting family?"

Vincent hesitated, then nodded. "My mother. I haven't seen her in years."

"Oh, that's wonderful," she exclaimed, her face lighting up. "Reunions can be so healing."

He looked at her, the words 'healing' and 'reunion' resonating within him. "I hope so," he said, his voice tinged with a mixture of hope and uncertainty.

"There's something about returning home, isn't there? It stirs up all sorts of emotions," she mused, her gaze drifting towards the window.

Vincent found himself drawn into the conversation despite his internal struggle. "Yeah, it can get complicated," he admitted, feeling a rare sense of connection, however fleeting.

The woman nodded, her expression empathetic. "Life is rarely simple, my dear. But sometimes, facing our past can open doors to the future."

As the flight continued, Vincent continued to engage with the woman, her words offering brief interludes from his thoughts.

***

As the plane began its descent, Vincent felt a subtle shift within him. The woman's kindness, though a small gesture, had pierced his isolation, offering a glimpse into a world where connections, however brief, mattered.

The terminal buzzed with activity as people moved around him, each wrapped up in their own world. In the middle of the crowd, Vincent felt an uncanny detachment, but also a burgeoning connection to the world he had kept away. With each step he took through the terminal, Vincent felt the pull of his past growing stronger, drawing him back to a time and place he had left behind. The hunger that gnawed at him was a constant companion, yet now it was joined by an increasing curiosity about what lay ahead. His mother, the town he had once called home, the unresolved feelings he harbored, all awaited him, and he felt a mixture of apprehension and a newfound resolve to face them.

VII

The rural landscape, once a picture of beauty and serenity, now carried a hint of melancholy. Vincent stepped off the bus onto the familiar dusty roads of his Kansas hometown. The expansive sky stretched endlessly above, and the scent of dry grass filled the air, transporting him back to his childhood days. The town, with its sparse collection of buildings and the wide, open fields beyond. He walked down the quiet main street, his footsteps kicking up small clouds of dust. The old general store, with its faded paint and creaky wooden sign, stood just as he remembered.

A few heads turned, notices Vincent's presence. Curious gazes following him from the porches of weathered houses. In a place where everyone knew each other, his return after so many years was an unusual sight.

"Vincent?" came a voice from behind. Turning, Vincent saw Mr. Jacobs, the elderly owner of the local hardware store his father Thomas used to frequent. His face was lined with age, but his eyes were still sharp. "Never thought I'd see you back here."

"Me neither," Vincent admitted. "I heard my mom is not feeling good."

Mr. Jacobs' expression softened. "Ah, yes. She's at Via Christi Hospital. Been there a few weeks now."

The news struck Vincent harder than he expected. His mother, hospitalized and alone, had been waiting for him. Guilt gnawed at him more than his hunger ever could. Memories flooded back – the smell of his mother's cooking, the sound of her laughter, the warmth of her hugs. He also remembered the harder times, the arguments, and the day he left, driven by a hunger he couldn't understand or control.

***

Vincent steps out of the Uber that parked in front of the Via Christi Hospital St. Francis. With every step towards the hospital, Vincent's heart raced with a blend of apprehension and an urgent need for reconciliation. The modest building, with its faded brick facade, stood in stark contrast to the sprawling urban hospitals he had seen in New York. Here, in the heart of rural Kansas, everything seemed smaller, more intimate. The heaviness of his emotions made every step he took feel like a monumental journey.

Upon entering, the hospital's interior was quiet, almost hushed, as if in recognition of the gravity of his visit. The fluorescent lights flickered overhead, casting a sterile glow on the linoleum floors. Vincent's footsteps echoed down the empty corridor. He paused outside the door to his mother's room, his hand hovering over the handle. His heart was a mix of emotions - guilt for the years lost, fear of what lay on the other side of the door, and a deep, aching love for the woman who had given him life. This was more than a threshold. It was a bridge to a past he had left behind and a future he was yet to understand.

Taking a deep breath, Vincent opened the door. The room was dimly lit. The only sound was the soft beeping of medical equipment. There, lying in the bed, was his mother. Her appearance was frail, a shadow of the vibrant woman he remembered. In that moment, Vincent knew that no matter what had passed between them, the bond between mother and son remained unbroken.

"Mom," he whispered, his voice thick with emotion.

At the sound of his voice, his mother's eyes fluttered open. Despite the weariness etched on her face, her eyes lit up with a recognition that transcended her illness. "Vincent," she breathed, a smile touching her lips.

Vincent moved closer, taking a seat beside the bed. He reached for her hand, feeling the fragility of her grip. "It's me, Mom." he said, mouth quivering. "I'm home."

His mother squeezed his hand, her gaze studying his face. "Look at you," she said, voice soft. "You've grown so much."

Their conversation unfolded slowly, bridging the gap of years with stories and memories. Vincent spoke of his life in New York, the struggles he faced, and the overwhelming hunger that had dominated his existence. His mother listened attentively, her eyes mirroring a vast ocean of emotions - sorrow, empathy, and unconditional affection.

"I can't believe I let your father send you away," she said, her voice weak but resolute.

"No, Mom, it's okay. I'm here now."

"But I won't be," she said, eyes welling up.

Vincent's eyes brimmed with tears as he absorbed her words. This was the acceptance he had craved, the understanding he had missed. "I wish I had come back sooner," he confessed.

"There's no right time for anything," his mother replied gently. "What matters is that you're here now."

They spoke of her illness, the reality of her condition hanging heavily between them. But even in the face of this, there was peace, a feeling of coming full circle.

As the hours slipped by, Vincent felt a transformation within himself. This reunion, fraught with emotion, was also a balm to his long-tormented soul. In his mother's presence, he felt a deep sense of belonging, like a sturdy anchor in the chaotic sea of his life.

Eventually, his mother drifted into a light sleep, her breaths shallow but steady. Vincent sat beside her, watching over her. He reflected on the journey that had brought him here, on the roads he had traveled both physically and emotionally.

This homecoming was not just a return to a place or a person. It was a return to himself, to the parts of him he had lost along the way. As he sat there, the pangs of hunger seemed less oppressive, like it's no longer in control. For the first time in a long while, Vincent felt a flicker of hope, a sense that maybe, just maybe, he could find a way to heal.

SLOTH
TIK TOK TIK TOK...

I

Sophie's thumb flicked upwards unconsciously, each swipe on her phone a bridge from one video to the next. A dog wearing a superhero cape tumbled into a pile of leaves — a brief chuckle.

Swipe.

A teenager with a spotty face and hopeful eyes danced awkwardly in a cluttered bedroom, seeking fleeting online fame – a momentary smirk.

Swipe.

An ad for a vibrant, cartoonish mobile game – a vacant stare.

Swipe.

An endless stream of dogs.

Swipe.

More stupid dances.

Swipe...

As she lay sprawled on her bed, the artificial light from the screen cast a glow on her detached expression, standing out against the commotion in the living room. The sudden crash of shattering glass jolted her. Her heart raced. She hesitated, the dreamlike trance of her digital world breaking. Reluctantly, Sophie turned her head towards the open door.

Her parents' voices, sharp and loaded with frustration, cut through the air. "No money!" her father's voice boomed.

"We have bills! We have rent!" her mother retorted. Each word, a dagger, twisting in Sophie's gut, amplifying a worry she tried so hard to ignore. She shut her door quietly, the muffled sounds of the argument seeping through, a constant reminder of a reality she wished to escape.

She turned to her desk. A fortress of unfinished homework and crumpled notes stood as silent sentinels of her academic neglect. She rummaged through a torn folder, her hands trembling slightly. The deadline wasn't due till next week, she reassured herself. But even this small relief was short-lived. The familiar ping of a TikTok notification beckoned her back. Just one more video, she thought, as minutes turned into an hour lost in the digital abyss.

***

The next morning, the consequences of her digital escapism greeted her harshly. She missed the bus, arriving at school just as the first-period bell rang. In English class, Mr. Brighton stood at the front, his tall frame casting a long shadow over the whiteboard, where "Fahrenheit 451" was written in bold letters.

Sophie slumped into a seat at the back, her mind foggy. Under the desk, she resumed her ritual, swiping through TikTok, disconnected from the lesson. A text bubble from Jessie popped up: "LOOLLLLLLL." Sophie flicked it away, her attention snagged by a clip of the Russia/Ukraine conflict. She swiped on.

"Ms. Sophie Williams!" Mr. Brighton's voice sliced through her daze.

Sophie fumbled, almost dropped her phone, stuffing it into her backpack. "Uh, yes, Mr. Brighton?"

"I saw you on your phone." His tone was calm but firm.

Sophie's cheeks burned with embarrassment. "No, you didn't," she mumbled, avoiding his gaze.

"Fine. Then can you tell me about the mechanical dog in our book?" he asked.

Sophie's mind went blank. "The what?" Panic fluttered in her chest.

Mr. Brighton sighed, disappointed. "You haven't read the chapter, have you?"

Sophie's eyes darted around the room, her classmates' stares prickling her skin. "S-sure I did," she lied.

"Then you should be able to answer."

Her voice was a faint squeak, words failing her. But the bell mercifully rang, signaling the end of the ordeal.

As her classmates hurried out, Mr. Brighton called out, "Remember, five chapter summaries due Monday!" Then, turning to Sophie, he added, "Could you stay for a moment, Ms. Williams?"

Sophie lingered, her heart pounding as the room emptied. Mr. Brighton looked at her, concerned and frustrated. "How are you doing in your other classes?"

"Fine," Sophie lied again, staring at her shoes.

"That's not what I've heard," Mr. Brighton said, pulling out a document from a file on his desk. "You've failed exams since January." He handed the paper to her, a concrete record of her academic decline.

Sophie glanced at it, then away, feeling a knot of anxiety in her stomach. "It's nothing," she mumbled.

"If it's 'nothing,' then I assume you won't have any trouble with a special project I have in mind." Mr. Brighton's voice was stern now.

Sophie's eyes widened. "What project?"

"I'm assigning you a presentation on *Fahrenheit 451*. Summarize the chapters, present to the class, and I'll consider waiving your failed grades."

"Oh, come on, Mr. Brighton. That's not fair," Sophie protested weakly.

Mr. Brighton raised an eyebrow. "Not fair? I'm offering you a chance to turn things around."

"It's a lot of work," Sophie said, her voice a mixture of desperation and defeat.

"Ms. Williams, you need to decide what's important. Your future or your phone?" Mr. Brighton's words struck a chord, but Sophie remained silent, lost in thought. But it was really because her mind was drawing a blank. "You're dismissed," he said finally, turning away.

Sophie snapped out of it and shuffled out of the classroom, her feet dragging against the linoleum floor. Each step felt heavier than the last, as if she were wading through an invisible swamp. Mr. Brighton's words hung heavy over her, an inescapable, looming specter. Inside, a tumult churned: dread mixed with a faint, flickering spark of challenge, one she felt unprepared for. Pausing outside the classroom, she leaned against the cool wall. Thoughts and feelings crashed within her like a tumultuous sea. The corridors echoed with the laughter and chatter of her peers. She closed her eyes for a moment, taking a deep, shaky breath. The familiar ping from TikTok in her pocket tempted her, promising a quick escape to her digital haven. But this time, Sophie hesitated, her hand hovering over the device.

There was a new awareness within her, a nagging voice whispering of change, of possibilities beyond the screen. Sophie remembered how her phone had become a refuge, an escape from the endless arguments at home and the feeling of inadequacy at school. With a reluctant sigh, she pushed the phone back into her pocket and pushed off the wall. Her eyes, once glazed with indifference to hide her pain, now flickered with a glint of determination, however uncertain. "Where to begin?" The question, once drowned out by the noise of viral videos and endless scrolling, echoed in her head, no longer rhetorical but a challenge to be embraced.

II

Sophie's bedroom was a chaotic mess. Clothes lay in unruly piles, like forgotten islands in a sea of clutter. Stacks of paper, unsorted and neglected, adorned her desk. Makeup kits and supplies sprawled across the floor and dresser, some of the contents staining the mirror. Socks dangled from the dresser, intermingled with bras hanging limply, as if in defeat.

She collapsed onto her unmade bed, the mattress sighing under her weight. The weekend was here, a time for rest, yet restlessness gnawed at her. Sophie's gaze swept over the room – her sanctuary and prison all at once. Her fingers instinctively reached for her phone, her escape hatch from reality. As she flicked through TikTok, the laughter and music from the app filled the room, drowning out the silence of her disarray.

A text message from Jessie popped up, snapping Sophie back to the world outside her digital bubble. "Sophie!! Did you see what I sent you?" Jessie's excitement was obvious even through text.

Sophie's lips curled into a half-smile as she watched the video Jessie had sent – a staged kidnapping on Zoom for a class. She texted back, half-joking, half-serious, "Girl, I wish that happened to me."

Jessie's response came with a wide-eyed emoji, "You want to get kidnapped?!"

"Brighton is trying to ruin my life," Sophie replied, her fingers tapping the screen with sarcasm.

"Wanna meet up at the park?" Jessie suggested.

Sophie hesitated, her eyes drifting to the pile of unopened books. "I feel lazy tonight," she texted back, though a part of her yearned for a change, a break from the endless scrolling.

Jessie was persistent. "C'mon please. It'll be fun!"

Sophie stared at the glowing screen, her thumb hesitating over the keyboard. The invitation from Jessie flickered on the display, captivating like a distant lighthouse in a foggy sea, offering companionship, yet surrounded by uncertainty. The comfort of her digital world enveloped her, a familiar haven in a tumultuous sea of thoughts. However, beyond the confines of her room, through the window, the real world loomed – a landscape brimming with unpredictable adventures and chaotic beauty.

With a hesitant sigh, Sophie started typing, her decision feeling like stepping off a cliff. She tossed her phone onto the bed and stood up, her movements mechanical. As she rummaged through her wardrobe, her mind raced with conflicting thoughts. The soft fabric of her favorite hoodie brushed against her fingertips, a tactile reminder of her usual evenings spent cocooned in her room, lost in the endless scroll of TikTok.

But tonight would be different.

She pulled out a pair of jeans and a simple t-shirt, clothes that felt like a costume of normalcy. As she dressed, the disorder of her room seemed to close in on her, the piles of clothes and scattered belongings compared to the curated perfection of the TikTok world.

Sophie glanced at her reflection in the mirror, the smudges of makeup from days past staring back at her. A deep breath filled her lungs, and she attempted to smooth her tangled hair, trying to muster a semblance of the carefree spirit her friends always seemed to radiate. Yet, beneath her attempts, lay a tangle of emotions. Her shoulders sagged under the burden of her family's discord, the constant pressures of school, and the isolating embrace of her social media world. Each aspect fought for space, adding to the oppressive feeling that seemed to keep her stuck. The recent arguments between her parents haunted her thoughts, darkening her once vibrant demeanor.

Grabbing her phone, Sophie slipped it into her pocket, its presence a lifeline back to her sanctuary. With one last look at her chaotic room, she stepped out into the night.

She pulled her hoodie tighter around her. Her hair, usually a cascade of unruly curls, was pulled back in a hasty ponytail, a few strands escaping to frame her face. Her deep brown eyes, often hidden behind a screen, now observed the world with apprehensive curiosity.

***

The park was a mixture of teenage life. There was laughter, chatter, and excitement with their phones ever-present as they recorded themselves trying to be TikTok famous. The air was crisp, carrying the sounds of music and youthful exuberance.

Sophie scanned the crowd, spotting Jessie, her platinum blonde hair reflecting the park lights, her laughter ringing clear above the din. She was the unspoken leader of their group, always full of ideas and daring challenges.

Nearby, Heather leaned against a tree, her long brunette hair flowing down her back. She had an air of nonchalance, her wittiness hidden behind a facade of indifference. In her black leather jacket and ripped jeans, she exuded a cool confidence that Sophie often envied.

Kate, the smallest of the group, buzzed around like a hummingbird, her movements quick and full of life. Her short stature was no indication of her presence. Her vibrant personality filled the space around her. The bright shade of red that she dyed her pixie cut matched her fiery spirit flawlessly.

Sophie approached them shyly, feeling akin to a forgotten book being rediscovered on a familiar shelf — present yet distinctly out of place. Jessie spotted her first, her face lighting up with a welcoming grin.

"Sophie! You made it!" Jessie exclaimed, pulling her into the group.

Sophie's smile was hesitant, yet genuine. 'Yeah, I'm here,' she replied, her voice weaving a delicate balance between nervousness and excitement. The departure from her usual solitude in her room, her safe haven, filled her with relief.

The girls huddled together, their animated conversation creating a vibrant atmosphere of friendship. Sophie looked at her friends, seeing them afresh, beyond the confines of a phone screen. At this moment, they were more than just profiles and posts. They were vivid, real, and beautifully complex.

As the laughter and chatter of her friends continued, Sophie's gaze wandered across the field. The park was alive with clusters of teens, each group in their own world. Her eyes then fell upon another group, distinctly different from the rest. They were the school athletes, and among them was Megan.

Something about Megan stood out, not just for her athletic build, but for the air of focus and discipline that seemed to surround her. Her hair was pulled back in a sleek, no-nonsense ponytail, and her posture exuded a confidence that came from physical prowess. She was laughing at something one of her friends said, her face lighting up in a way that showed her genuine enjoyment of the moment.

For a brief instant, as Megan turned, her eyes met Sophie's. It was a fleeting connection, a momentary crossing of paths in a sea of people, but it left an indelible mark on Sophie. In Megan's gaze, there was no recognition, just the casual glance of a stranger, but for Sophie, it felt like a glimpse into a different world.

Sophie turned back to her friends, but part of her mind remained on Megan. She couldn't help but admire Megan's athletic grace, so different from her own haphazard way of moving through life. Sophie admired Megan's ability to embody focus and intentionality, qualities she desperately desired in her own chaotic existence.

Jessie's voice brought Sophie back to the moment. "Sophie, you there?" Jessie teased, waving a hand in front of her face.

Sophie blinked and smiled sheepishly. "Yeah, Jess, sorry. Blanking out."

"Girl, you always do." Jessie laughed. "You need to start focusing more."

As the night carried on, Sophie found herself stealing glances at Megan and her group. They were practicing some kind of drill, their movements synchronized and fluid. Then Sophie turned to the aimless wandering and dancing of her own group. There was something within her. There was admiration and a faint spark of aspiration. Could it be something Sophie wanted?

Jessie was in her element, dancing in front of her friends, who filmed her with their iPhones from different angles. "I feel weird," she confessed after a few takes.

Sophie watched from the sidelines, her friends' voices blending into the background. She observed their interactions, their carefree attitudes. It was a world she felt a part of, yet detached from at the same time.

Heather, always the outspoken one, commented on Jessie's dance. "Maybe you should put your hair in a bun," she suggested. "That way, it doesn't flail around hitting your face."

Sophie remained silent, lost in the maze of concerns stirred by Mr. Brighton's assignment. With a sharp exhale, she muttered almost to herself, "Maybe if I start early, it won't be so bad." Her friends responded with collective groans at the mention of schoolwork, underscoring the gap between her worries and their carefree enjoyment.

As the evening progressed, the discussion shifted towards more personal matters.

"So, what's everyone's plan after graduation?" Heather asked, her tone tinged with both curiosity and a hint of anxiety.

Jessie kicked at the grass, her gaze thoughtful. "I'm thinking of taking a gap year, travel maybe. There's so much out there to see."

"I just want to get into a good college," said Kate, her voice steady but her hands fidgeting with the hem of her shirt. "My parents are expecting it."

Sophie listened, her own thoughts a jumbled mix of uncertainty and dreams yet to take shape. She remained quiet, her response lost in the labyrinth of her own worries about the future.

Heather glanced at Sophie, a slight frown on her face. "Any big plans, Sophie?"

Sophie hesitated, thinking about the assignment and her broader uncertainties merging. "I... I'm not sure yet," she finally admitted, her voice barely above a whisper, reflecting the chaos of her inner world.

The group fell into a thoughtful silence, each lost in their contemplation of the future, the night sky above them a vast canvas of possibilities.

Sophie lay on the field, staring up at the vast expanse of sky, her friends' voices a distant echo. "I just want to be rich and say fuck everything," she murmured, a blend of jest and earnest desire.

Jessie, ever the optimist, pulled Sophie to her feet. "We now have TikTok to help us all get famous and rich," she declared.

The conversation drifted to finding a unique angle for their videos. "Everyone is doing dances, though. We need to do something new," Heather pointed out.

Sophie, inspired by a sudden spark of creativity, suggested, "Let's do all four of us. Four different hairstyles doing the same dance or something."

The girls rallied around the idea, excitement building. But as they set up their phone to record, it tilted over. "Goddamn it," Kate muttered, a moment of frustration in an otherwise spirited night.

***

Finally, after arriving home from a fun night without the worry of responsibilities, Sophie lays in bed. The image of Megan's focused expression lingered in her mind. It was a silent call to something she couldn't quite name, a challenge to step beyond the familiar confines of her current existence.

Sophie felt a yearning to break free from her routine. Inspired by Megan's discipline, she contemplated a different path, one filled with intention and growth. As she drifted off to sleep, an idea took root in her. Tomorrow would be the start of something new, a step towards a self she longed to discover.

III

Sophie sat at the kitchen table, her attention torn between the low view count on her latest TikTok video and her half-eaten bowl of cereal. The video from last night – her and her friends awkwardly dancing to "7 Rings" – played on a loop, watching her attempts to fit in. Her mother's weary voice cut through the silence, bringing her back to reality. "How was your night, sweetie?"

"It was fun," Sophie mumbled, the word feeling hollow as she scrolled past the video.

"I didn't want to bother you, but Mr. Brighton called," her mother continued, her hands busy washing dishes, her back to Sophie.

Sophie's heart sank, guilt welling up inside her. "Mom, he's lying. Whatever he's saying."

Her mother paused, turning to face her with a furrowed brow. "He's lying about waving your failed exams? That doesn't sound like something he'd lie about."

Sophie froze, her fingers tightening around her spoon. "Wait, he told you that? Why?"

"To make sure you get the homework done," her mother replied, her voice laced with concern.

Sophie's emotions churned – a blend of reluctance and the dawning realization that things couldn't continue as they were. "It's just... I don't know, Mom. I'll do it. But presenting in front of everyone..." Her voice trailed off, the thought alone was enough to quicken her pulse.

"You're on TikTok all the time. How are you shy?" her mother asked, a hint of irony in her voice.

Sophie set her bowl down, unable to meet her mother's gaze. She didn't have an answer. After a silent mutual agreement, Sophie helped with the dishes. As she left the kitchen, she couldn't miss the worried look on her mother's face. "Hey, are you okay, Mom?" she asked, her voice softening.

Her mother's eyes lingered on the running water, her expression distant. "I'll be fine, sweetie. Just focus on yourself, and things will be okay," she said, managing a strained smile.

***

In her room, where the morning sunlight streamed through the window, the disarray seemed to mock her – clothes strewn like fallen leaves, papers in disheveled piles, and makeup scattered as if in the aftermath of a storm. The chaos of her life materialized before her eyes. With a hesitant hand, Sophie picked up *Fahrenheit 451*, its unturned pages looming before her like a rocky mountain to be climbed. The book felt heavy from the responsibility it represented.

Her phone buzzed with a familiar urgency, a notification from Jessie flashing on the screen. Sophie's instinct was to reach for it, to dive back into that digital world. But something stopped her. Her fingers, which usually swiped and tapped with mindless ease, now rested on the book's cover. She was at a crossroads, and for the first time, the path of escape wasn't the one she chose. Setting the phone aside, she felt a small but significant victory within her.

Opening the book, Sophie began to read. Ray Bradbury's complex and unfamiliar words cast their spell, gradually. The world of *Fahrenheit*

451, with its intense imagery and haunting foresight, captivated her. She found herself drawn into the narrative, the dystopian world mirroring her own sense of entrapment in a digital age.

The further she went, the more the task of the presentation consumed her thoughts, like a vine slowly wrapping around her mind. What had seemed like an insurmountable obstacle took on the shape of an opportunity. With each chapter, her understanding grew, and with it, her confidence. The themes of the book – censorship, losing intellectual freedom, the power of knowledge – resonated with her, sparking thoughts and ideas she didn't know she had.

The process was a stark contrast to her TikTok endeavors. Where creating videos often felt fleeting and superficial, this was different. It required a deeper level of engagement and critical thinking, something that her hours on social media rarely demanded.

By the time she closed the book, the sun had shifted in the sky, casting long shadows across her room. The mess around her remained, but something within her had changed. The initial dread of presenting had evolved into a budding curiosity. How would her own interpretations and perspectives be received by her classmates?

Sophie fights the urge to reach for her phone that sat next to her book. Instead, she moved her phone to her nightstand, that sits far from her computer desk. Then she reached for a notebook, her hand steady. Ideas flowing, words spilling onto the page with an ease that surprised her. This was a change to the rigid creativity she often felt while crafting TikTok content. This presentation was no longer just a school assignment; it had become a canvas for her ideas, a platform to articulate not only her insights on the book but also her reflections on herself. It was a realization that perhaps true creativity and expression lay beyond the confines of her phone screen.

In her quiet room, with the last rays of sunlight fading, Sophie gained a newfound sense of purpose. The journey ahead was still uncertain, but she was no longer the same person who had feared to take the first step.

***

Come Monday, with a fresh start but a heart heavy with apprehension, Sophie approached Mr. Brighton. "I'll do the presentation," she declared, her voice more confident than she felt.

Mr. Brighton looked at her, a glimmer of surprise in his eyes. "Good," he said, offering a small nod of approval.

A fleeting glimpse of Megan, the school's track star, through the classroom window became a moment of quiet revelation for Sophie. She watched as Megan moved with a purposeful grace across the field.

Later, as Sophie walked down the school corridor, her eyes were drawn to a brightly colored flyer pinned to the bulletin board. "Track and Field Team Tryouts," it announced boldly. She stood there for a moment, lost in thought. The image of Megan's effortless athleticism played in her mind, a stark contrast to her own uncoordinated attempts in gym class. Yet, there was an undeniable pull, a curiosity about what it would be like to move with such confidence and control.

Acting on a whim, Sophie pulled out her phone, not for the habitual dive into TikTok, but to capture a photo of the flyer. The tryout details, now saved in her phone, leading to a potential path – one that could mirror the poise and strength she saw in Megan.

That evening, Sophie's usual routine of endlessly scrolling through TikTok was replaced by a different kind of screen time. She found herself absorbed in videos of track athletes, their bodies in motion demonstrating strength and agility. Their dedication and discipline, so vividly displayed in each clip, struck a chord with her. It was a world she had never given much thought to, yet now it fascinated her, offering glimpses of what discipline and commitment could look like. Lying in bed, Sophie felt a gentle stirring of hope, an unfamiliar but welcome sensation. The relentless cycle of aimlessness and distraction that had defined her days was beginning to crack, making room for new aspirations. Instead of scrolling through her phone, she drifted off to sleep, her mind filled with dreams of uncharted paths and endless opportunities.

Sophie woke up refreshed and began to tidy her room, finding solace in bringing order to her space. Each book placed on the shelf, every paper neatly stacked on her desk, felt like a small triumph against the persistent chaos that had engulfed her life. But this sense of control was short-lived. As she stepped out of her room, the remnants of a heated argument between her parents hung heavy in the air. Her mother, standing in the kitchen with eyes brimming with tears, was a silent testament to the strife. The argument, Sophie knew, was about their precarious financial situation – a recurring theme that had become the soundtrack of their family life.

Her father, a figure of frustration and despair, had been grappling with unpaid bills and looming debts. He had been working at Summit Auto Manufacturing for years, but the plant had recently been hit hard by economic downturns. The threat of layoffs and cutbacks at the factory had become a constant source of tension. The problems at work had infiltrated their home, creating an atmosphere of despair and hopelessness.

Sophie had overheard fragments of their conversation – the missed mortgage payments, the rising costs of living, and the dwindling savings – each word a strike against the fragile stability of their family. And today, it seemed, her father had reached his breaking point.

The sound of the front door closing behind him was jarring. It reverberated through the house, echoing like the final, dissonant note in the long symphony of their strained family life. Sophie stood frozen, the resonance of the door closing mirroring the fracture in her family's foundation. The sad reality of her father's departure marking a turning point she couldn't yet fully grasp.

Her mother's face, usually a mask of resilience, had crumbled under the weight of the moment. Each tear that streaked down her cheek was a silent echo of years of strain and struggle. Sophie felt helpless watching her, the matriarch of their little family, so vulnerable and defeated. The mounting family tensions, the sound of her father's car fading into the distance, coupled with her own academic struggles, now seemed to form a relentless tide, threatening to pull Sophie under. The walls of the only world she had known seemed to be crumbling around her.

She retreated to her room and sank onto her bed. The reality of her father's departure settled in like a heavy fog. Her thoughts were all over the place once again, each one colliding with the next – the pain in her mother's eyes, the uncertainty of what lay ahead for their family, her own struggles with attention and focus that now seemed insignificant in the grand scheme of things. She grabs her phone, scrolls through TikTok for a brief escape, watching cute dog videos and funny dances. Then she hears the ticking of the wall clock above her desk.

In that moment, surrounded by the clutter of her life, Sophie realized the gravity of the change she had undertaken. It wasn't just about tidying her room or doing well in a presentation. It was about learning to swim against the tide that threatened to overwhelm her. With a deep, shaky breath, Sophie tossed her phone aside and stood up. She continued to pick up the clothes from the floor, each piece folded a small step toward bringing order to her world.

IV

Sophie stood on the edge of the track field, her heart pounding in her chest. The plaid surface stretched out before her, its lanes like ribbons unfurling into the distance. She was surrounded by the electric energy of athletes, their warm-up routines executed with fluidity and confidence. She felt out of place in her new running shoes, which still felt stiff and unfamiliar.

As the coach blew the whistle, signaling the start of practice, Sophie took her place hesitantly at the starting blocks. She watched the other runners crouch, their bodies coiled. The whistle sounded again, piercing the air, and the group exploded forward in a burst of speed. Sophie pushed off awkwardly, her limbs uncoordinated and out of sync.

The first lap was a revelation of her own physical limits. Her breathing grew ragged almost immediately, her lungs straining for air. Her legs, unaccustomed to the rigorous demand of sprinting, burned. Around her, the other athletes, including Megan, seemed to glide effortlessly. Megan's stride was long and steady, her breathing controlled compared to Sophie's labored gasps.

As they transitioned to middle-distance running, Sophie's initial burst of adrenaline waned, and fatigue set in. Each step felt heavier, and the track seemed to stretch endlessly. She watched Megan and the others rounding the curve, their forms becoming distant blurs. The sound of their spikes striking the track in rhythmic unison was disheartening. Sophie faltered, her pace slowing. She could hear the coach's voice, distant but insistent, urging the runners on. "Keep your form, drive with your arms, stay on the balls of your feet!" The words swirled around her, a litany of techniques that she couldn't seem to translate into action.

As practice drew to a close, Sophie's muscles ached and her body felt drained. Sweat spilling from her face to the tracks. She collapsed onto the infield grass, her chest heaving, every breath more painful than the last. At least she had completed the practice. Maybe not gracefully, nor effortlessly, but she had endured.

Megan approached, a water bottle in hand, and offered a small smile. "First days are the hardest," she said, sitting beside Sophie. "I'm Megan."

Sophie looked up at Megan, her face flushed and sweat-drenched. "I'm... Sophie." her voice heaved with exhaustion, knowing damn well that track was more than just physical exertion. It was a test of willpower and determination.

As they rested on the field, Sophie and Megan chatted casually, the conversation flowing more easily than Sophie had anticipated.

"I've got this big presentation for English," Sophie confessed, picking at the grass. "It's on *Fahrenheit 451*. I've just started it, but it's kind of overwhelming."

Megan's interest piqued. "I love that book. We had it last year."

Sophie looked at her, surprised. "You read it? I just started."

"Yeah, it can be a bit much at first," Megan agreed, sitting up. "But once you get into it, it's fascinating. The whole idea of censorship, the value of books. I can go on and on about it."

Sophie felt a glimmer of relief, the daunting task of the presentation seeming slightly less intimidating with Megan's enthusiasm. "Maybe you could help a girl out," she admitted, half-joking.

Megan's response came with a genuine smile. "I'd be happy to. Sometimes just talking about it helps."

Sophie's gratitude was immediate and immense. Megan's offer was a lifeline, a connection she hadn't realized she needed. "That would be amazing, Megan. Thank you."

Sophie sensed a profound unity with Megan as they both rose to their feet, their connection surpassing their shared experience on the track. Megan was not just a peer but someone who could guide her, not only in navigating the physical challenges of track but also the intellectual challenges of her studies.

V

In the quiet corner of the school library, Sophie and Megan sat huddled over a scattered array of notes and copies of *Fahrenheit 451*. What once seemed a daunting task of preparing for the presentation had transformed into an engaging challenge, thanks largely to Megan's insights. Sophie leaned over her notebook, her pen moving swiftly as she jotted down ideas. "So, Bradbury is highlighting the dangers of being perpetually distracted, right? How it leads to a society disconnected from reality and lacking depth?" she asked, looking up at Megan after pondering one of Mr. Brighton's questions.

Megan nodded, tucking a strand of hair behind her ear. "Exactly. Think about how that relates to today's world, especially with our obsession with technology and social media."

Sophie's eyes lit up with understanding as she drew connections between the novel and her own life. "It's crazy how a book written so long ago can say so much about what's happening now," she mused. The novel's themes, which centered around the attraction of shallow entertainment and the gradual decay of genuine interactions, resonated deeply with her when she realized how often she mindlessly scrolled through social media.

As they pored over the pages of *Fahrenheit 451*, the conversation gradually shifted, branching out into more personal territories. Sophie is curious about Megan. "So, what are you looking to do after you finish high school?"

Megan leaned back in her chair, her eyes reflecting enthusiasm. "Well, I would like to go far in track. Maybe compete at an Olympic level. It depends."

Sophie listened, intrigued. "Depends on what?" she asked.

"If I do well enough to get a scholarship for college." Megan said, gaze drifted towards the window, as if visualizing her aspirations.

"I think you'll get it. You're amazing." Sophie said genuinely. She felt the admiration for her friend's clarity of vision.

Megan blushes, looks away, but is thankful for the compliment. "And what about you? What are your dreams, besides finishing this presentation?" Megan asked, turning the focus back to Sophie.

Sophie hesitated. Her dreams had always been a blur, obscured by the fog of her daily struggles. "I don't know," she admitted. "Just been so caught up in the craziness at home and trying to keep up at school. I haven't really thought about the future, to be honest."

Megan nodded understandingly. "What craziness at home? What's going on?"

Sophie fidgeted with the corner of a page, hesitant. After a moment, she looked up, meeting Megan's concerned gaze. "It's my parents, mostly. They've been fighting a lot... about money, future stuff. And now, my dad has left. It's just... a lot to handle."

Megan's expression softened with empathy. "I'm so sorry, Sophie. That sounds really tough."

Sophie shrugged, a bitter-sweet smile touching her lips. "Yeah, it's been rough."

Megan reached across the table, offering a reassuring squeeze to Sophie's hand. "You're stronger than you think. And hey, you've got me now. We'll get through this presentation, and who knows? Maybe we can figure out the rest together."

Sophie felt a warm sense of gratitude wash over her. Megan's words, simple yet sincere, offered a glimmer of hope in her muddled world. "Thanks, Megan. That means a lot," she said, her voice steadier than before.

Megan smiled, her eyes twinkling with encouragement. "Anytime. Now, let's get back to this. We're going to ace it!"

Sophie pondered Megan's words, thinking about the different pieces that formed the puzzle of her life: her family's struggles, her own battles with focus, and her newfound venture into track. Megan, with her well-defined goals, stood as a symbol of resilience. Yet, Sophie knew there was more beneath the surface. She glanced at Megan, her curiosity piqued. "What about you? You seem so focused, so sure about your future. Is your family like that too?"

Megan let out a small sigh. "Not exactly. It's mostly just me and my dad. He's... well, he's pretty tough. He was an athlete, played all kinds of sports and was an Olympic wrestler, and he never really got over his career ending early. So, he's kind of living through me, I guess."

Sophie's eyes widened slightly, understanding dawning. "That sounds really hard."

"It is, sometimes," Megan admitted. "He pushes me a lot, which is great for track, but it's a lot of pressure. I'm trying to find my own path, you know? One that's about what I want, not just what he didn't get to do."

Sophie nodded, a new sense of connection blossoming between them. "I guess we all have our stuff to deal with, huh?"

Megan smiled, a touch of warmth in her eyes. "Yeah, we do. But I believe we'll get through it as long as we help each other."

Understanding the challenges Megan faced with her father — his strict discipline and high expectations — painted a more complex picture for Sophie. It wasn't just about natural talent or ambition; Megan's achievements were also a response to the intense pressure from her father, a way to seek his approval and fulfill unmet dreams. This realization showed Sophie that everyone has their battles, some visible, others hidden beneath the surface of apparent success. Sophie found their conversation to be a sincere and comfortable exchange. It felt natural to tell Megan her problems as she offered an ear to listen, unlike her best friend Jessie.

As the afternoon ended, Sophie packed up her notes, feeling accomplished. "Thanks, Megan. I don't think I could've made these connections without your help," she said.

Megan smiled. "Girl, it was all you. I just helped you see what was already there."

Sophie felt a surge of gratitude.

The girls made their way to the track field for practice. The air was crisp, signaling the onset of evening. With her running gear on, Sophie felt a surge of determination as she made her way onto the track. Her body was ready for the physical challenge, her mind still hectic with the ideas from their study session.

As they began their warm-up laps, Sophie felt the strain from her previous session; her muscles were sore, her movements slightly stiff. Despite the discomfort, she pushed through, each stride gradually growing more confident. The initial awkwardness of her first day lingered, but there was a budding sense of determination in her steps.

During the grueling set of intervals, Sophie's muscles ached with the effort, a stark reminder of her body's adaptation to this new challenge. She leaned on the mental resilience she had started to develop during her presentation preparation. Each lap felt tougher than the last, mirroring the complexity and challenges she encountered in *Fahrenheit 451*. The physical exertion, while daunting, was becoming a metaphor for her journey – each step a testament to her growing endurance, both physical and mental.

As practice ended, Sophie bent over, hands on her knees, catching her breath. She had pushed herself harder than ever before. Her thoughts were a mix of Bradbury's dystopian imagery, like the Mechanical Hound prowling the streets with its needle of poison, and her own aspirations for a future beyond the confines of her current existence.

Sophie's heart swelled with pride as she walked off from the track. She had not only survived the practice, but had also found a rhythm in her running that echoed the newfound rhythm of her life. Rather than an obstacle, the presentation was seen as an opportunity to showcase her progress.

In the dimming light of the day, Sophie realized how far she had come. The presentation, once a source of dread, was now a project she looked forward to. And in Megan, she had found an unexpected ally, a friend who saw the potential in her that Sophie was only just beginning to see in herself. After parting ways with Megan, Sophie walked towards her home and felt a familiar tightness of anxiety in her stomach. There was strained silence. Then her phone buzzed — a message from Jessie. Opening it, Sophie's heart sank. "Heard you're hanging with Megan now. Too cool for us?" the message read.

Sophie's fingers hovered over the keyboard. She wanted to explain, to tell Jessie about her struggles and her efforts to change, but the words seemed laughable. She typed a response, trying to bridge the growing gap. "It's not like that. Just trying to sort some stuff out. We're still friends."

Jessie's reply was swift and cold. "Don't care. You need to get back to the real world with real friends." The message stung. Sophie felt a painful lump form in her throat. Her efforts to improve herself were costing her friendships. The very connections she once relied on.

As she pocketed her phone, her mother's voice cut through the silence. "Sophie, we need to talk about your father." The words hung heavy in the air. Her mother looked tired, her eyes reflecting a deep sadness. The conversation that followed was a blur. Her father wasn't coming back anytime soon. The family dynamics they once knew were changing, and with it, their financial stability was in question. Sophie felt as though the ground was shifting beneath her feet. The reality of her family falling apart was overwhelming.

Feeling suffocated by everything, Sophie retreated to her room. She sat on her bed, the walls of her sanctuary closing in on her. Her mind raced as she thought about the family crisis, the presentation, the fallout with Jessie. It was all too much to bear.

In a moment of desperation, Sophie reached for her phone. The moment she opened TikTok, she was instantly transported to a different realm where her worries seemed to fade away. As she scrolled through video after video, time slipped away unnoticed. Laughter, music, and mindless content filled the void, numbing her.

Hours passed. Darkness filled the room, leaving only the faint illumination of her phone. Sophie was lost again in the digital world, the one place where the complexities of her life seemed to vanish. But as the night wore on, guilt crept in. She had slipped back into old habits, wasting more precious time that she knew should be spent working on the presentation.

VI

The morning sun streamed through the classroom window, casting long, warm beams across the rows of desks. Sophie sat, her hands clasped tightly under the table, as Mr. Brighton's words echoed through the room. "Remember, today is the deadline for your summaries. And Sophie, I expect you to be ready to present them to us." His gaze settled on Sophie for a moment.

Her heart sank. The deadline. In the chaos of the past few days, it had slipped her mind entirely. Panic rose like a tide within her. The consequences of her previous night's escape into social media now loomed large, consuming her with regret.

As the bell rang, signaling the end of class, Sophie's classmates rushed out, but she remained seated, frozen in her realization. She watched as Mr. Brighton began to gather his papers, his expression focused and stern. Gathering every ounce of courage, Sophie approached him, her voice barely above a whisper. "Mr. Brighton, I... I need to talk to you about the presentation."

He looked up, his expression softening slightly at her distress. "Yes, Sophie? What about it?"

"I... I missed the deadline," she admitted, her voice shaking. "But I have it prepared. I just lost track of time."

Mr. Brighton's face hardened. "Sophie, this presentation is a significant part of your grade. You knew the deadline weeks ago."

Sophie's eyes filled with tears, the gravity of her mistake weighing heavily on her. "I know, and I'm so sorry. Things at home have been difficult, and I..." She trailed off, unable to articulate the issue that had led her to seek refuge in the hollow comfort of her phone.

Mr. Brighton regarded her for a long moment, the lines on his face etching deeper in contemplation. Finally, he sighed, his demeanor reflecting a battle between his disappointment and his empathy. "Fine, Sophie. I'll give you one more day. But this is it."

Sophie's relief was immediate, a relief. "Thank you, Mr. Brighton. Thank you so much. I promise I'll have it tomorrow."

He nodded, his gaze lingering on her a moment longer.

As Sophie left the classroom, she couldn't help but feel a rush of gratitude. Mr. Brighton's willingness to give her another chance was more than just an extension of a deadline; it was a belief in her potential. She knew she couldn't let this opportunity slip through her fingers.

After speaking with Mr. Brighton, Sophie found Megan in the busy cafeteria. Sophie appeared urgent and quickly shared her situation. Megan's response was immediate and supportive. "Okay, let's find a quiet place and get to work," she said, her tone firm.

They settled into a secluded corner of the library, surrounded by a fortress of books and notes. Megan listened intently as Sophie outlined what she had prepared so far, her eyes scanning the pages of scribbled text. "You've got a solid start here," Megan encouraged, pointing to a paragraph. "But let's get deeper into Bradbury's symbolism. Think about how it reflects our society today, the dangers of complacency."

Sophie leaned forward, her mind igniting with ideas as Megan spoke. They discussed the novel's themes, Megan gently guiding her to make connections between the dystopian world of *Fahrenheit 451* and the realities of their digital age. The parallels to Sophie's own life weren't lost on her. The lure of screens, the numbing comfort of endless scrolling. It was all a modern echo of Bradbury's warnings.

As the day faded into evening, Sophie's presentation began to take form, guided by Megan's insights. She found herself drawn to the character of Clarisse in 'Fahrenheit 451' - a young girl who questions the world around her, much like Sophie had begun to question her own reliance on social media. Clarisse's curiosity and willingness to see beyond the surface resonated deeply with Sophie, reflecting her newfound desire to engage more meaningfully with the world.

Rehearsing her speech, Sophie's voice grew steadier, her words imbued with conviction. Megan nodded along, occasionally interjecting with suggestions and praise. "See, you're getting the hang of it," Megan encouraged, her smile reinforcing Sophie's growing confidence.

Another parallel struck Sophie as she spoke about Guy Montag, the book's protagonist, whose transformation from a complacent fireman to a questioning rebel mirrored her own shift from passivity to action. Montag's awakening to the hollow nature of his society and his subsequent quest for knowledge echoed Sophie's journey from the distraction of TikTok to the pursuit of deeper understanding.

The concept of the Mechanical Hound in Bradbury's narrative, a symbol of mindless conformity and control, now took on new meaning for Sophie. She likened it to the relentless pull of social media algorithms, designed to keep users engaged but not enlightened.

With each rehearsal, the themes of 'Fahrenheit 451' intertwined more closely with her own experiences. The words of the novel, once just a story, now became a reflection of her path from mindless consumption to mindful action, from being a passive receiver of information to an active seeker of knowledge.

Sophie felt a swell of confidence, a far cry from the uncertainty that had gripped her that morning. As she spoke, the world of 'Fahrenheit 451' ceased to be a distant dystopia and transformed into a mirror of her own awakening.

They packed up their things as the library announced closing time. "Thank you again, Megan," Sophie said, a genuine warmth in her voice. "You're saving my life right now."

***

The next day was the day of the presentation. Sophie stood at the front of the classroom, the familiar faces of her peers before her. She took a deep breath, feeling a surge of purpose coursing through her. This was her moment to share not just an analysis of a book, but a piece of her own journey.

"As many of you know, Ray Bradbury's *Fahrenheit 451* is not just a story about firemen burning books. It's a warning," Sophie began, her voice steady and clear. "A warning about a society that's lost its way, where censorship was in control and independent thinking a thing of the past." She paused, making eye contact with her classmates. "But how relevant is this today, in our world?" she asked rhetorically. "In the digital age, we don't have firemen burning our books. Instead, we have something far more insidious. The endless stream of content on social media, numbing our minds, and dulling our capacity to think critically." Sophie felt a personal connection to each word she spoke. "I'll be honest, I was a victim of this digital dilemma. Hours and hours spent scrolling through TikTok, losing myself in an ocean of mindless content. It was my way of escaping reality, but in doing so, I was censoring my own ability to engage with the world around me, to think deeply and independently." The room was silent, her peers absorbed in her words.

Sophie then spoke about the symbolism of Bradbury's world, the nuanced portrayal of its characters, and the unnerving similarities between the fictional society and our own. She spoke of the salamander and the phoenix, symbols of rebirth and resilience, drawing parallels to her own awakening from a digital trance. She analyzed the characters' complex motivations and the chilling relevance of their actions in a world increasingly dominated by technology.

Sophie took the moment to drive her point home. "Bradbury feared a future where people would willingly give up on reading, on being informed. Today, we might not be burning books, but we're at risk of something similar. Every hour we spend lost in our phones is an hour we're not spending learning, questioning, growing." She looked towards Mr. Brighton, then back to her classmates. "It's time to wake up, to choose how we use our tools. Let's not walk blindly into the dystopia Bradbury feared." As she concluded, Sophie felt a gentle breeze of relief and pride brush over her. "Thank you," she finished, her voice a whisper of triumph.

The class erupted into applause, louder and more genuine than she had ever heard before. Mr. Brighton gives a nod of approval.

Sophie took her seat, her heart still racing, but her mind was now clear. She had not only delivered a presentation. She had shared a part of herself, and in doing so, had taken another step in her journey of self-discovery and change.

As Sophie approached the track field, the pounding of her heart echoed in her ears. She could feel her nerves tingling and her excitement building up inside her. The stands were packed with students and parents, their enthusiastic cheers adding to the vibrant atmosphere. She could see her mother, classmates and teachers, some with phones in hand, ready to capture the highlights of the meet. The entire school seemed to buzz with anticipation, the rivalry with the neighboring school adding to the fervor.

Sophie arrived just in time for her event. She quickly changed into her running gear, tying her shoelaces with steady hands. Her mind focusing on the race and determination to prove herself on the track.

As she stepped onto the track, the noise from the stands seemed to fade into the background. She was in her zone now, every sense attuned to the race ahead. Taking her position, she felt the familiar texture of the track beneath her spikes. The lanes stretching out before her like paths to potential victory.

The starting gun fired, and Sophie exploded forward. Her strides were stronger than ever, the result of weeks of rigorous training and newfound mental resilience. She could hear the crowd, a distant roar, but her focus was solely on the track, on the rhythm of her breathing, and the steady beat of her heart.

Surrounded by the swift motion of more experienced runners, Sophie held her own pace. She felt every muscle engage, a testament to her newfound strength and endurance. Each lap was a challenge, but she met it head-on, pushing beyond the limits she once thought insurmountable.

As she rounded the last curve, Sophie's focus was not on outpacing the others but on beating her own best time. The cheers from the stands melded into a distant roar, spurring her on. She tapped into every reserve of energy, her strides determined and strong. Crossing the finish line, she didn't come first, but that wasn't her goal. Instead, she shattered her personal record, coming in fifth — a remarkable achievement for a newcomer.

Sophie slowed to a stop, gasping for breath, a surge of pride welling up within her. She had competed against herself and had come out stronger. This race wasn't just about her position; it was a testament to her growth, a breaking free from the doubts and fears that once crippled her. As her teammates came over to congratulate her, Sophie knew this was just the beginning of her journey, a journey marked not by victories over others, but by the triumphs over her past limitations.

For a moment, time stood still. Sophie had done it and turned to see her teammates rushing towards her, their faces alight with joy and pride.

In the stands, the crowd was ecstatic in celebration, with their phones capturing the victorious moment, immortalizing it in digital memory. Sophie, once lost in the world of social media, now stood at the center of a real-life moment of triumph, a moment far more rewarding than any online validation.

***

As the evening settled in, the track team found themselves seated in the lively ambiance of a local restaurant, a celebratory dinner courtesy of the school. The air was filled with the clatter of dishes and the buzz of excited conversation. The team, still riding the high of their victory, shared stories and laughter over plates of food.

Sophie and Megan sat side by side, their conversation turning reflective amidst the celebratory noise. Megan nudged Sophie, a playful grin on her face. "You know, it's incredible how far you've come in such a short time," Megan said.

Sophie nodded, feeling quietly satisfied. "Yeah, it feels surreal. I am feeling more alive than ever."

Megan's expression turned thoughtful. "It's funny how life works, isn't it? We get so caught up in what's on our screens that we miss what's happening right in front of us."

Sophie smiled. "Exactly. I'm just grateful I found my way here, to this moment."

Megan agrees with a nod. She sips a cup of seltzer, turned to Sophie with a curious look. "So, after today, have you thought about what's next? Like, what do you want to do in the future?"

Sophie paused, her fork idly spinning in her hands. The question had been lingering in the back of her mind, but the events of the day had brought it to the forefront. "I've been thinking about that a lot lately," she admitted. "Today made me realize I'm capable of more than I ever thought. Maybe I could aim for something in sports, and media. After doing this presentation on Bradbury's book, I was thinking maybe journalism or communication studies," Sophie mused, her voice tinged with newfound aspiration.

Megan's eyes lit up. "I think that's perfect for you."

Sophie's smile revealed a promising sense of possibilities. "I guess it is. I think I'm ready to start exploring that path wherever it leads."

Their conversation drifted to plans for the summer, training regimes, and classes for the next school year. As they talked, Sophie felt a deep sense of gratitude for Megan's presence in her life. Her friend had become a guiding force, helping her see her potential and encouraging her to pursue her passions.

The team's laughter and chatter around them were a reminder of the journey she had undertaken. From a solitary figure lost in the digital world to a young woman discovering her place in the real one. The night was a celebration of her personal victories, of battles fought and won within herself.

As the night ended and the team bid farewell, Sophie experienced a profound feeling of serenity. Walking home under the starry sky with Megan by her side, she reflected on her journey.

WRATH
UNFINISHED LESSONS

I

Catholic school was hell. Divine Grace Catholic School, to be exact. I adjusted my position in the tiny chair in the back of the last row of five. Seven desks lined up in a row, each one perfectly spaced. Each student at the school wears identical maroon uniforms and spends most of their time talking about current pop culture trends. The girls would argue which Spice Girls they can relate to, the popular boys would argue about who was a better rapper, DMX or Ja Rule; others would talk about *The World is Not Enough* or *Sleepy Hollow*; the nerds would brag about who caught what Pokémon and how one would kick the other's ass if only they had a link cable. I felt a wrench of disappointment as I listened to everyone's conversations. The sound of joy in their voices, laughing, and conversing made me feel like I didn't belong. It felt lonely.

My eyes felt so heavy and sticky, I had to fight to keep them open in the early morning. I couldn't even mumble a word to my buddy David Khoury, who kept asking about *Pokémon Yellow*.

"Tony, did you hear me?" David asked.

I snapped out of it and turn to him. "What?" I replied.

"Did you catch Mew, yet?"

"Don't you need GameShark for that?" I asked after a second of genuine confusion.

"No, man, there's a strategy. It's on the internet."

"I don't have internet, David, remember?" This is my hundredth time telling him.

Christina O'Neil waltzed into the classroom, her perfume filling the air, and her blonde hair perfectly coiffed. Her neat attire comprised a white blouse paired with a plaid skirt that incorporates the school's maroon and gray colors. The skirt falls to just above the knee, in line with the school's modest guidelines. Then she showed off her perfect teeth that didn't see braces once and wore a gold bracelet that cost more than my mother's rent. Everything about her screamed, 'I'm privileged.' Her only flaw was her high-pitched voice that would cost me another pair of glasses. Although, I wouldn't mind. Putting on these glasses made me look like a budget-friendly version of Harry Potter. Christina gently placed her pink Barbie bookbag under her desk, then pulled out her math workbook. The rest of the class followed. The sheer power she had because everyone wanted to be like her. No one could even come close to matching her academic excellence.

I shoved my hand into my black JanSport backpack, rummaging through the crumbled failed exams and torn workbooks. My eyes darted awake. I dug deeper through the paper caverns, nearly about to puke out my fast-beating heart. The one workbook I needed the most was not there. Dread consumed me as I observed everyone else engrossed in their math workbooks, my chest tightening and my heart pounding in response. "What's wrong, Tony?" David asked, his tone worried.

"I-I forgot my workbook," I said, voice breaking.

"I knew I should've reminded you."

How can I get out of this? I had to escape. The window was large enough for me to climb out of. Wondered if I could make a move with no one noticing. The door screeched open and my stomach dropped, heart pounding in my ears. I nearly shook in place. Walking into the classroom was the devil herself, Ms. Marie Moffat. The cold, windy weather had left her flat, skinny face bright pink and her lips chapped and blue. Her makeup was a mess, and her hair tangled from her wooly winter hat. She swiftly covered her bruised cheekbone with her brown hair, then tossed her purse behind the leather chair.

The room fell into a hushed silence as Ms. Moffat took her seat behind the enormous desk. "Good morning, class," she said.

"Good morning, Ms. Moffat." The class responded in unison, except for me and a few others.

"Sorry, I'm late. Had to deal with something real quick. Please stand for prayer."

All the students rise and follow Ms. Moffat, performing the sign of the cross, and together we pray the "*Our Father.*" I'm wondering if I pray and actually mean it – will she skip the homework and move on to the lesson? My jittery hands gave away my lack of confidence as I folded them.

"Relax," David quietly told me as we sat back down. "Just bring it in tomorrow."

"She won't accept it. Remember what she did last week with my English homework?" She humiliated me by announcing to the class sarcastically that I finally did the homework. Then she tossed it in the bin and said it wasn't worth it since we're starting a new lesson. Still got an F.

Ms. Moffat sat down and pulled out a math textbook. "Take out your math textbooks and open up to chapter three, page forty-five. Today's lesson we'll be going over fractions."

I hate fractions, but wait... It looked like she won't go over the homework. That's usually the first thing she checked every morning. The Lord answered my prayers. I finally relaxed and opened the math book to chapter three with the biggest grin on my face. Fractions you say, Moffat? All good to me. As I looked up, I double took and saw Christina, waving her hand at Ms. Moffat. "We had homework, remember?" This bitch.

Ms. Moffat slapped her own forehead, knowing her carelessness, and shoved the textbook back in her desk. "Open up to your homework so I can come around and look."

Now, I'm pissed. I hate Christina for this. Even David shook his head.

Ms. Moffat brought her red pen and went to each row, marking a checkmark on the page of the workbook. My heart pounded once again. I hoped the bell would ring or something. With each glance out the window, I was met with the unsettling sight of a few crows, their unwavering gaze locked onto mine. I wanted to take Christina by her pretty little hair and fling her out the window so the crows could rip out her tongue, so she could never, ever speak again. I kept my attention on that scenario until the sound of someone clearing their throat interrupted my thoughts.

There she was as I slowly turned to face the menacing demon towering over me. Her foot tapped on the linoleum tile with her hands over her hips. "Mr. Aoun." She said with a poor attempt to say my last name by pronouncing it as *A-Wan*. I wish I had the balls to scream at her. *It's A-Yoon, you fuckin' bitch!*

She continued, "Where is your homework?"

My words jumbled and rushed, stuttering and mumbling.

She chuckled and shook her head. "Typical, typical, typical. What else is new with you? I even made a bet knowing you wouldn't do it. Looks like I won."

"B-but I did the homework. I just... left it at home."

"B-b-b-but that doesn't matter. It's not here." She said, voice mocking mine.

I really did. But since I missed most of the homework at the beginning of the school year, she'll never believe me.

"You know what? I want to see your backpack." Ms. Moffat snatched my backpack, unzipped it, and dumped the mess of books and crumbled paper onto the floor. She angrily kicked the contents, as if the math workbook would appear. She glanced at the unsigned exams and scoffed disdainfully.

The class observed the situation. The heat in my cheeks was hot enough to keep your hands warm during this brutal season. My eyes welled up.

"Guess I'm going to have to give you detention for a week." She said proudly. "Maybe that'll teach you a lesson not to forget. I'm also going to phone your mother and tell her about all these failed exams you didn't show her. Stupid child."

I heard Christina chuckle. My eyes shot daggers at her. Ms. Moffat suddenly smacked the back of my head with her notepad. My classmates gasped.

"Don't be mad at her because she did her homework. Be mad at yourself for being stupid and incapable of doing anything. If only you could focus on your homework as much as you do on video games, maybe you'll be just as capable. Worthless as usual." With an apathetic gesture, she carelessly tossed my empty backpack to the floor. She turned to David. "Don't help or you'll join him."

I stuffed my books in the backpack one by one, fighting back tears. David felt helpless, which is understandable. I sat back down, buried my face in my arms, and attempted to hide the embarrassment, hoping no one saw. I felt multiple eyes staring at me from each corner. Even though I was only turning ten that month, all I could ever think about was how I was going to kill that bitch.

II

Just thinking about fourth-grade makes me cringe. As I browsed through my old HP Pavilion, I could hear the rumbling engine of Henry's beige 2004 Hyundai as it pulled up on the sidewalk. Through the paned glass of the condominium, I watched him gestured with his hands, mockingly pushing the air in my direction, asking me to bring the trolly. Nothing feels more humiliating than being demanded to get something like a little monkey. But this is what's it like being a doorman. I begin my afternoon duties and assist the asshole with his groceries. "Good afternoon, Tony!" He said. "Finally, they're going to impeach the bastard."

"What?" I said.

"Trump. The impeachment process entering a new phase. The House is strong on this one."

"Oh." I said, just trying to kill the political talk.

"How was your weekend? Do anything fun?"

"Not really. Stayed home with my mom and the pup. What about you?"

"Took the grandkids to see *Frozen II*. You should take your mom to watch it. It's a good movie."

"We'll see." I load up the heavy plastic bags onto the trolly while the chilly wind chips away the dry skin off my knuckles. It's eczema, they say.

"I'm going to look for parking. Send up the trolly to my wife. She's waiting." Henry trekked back to his car as I hurried the trolly back to the seven-story condo and sent the trolly up to the sixth floor. There was a faint sound of Susan's nagging coming from the elevator shaft.

I warm my hands with my garlic breath and raise the thermostat to eighty degrees Fahrenheit. On the security footage showing the sixth floor hallway, a tiny old woman yanks the trolly and drags it to her unit.

Now back to browsing. The laptop screen shows a history of Google searches. *Moffat teacher; Margarette Moffat; St. Anselm's Catholic Academy of 99; Yearbook 1999 St. Anselm's staff.*

It's frustrating to search for hours and still be unsatisfied with the results. Unless she's dead, which I doubt. After all these years since the time this bitch taught my fourth-grade class; did she retire? I don't think I'm being specific enough in my hunt. I know this is her name because it's the only full name I remember while attending that godforsaken school.

Apparently, the name Moffat is a common Scottish surname. Even the full name "Margarette Moffat." Which is weird because this bitch is the only person I know with that specific name. Figured she's unique. Maybe if I search on LinkedIn for "*Margarette Moffat grade-school teacher*" and hit search.

Results show there are three people with that exact name and that exact occupation. One of them is definitely not her because she looks way too old. The cobwebs were showing beneath her eyelids. Another is a high school teacher in New Brunswick with bleach blonde hair, pearly white teeth, and a small nose. In fact, she's actually pretty. Really pretty. Then, the final one is a professor at Miami University. Strangely enough, she looks almost exactly how I remember. A middle-aged shrew with shoulder length hair, a triangle face, and a pointy nose. She definitely aged and put on a few pounds. My hands were shaking as I clicked on the thumbnail to expand it.

This is it. This is the woman. Holy shit. After all these years looking for her. I found her. Her full name is Margarette Lynch-Moffat. I did a deep dive Google search on her. Her Facebook page is the top result. Her profile picture shows her with her two freckled teenage daughters and a thin, bald man in a red plaid shirt. As my heart races, I return to browsing and search "*gun laws in Florida.*" Lo-and-behold, nothing as serious as New York.

At the stroke of midnight, the Upper East Side is much calmer and quieter. Nothing is more peaceful than leaving the building, hearing no traffic coming from the Queensboro Bridge. I still can't contain my excitement about the results earlier today. I give a nod to Greg, the overnight shift doorman who relieved my shift, and head out as I swing my North Face bookbag to my back.

The Q train moves at a slow pace and hasn't had its heating system fixed yet. *Homicide* by Logic blares into my ears as I search through my Samsung Note 10 for gun stores in Florida. There's one near the hotel

I'll book. Should get things done and easier. This bitch won't know what hit her.

I get home, and suddenly I hear a rapid tapping on the hardwood floor. My black and white pit-bull, Baily, jumps on me with joy, tail wagging wildly. His zoomies kick in just like the first day when I found him in the streets of Crown-Heights while I was doing food deliveries for Uber Eats. The worst job with the worst customer service. Baily almost knocks down the colorfully lit Christmas tree my mother worked so hard on. She wakes up for the hundredth time because of the noise he always causes.

Under the dim light in the cozy alcove section of the apartment, I set my bookbag next to the large oak wood dining table and pull out my laptop. I begin my search for cheap airline tickets to Florida while Baily snores away next to me. The rush of adrenaline makes me all jittery. Suddenly, my mother makes her way to the dining area. I quickly shut my laptop, feeling like a fourth-grader that almost got caught searching porn. Though, it's something easier to explain than what I'm doing currently. My mother questions nothing anymore, nor does she care. I'm almost thirty-two. She sits down across from me and takes a sip from the glass cup of ice-cold water.

"I like the tree." I said.

My mother smiles. "Thanks." She turns, admiring the multi-light-colored tree. She doesn't seem conversational now. I mean, it is two in the morning. She rests her head over her knuckles on the dining table, then moves her gray hair away from her light brown eyes. "What are you doing?" She asked.

"Planning my vacation."

"When?" She gives me this what-the-hell look.

"Two weeks from now."

"Where to?" She said, voice concerned.

"Florida, Mom."

She shrugs it off, probably thinking it's over a woman. Something I did a couple of years back when I went to Los Angeles for the first time just to sleep with someone I met off Tinder. My mother heads back to bed. "Just be back before Christmas. We're celebrating your twin cousins' birthday."

I almost forgot about them. I book a flight that will occur two weeks from now, then grab the Switch to do my routine online challenges in *Super Smash Bros. Ultimate,* a game that causes more frustration because of tea-bagging cheaters. If only I could get my hands on those fuckers.

III

The weather hurts. The chilling wind blows against my face, nearly breaking the skin around my nose. On a windy day, the winter spirits never show mercy as the wind whistle past my ears. For once, I'd like the ride with the wind. But, no, it's a fuck you from God himself... if there is one.

I finally make it to the condo after getting off Lexington and 62nd Street at the Upper East Side, where I arrive an hour early as usual. Matt, the morning shift doorman, always greets me with a smile and tells me his long-winded conspiracy theories about the government. Not that I care, but he always has to exaggerate when he talks. For someone who has such a small mouth, he has a lot to say. It's annoying. But I'm a professional and have to nod and smile because of his history of snitching. "I'm telling you, the government killed Epstein," he said, trying to convince me like I care. "Look who he was testifying against. Tell me it wasn't a murder."

"Bro, I just woke up." I said, voice low and tired.

"Fine, fine. But I just had to say it. That's all."

"Let me get ready. We'll talk soon." I said, lying about it. I'll definitely wait till he leaves. I legit don't care about what he has to say. All I care about is how I'm going to plot my mission against Moffat.

Omar, the superintendent, welcomed me into the office with the brightness of his cracked iPhone 6 screen playing Tetris. "When are you getting the iPhone Eleven?" I asked, pointing at the beat up phone.

Normally quiet, he replied, "If it still works, I don't need a new one. Plus, that shit is expensive."

"I hear you. I'm just surprised it didn't shut off on you yet. Doesn't Apple have a chip to shut down your phone if you use it for too long?"

"Now you sound like Matt." Omar remembers something. "Oh, just a heads up. No one can cover your days. You'll have to find someone." Omar returns to his Tetris game.

"Why am I not surprised?" I said.

"See if Matt will cover at least two days." Omar said.

"He'll be working seven days then." I said, knowing this is impossible.

"I would've done it since I'm not working, but you know how the Board is." Omar has always been generous, but his job is to be a porter. Management got in trouble for allowing Omar to cover Matt one day. The Board he speaks of paid time and a half for his day and then they rewrote the rules about employment's schedule and job descriptions.

So far, so quiet. I get the contact information of Professor Moffat from the Miami University's website. As I'm dialing in the number on my smartphone, the lobby desk phone rings. It's management. I answer politely, "Hello, this is Lexington Condos, Tony speaking."

"Tony, it's Paul. What's going on?" Paul said, voice hoarse, like he smoked a pack of cigarettes. He's the property manager who hired me. He's also a big time conservative who Henry, the fat tenant, isn't a fan of.

"I was concerned about my vacation leave." I replied. "I heard no one can cover for me."

"Sorry, unless you can get someone yourself to fill in for you, I don't mind."

But I do mind. Shit like this shows I'm inches away from quitting this poorly run company, but I need the money despite the lack of benefits I'm getting. Fucking credit card debt and student loans. "I'll see what I can do, but to be honest, this vacation is important to me." Here's hoping he understands and will insist on looking for someone as well.

"You know that you're supposed to hand in your leave form a month prior, right? I'm doing you a favor to get someone for the time being."

He's right. But I'm impatient and don't want to wait longer than a month to visit the wicked witch of Florida. I definitely don't want her celebrating Christmas after ruining mine in 1999 by loading me up with tons of schoolwork. Paul and I come to agreeable terms, and now I must look for someone to cover. Meanwhile, I stare at my large smartphone with Moffat's contact info and decide I should call later. I'll just have to ask her if she remembers teaching at St. Anselm's another time.

IV

I take a seat inside the diner, the smell of breakfast wafting in the air, as I try to make out what's beyond the foggy window. This mocha doesn't taste as good as I hoped, but whatever. It's keeping me warm. A black Nissan Altima pulls up. A tall, thin man, my best friend David, dressed in scrubs that probably still smelled of antiseptic, thanks his Uber driver and rushes into the diner. The chilly wind making him shiver and blow warm air into his hands.

We hug it out, then he takes a seat across from me and orders a cappuccino. Then the usual small talk. Asks about my day, how's my mother and Baily, how I'm managing with stress during work. I repeat it back to him and ask about his wife of seven years, who he can't stand. His main concern is my significant weight loss over the course of a few months, haven't been eating as much, nor did he see me at the gym anymore. Maybe it's stress. But I don't think stress would keep me more mellow.

The blonde college-aged server brings the cappuccino, and of course, David flirts with her with confidence that his wife won't find out. He is a good-looking man but is still insecure if he's desirable. His jawline would make any man jealous just to have that feature. I remain quiet, minding my own business until they're done. The server smiles and giggles as she returns to the dark world of minimum wage and Karens. David turns to me with his cheesy smile, pointing out that he still has game. I sarcastically smile back, can care less if he's still got it or not.

"Are you still off next weekend?" I ask.

"I am for the rest of the month." He said before sipping his cappuccino. "Why, what's up?" He leaves the white foam mustache above his lips, thinking it's comical.

"Uh, I'm having trouble at work. I'm going on vacation, but no one can cover for me. I was hoping if you're not doing anything—"

He puts his head down, disappointed. "I don't want to go back doing Paul favors." He said, shaking his head. "When are you going to leave that company, man?"

Here we go with the lecture. I've been working there for almost four years and nothing has changed but more disappointment and annoyance. It's not a future, but no one was hiring at the time, so I took the job when the opportunity presented itself.

David continues, "You should go back to school, do something better. Look at me. After I left that shithole management, I'm in a much more respectable position. I like Paul, don't get me wrong, but the tenants are pieces of shit. How much longer can you take seventeen an hour?"

"You're right. I have thought about it and I do want to leave. But I'm balls deep with creditors."

"Why don't you be a teacher? You have a degree in English."

Goddamn, if he doesn't want to cover, just say so. "I'll consider it." I said, just to get the conversation over with.

David gives a nod, "Look, I got you. Just this one time and one weekend." He said this only because he's feeling guilty. He probably just remembered that time I helped him write his psychology essay last minute, which got him an A and a passing grade on the final. But the real reason is so he can fuck his MILF neighbor before she moved out of state.

"Thank you." I reply. "This means a lot."

Then he asks, "So, where are you going?"

"Florida." I said as I sip my mocha.

"Oh, nice. Yeah, it's much better than here. So much warmer."

"Exactly."

V

The suitcase is ready, my flight is tomorrow, and I'm nervous as fuck. Eating the last meal before I head out. The most delicious grilled chicken and broccoli with garlic lemon sauce drizzled over it. Nothing better than mom's home cooked meal. She would make food inspired by other restaurants so much better that I refuse to order out anymore. It's that good. As I mention seeing David the other day, my mother's eyes lit up with delight. It's been a while since she saw him and his mother. "How's he doing?" She said.

"He's good." I said. "He's a radiologist for NYU Langone now."

"Oh, good for him." She said as she chews on a broccoli. "Why don't you invite him for Christmas?"

"You know, I should." I said, without realizing that David's wife is an atheist. She's a sweetheart, though. Maybe she'll get along with my mother. Then I continue, "He's covering me during the vacation."

"Oh, and Paul doesn't mind?"

"Nah, Paul doesn't care if a bum is covering my shift." A bit exaggerated there, but I don't doubt Paul's thoughts. "As long as someone is at the front desk."

"That's nice of him." Then my mother's smile fades. "David has always been loyal to you. He was with you at St. Anselm's, where your fourth-grade teacher—"

I cut her off because whenever I hear "fourth-grade" or "Ms. Moffat" shivers down my spine. To hear my mother's voice break when she brings it up is the reason I'm heading to Florida. I take my mother's hand and I tell her as I look straight into her watery eyes, "I'm still here, I'm working, and I'm a college graduate. I made it."

"You're right." She takes her other hand and covers mine, warmly wrapping it around her own. "Have you ever thought about forgiving her?" She asks.

I stare at my mother for a moment, processing the question. Did she just ask if I thought about forgiving the monster? I had to ask to make sure. "What?"

"To forgive her. Ms. Moffat."

"Hell no," I said, voice striking, aggressive. "Do you not remember what she did to us? She put us through hell. She humiliated us." My voice almost cracked.

"It was just a thought... maybe that's why I'm stressed. There's this hatred in my heart for her and only her. I thought maybe if I forgave her. I don't think I'd be this angry anymore. You understand what I'm saying?"

"No, Mom, I don't. You're probably stressed because you keep depending on ghost clients in your real estate deals." Clients that claim to present an offer to a house she showed and never show up again.

"My clients are renting the house. We're signing the lease this Sunday."

"Then you'll be fine after that. Just give yourself some time."

"Maybe I am overthinking. It's weird that whenever I get angry, Ms. Moffat first comes to mind." My mother gets up and grabs a cup of water. She drinks it down and takes a deep breath. She is stressed because she hasn't heard from the property owner to set up the lease. I need to sleep and get ready for my flight. I kiss my mother and wish her a good night and good luck.

VI

Class is in session. My classmates and I are making Christmas props for the school play. A Christmas musical of Silent Night. David sits in front of me doing decent work. Meanwhile, Christina, the kiss-ass, cuts the red construction paper with precision. She flaunts about her creativity and plans to be an artist when she grows up. I just wish I could pull her by her ears and shout at her that no one cares, but I'm not an asshole. She shows off her artwork like it's a prize she won just so people can shower her with praise.

David turns to my desk to show me his what's supposed to be a wreath with red crayon scribbled in to be ornaments. He sees my attempt at a Christmas tree. It's not bad, but not perfect. Just decent enough for a B- or C+ but I never cared. All I kept thinking about was that long holiday break we're going to have next week. The gifts and new video games I'll get to play. It really is the most exciting time of the year. I notice Christina looking towards me and at my artwork. Her eyes rolled in disbelief and her head shook in disapproval.

Bitch.

The classroom doors open and the demon woman, Ms. Moffat, walks in. She gingerly touched her cheeks, which were clearly swollen and tender, a sign of her tooth being pulled. At least, that's how I see it, because that shit happened to me when the dentist pulled out my infected molar. Halloween was almost two months ago, yet I still get anxiety as she makes her way to each student, checking on their projects. I quickly picked up some of my broken crayons, their colors mixing as I start drawing some ornaments in my tree. It's still an attempt, just care for the grade. I hear Christina's ear-ringing, high-pitched voice calling out to Ms. Moffat to see her artwork and why it should be "lead prop" whatever the hell that means. Of course, Ms. Moffat smiles enthusiastically and agrees with the spoiled brat.

I'll show her. I cut out yellow construction paper and attempt to create a ten-pointed star, then glued the star at the top of my somewhat decent tree. David noticed this and gave a nod of approval. Looked like the star was my best artwork to date. I was proud of this star. The tree, eh, not so much, but it was doable.

Ms. Moffat went around and observed the artistry of the class. The anxiety was building up. Ms. Moffat got closer and closer. Her eyes flicking back and forth between me and the next student. I took a deep breath as she approached David and his prop. She gives a nod of approval and then she comes over to my desk. "Mr. Aoun." She announced.

"Ms. Moffat." I noticed the class was awkwardly quiet.

She observed my prop. Picked it up, examined it like some kind of art critic. It's like she's looking for a mistake. Some of my classmates had a worried look on their face, some just observed out of curiosity. Christina, herself, had a look of worry. Ms. Moffat just drops the prop on my desk. "It sucks." Just like that. Not "it's okay" not "fix up the ornaments" not "the tree is too thin" just "it sucks."

I looked at the prop, then back to her and genuinely asked, "What's wrong with it?"

"You're really going to ask me 'what's wrong with it?'" She snatched the prop and waved it to the class. "Look at this prop, class. Tony would like to know what's wrong with it?"

I knew this was going to happen. I can sense the stares of disapproval, like a heat wave running through me. Nobody wanted to answer, though. Not even David, who I don't blame. He's in it for the grade and doesn't want to get himself in trouble. I forgave him for not defending me. He felt hopeless. We all did.

Christina abruptly stood up, her voice echoing off the walls as she shouted, "IT SUCKS!"

Ms. Moffat laughed and tore up the prop from the star down. She tossed them in the air, and I saw the pieces of disappointment fall around me like confetti. My eyes well up, my lips quivered as I attempt to hold in my sadness. But tears burst out. Christina was laughing with her entourage of secondary ass kissers. All I could do was bury my face in my arms, let the tears stream down to my cheeks, as they drop on the torn yellow pieces of paper.

Today, as I stare at the lit 10-pointed star, I watched the multi-colored lights dancing off the walls from the Christmas tree. I'm snuggled up next to Baily, whose soft snores fill the room. Reminiscing about the past has got me overthinking of things I wish I could've done. Still can't figure out what was wrong with me, according to this bitch of a teacher. Did I not put in enough effort? What the fuck did I do wrong?

VII

I hate flying and it's been forever since I went to Lebanon to visit my cousins for the first time. When I'm not in control of my environment, my blood rush through my veins like they're in a hurry to reach my entire body. We humans have yet to evolve to such technology since its brand new compared to how old civilization is. The Wright brothers were madmen. Perched by the window, I look out, biting the cuticles off my fingers, becoming increasingly restive as I wait for the plane to take off.

A mother and her toddler son make their way to me. I hope they don't sit... never mind. Her son sits right next to me, and his mother smiles and politely greets me. I give a nod and return to the window and continue having a war with my dry skin on my cuticles.

"Are you scared?" The kid asked.

I turned with a stare, my eyes wide with surprise. "Do I look scared?"

The kid nodded so hard his head almost bounced off his shoulders. His mother is busy scrolling through her phone, laughing and giggling at whatever. "What's your name?" The boy asked.

I give a look and decide maybe I should talk to get my mind off things. "I'm Anthony, but you can call me Tony. What's yours?"

"I'm Frank, but my friends call me Franky."

"Nice to meet you, Franky."

"What's your last name?"

"Aoun."

"Huh?"

"It's Arabic." As soon as I said that, his eyes lit up with fright. He tugs on his mother, telling her what I said. He almost screams out terrorist, but his mother quickly covers his mouth. She apologizes to me, but innocent minded Franky here cries. I slowly turn back to the window, return to my insufferable anxiety-induced habit, knowing that this is going to be a long three-hour flight.

VIII

The PlayStation is hands-down Sony's greatest creation. *Metal Gear Solid, Resident Evil, Tomb Raider, Syphon Filter, Twisted Metal* are just a few examples of many brilliant games. I sat in my room on the recliner that my parents wanted to throw out and played my favorite, *Metal Gear Solid*. The story and gameplay made up for the boxy graphics. Before beginning, I heard in the living room my mother crying.

She curled up on the couch, her face buried in the cushions, and muffled sobs escaping her trembling lips. I don't know what to make of this, but gently tap her shoulder. She quickly glances at me, but can't hide the tears streaming down her face as she swipes them away. "What's wrong?" I asked.

"Nothing." She replied as she fixes her blonde hair. "Go to your room. I'll take care of it. Don't worry."

As I make my way back to my room, I stop and turn back. "Is it about school?"

My mother can't hide her white lies how she used to. So, she nods and bursts out crying again.

I approach my mother and hug her. "It's okay, Mom." I try my best to comfort her.

"You're getting held back." She said in her choked-up voice.

I look up at my mother, confused.

"Ms. Moffat said you failed the finals and will keep you in fourth-grade for another year. But don't worry. I'll fix this. I'll see what I can do. Okay? You'll make it to fifth-grade with your friends."

"Are you sure?" I spoke with an anxious tremor in my voice.

"Yes, Tony. I promise. I just have to figure out what to do. Enjoy the Summer with your friends. Okay?"

From there, I knew things weren't going right. I stared blankly at the home screen of *Metal Gear Solid* reflecting. How am I going to prepare for the embarrassment I'm about to endure in September?

As I made my way to my room, the news about school crept through my mind. I couldn't help but catch whispers of a conversation between my parents in the kitchen. The TV in the living room was still on, its screen flickering with the evening news. It was another story about 9/11, a tragedy that seemed to have changed everything, especially for families like ours.

"Ever since that day, it's been different for him at school," my mother's voice trembled slightly. "They look at Tony like he's... I don't know... responsible?"

My father's response had a hint of bitterness, a rare tone in his voice. "Even me at the site. From the contractors, they stare, and now aren't listening to my authority. I'm not being taken serious anymore. Our name, our heritage. Stained with this political bullshit."

"I know, but what can we do? We can't change who we are."

Those words struck a chord. I remembered the moments in the school's hallway, the way some classmates started avoiding me, and how even some teachers seemed more distant, more critical. I was just a kid trying to deal with school, with Ms. Moffat's constant disapproval, and now this - a shadow cast over me for something I didn't understand, let alone have anything to do with. The cruel irony didn't escape me; here I was, often escaping into *Metal Gear Solid* where terrorists were fictional villains, only to be unfairly labeled as one in the real world because of my race.

IX

I should've been more prepared for this weather. Not saying that this weather is bad, I'm just saying how much I underestimated its warmth. Miami feels welcoming but holy shit, the air is humid. The hotel is pretty decent, with full service. Three and a half stars, according to Google. I got lucky on a deal. It cost me about $500 for the seven days I'm here. The room is pleasant. It's quiet and cozy enough to just relax. What's more important is my mission. I start my search using my Note for the location of Miami University. After that, I continue researching on what this bitch, Moffat, has been up to.

She's quite popular among her colleagues. Many publications in biology and chemistry, along with prestigious prizes for some of her notable work. Fuck, that means if anything happens to her, the media will be all over it.

I lay in bed, wide awake, as the bright sun beams over my room. Random thoughts cross my mind, making me wonder if coming here was a mistake. If I did this out of impulse. If I should continue pursuing this. I look back and remember my mother crying. The rants Moffat would use against me, screaming and yelling at me over missing homework even when it wasn't that big of a deal. She failed me in almost every course she taught me, but I passed the ones she had no influence over, such as art, gym, and computer classes.

Fuck her.

X

There is a Beretta, a Glock, and a Smith & Wesson on the glass counter. I take each one of them and imitate a corny movie line. The gun clerk rolls his eyes. I feel powerful just holding something that can take a life away in a second. Just having control over the fate of someone's life when encountered. Then I look over and I see a Magnum revolver. Now that's a gun. I could feel the roughness of the handle as I tightly gripped the long nose barreled weapon. The clerk warns me that the recoil isn't one to mess with. People underestimate its power and can sprain or even break their wrist when fired. He used the word break, and that's without exaggeration. Before I'm even allowed to buy a gun, I must pass a background check, which will take up to three days. Well, I have a clean record. I never did drugs in my life, and I'm a United States citizen. Plus, I'm on vacation for seven days. Today is my first, and I'm getting a gun.

XI

Since it's my first time in Miami, might as well make the best of it. I visit the university and see my way around. Nice, vibrant place. Students swarm around in the middle of the day. I ask the security about the Biology Department and Chemistry Department. It's a few floors up.

In the halls, I see multiple classrooms in session and offices belonging to professors. My heart sinks to my stomach after reading Moffat's name on the plaque. *Prof. Margarette Lynch-Moffat.* My heart beats quicker than my hands quiver wanting to knock, but I turn away—BAM! I stumble into the witch herself. The documents in a file she carried fall to the floor with a thud. I help stack them up and hand them to her with shaky hands. Ms. Moffat stands there curiously as I step aside for her to go to the office. She's shorter than I expected, and her face looks more like a bulldog's as her cheeks droop down. She unlocks the door, then turns to me as I observe. "Can I help you with something?" She asked.

I shake my head. "No."

"Are you sure? You were about to knock before you almost knocked me down."

"I..." I take a big gulp. It was obvious. She giggles to ease the tension. I continue, "I was just curious about the biology program. Maybe you can spare a minute."

"I can spare two. Come in." She invites me to her office. It looks like she doesn't recognize me. Maybe it's the stubble beard or my thicker eye frames I got last year after breaking my last pair. I really need LASIK.

When I walk into her office, it's so orderly and precise that it's overwhelming. Prizes tucked away in glass cases, collecting dust on the shelves. Miss... Professor, I shall say, Moffat drops her files on the desk and sighs in relief. "You win awards, but the work just keeps piling on."

"I hear that."

She takes a seat and offers me to sit across from her. She clearly doesn't remember me. This is something I should take advantage of. I happily plopped my ass onto the chair, the sound of its legs grinding against the tile floor echoing through the room.

She breaks the ice. "So, are you a student here?"

"No, but I am thinking about getting my master's here." I said nervously. My palms are sweaty and with the back of my hand, I wipe off my forehead.

"Oh, a graduate student! What are you looking to do here?" She said, her voice enthusiastic.

I should've prepared myself for the questionnaire. I can feel the sweat beading on my skin as my blood speeds up. It must be the Florida weather. I take a deep breath and answer. "Something with biology and chemistry."

Ms. Moffat laughs. "Luckily for you, I teach both at graduate levels."

This bitch did not just say I'm lucky to have her teach those courses. Even though I'm not applying, I still feel appalled by her thought process in this. "Of course. Why wouldn't I be so lucky? You are clearly an achiever in your field." I say so as I gesture to the undusted trophies. However, I am curious about her teaching experience since she is teaching something at a high level compared to fourth-grade. "Quick question, have you, you know, taught other levels before?"

She sits back thinking and nods. "I have to say so. I wasn't a fan of it because most of my students were lazy and incompetent. At least with graduate students, I know they're career-driven."

Blah, blah, blah. Still didn't answer my question, though. "I'm talking about lower-level teaching, maybe high school or even, I don't know, elementary school."

This got her really looking back. Probably the first time someone has brought up the past that far back. As she's about to answer, an older professor walks in by surprise. This gray-haired jackass brings up how she's supposed to speak to a group of upcoming graduate students. It's obvious from her eyes that this is a task she doesn't want to do. She puts our brief meeting on hold and to pick it up another time. Before I let out another word, she hands me her business card and rushes out. I look at her card and slip it into my back pocket.

XII

The sky was ablaze with the colors of the setting sun. The hotel had a pool area where many guests hang around. It's breezy and humid. The sun is setting as I sit by the pool after having a swim, just thinking. I see beautiful women in their 20s in bikinis just enjoying themselves. I do fantasize about sleeping with them, but I'm too shy to even approach. Staring at them isn't helping either. Better not to look and continue observing the sunset.

The sudden splash of water against my body broke my peaceful state. One of the young women, a skinny, pale brunette, apologizes with a giggle. I offer a polite smile, my clenched jaw betraying my irritation as she swims back to her friends. She lifts herself up, revealing a light green bikini, and grabs a beach towel to dry off. Her beautiful body got me thinking of things I probably would never do, but I must remain focused on my mission. I think it's those luscious lips that make her innocent features look much more attractive. I quickly look away as she glances back in my direction. She and her friends talk among themselves and laugh. Are they laughing at me? Am I being too creepy? I'll be the bigger man and leave. I admired the sunset enough.

Room service is excellent. Food is great too. I had a full course meal from a salad to a decent size steak, medium rare because only psychopaths eat it well-done. Yet, it still feels pretty lonely here. I'm in sex town Miami and should be out there, going to clubs, having fun, getting laid. Instead, I'm at the hotel alone in bed. What am I doing here exactly?

I call up my mother because I am feeling just a tad home sick. It's been a while since I went on a vacation alone. My mother always holds down an engaging conversation. I miss her and Baily a lot. I discuss my future and how I plan to go back to school and getting my master's, but not here. God, no, not here. Thinking I should take David's advice and be a teacher. Hearing my mother's voice go ecstatic is the reason I'm still alive today. My mother wishes me a good night and to be safe. We hang up and now it's quiet again. I turn on the TV and look for something interesting. There is nothing. I guess it's best to call it a night.

XIII

Temperature drops to the fifties. Wind breakers, blue sky, and deciduous leaves. Summer is officially over. It's the first day at St. Anselm's Catholic Academy. All the students mingle with each other, catching up with what they've accomplished during the summer. All have smiles on their faces. I look around to find David, but he's nowhere around. Turns out, his parents moved him to St. Patrick's Catholic School on Staten Island. Even though there are about thirty-five students in the class, I still feel alone.

Ms. Moffat walks in with a document in hand as the class settles down. She reads through a list of names in alphabetical order of those who advanced to the fifth grade and what room they'll go to. I look away to the window, trying to hide my upcoming embarrassment. I can feel my classmates staring at me. They know Ms. Moffat skipped my name because she pauses after naming the last name that begins with A, stares at me, then starts with the B names. I can hear my classmates whisper amongst each other about how Ms. Moffat didn't call my name. It's like they feel bad for me. I can't help but observe the birds on the branches with admiration, longing for the same freedom they have.

The bitch clears her throat. I turn and notice the class is empty. "Wow, Mr. Aoun." She said sarcastically. "You're still here? You're brave."

I wish I can punch right in her pointy fuckin' nose.

"Oh, don't worry, I won't be your teacher this year. You'll be going to room four-two. Because if I had you again, you'd just waste your time." She said with a smirk on her crusty, chapped lips. She walks out and shuts the lights off, leaving me alone with just the sunlight beaming in the room.

I never saw her again.

XIV

The gun clerk greets me with a practiced, polite smile, masking any concern in his eyes with professional courtesy. After I paid him the three hundred dollars for the Glock, he packs the gun and ammo, then wishes me well. The bag is discreet, but people in Florida know you're carrying. They can sense I'm a first-timer. I can care less. The weather is hot, I'm feeling great. It's time to set up the plan.

I make it back to my hotel and see the same beautiful young woman from the swimming pool hanging with her friends. She glanced my way, her eyes crinkling with the corners of her lips in a mischievous smile, and I couldn't help but return it with a playful grin. Her friends grab her attention to something more interesting. There was a moment I almost forgot about my purpose here. I quickly come to my senses and then make my way to the hotel.

I drop the bag on the bed and head to the bathroom to release two bottle's worth of water out of my system. As I release, my doorbell rings. This concerns me. Housekeeper cleaned the room already. No one knows I'm here. I hastily zip up my jeans, rub some hand sanitizer on my hands, and move towards the door. It's the green bikini girl. She's much shorter up-close, but my God, she's a smoking ten. Maybe she's attracted to me—she hands over my wallet. "You dropped this," she said, her voice raspy.

"Oh." I reply as I take back my wallet.

"Check it out. The money is there."

"I trust you." I don't, but I don't want to appear rude in front of such a dynamite.

"Okay, whatever. Have a nice day." She giggles.

"Vacation?" I asked before she heads out.

"It's my best friend's birthday." She said after a nod.

"I'm here from New York."

"Really? That's so funny. We came from New York."

Sheer coincidence. "Where from?"

"Brooklyn. Bay Ridge."

"I'm... also from Bay Ridge. Are you stalking me?" I think I'm being followed. I look more concerned now.

"Maybe it's the other way around." She giggles.

"I'm Tony, by the way." I said.

"Robyn." She shakes my hand with her cold, boney hand and makes her way to her impatient friends. "See you around, Tony."

"Hope so, Robyn." That felt creepy to say. But she laughed it off and scurries away. I give a quick glance at her from behind. I might get lucky after all.

But back to my mission.

XV

New York City benches are definitely freezing someone's ass off tonight, but not mine. This bench is nice and warm despite getting dark out now. The sprawling campus of the university begins to quiet down, with students trickling out from various buildings. My focus, however, is intently fixed on one particular exit of the science building. This is where Ms. Moffat, carrying her day's burdens, emerges. She exchanges brief pleasantries with a fellow professor before passing by, oblivious to my presence. My disguise — a cap from a local discount store and a strategically kept mustache, not to mention the thick sunglasses I snagged from a nearby restaurant — seems to be doing its job. I watch her for a while, blending into the campus rhythms, before I start tailing her cautiously. There are many cars, perfect to hide behind as I stalk my prey. Ms. Moffat makes her way to the parking garage and approaches a navy BMW. I'm not familiar with models or year, but in my eyes it looks brand new. She opens the backseat and tosses her belongings in. Then she heads for the passenger glove compartment and pulls out from a rolled paper towel a joint.

That's right. Weed.

Based on my knowledge, marijuana remains illegal in the state of Florida, unless medically prescribed. I'm sure that's not the case here, since she's furtively glancing around like a frightened primate. She lights up and puffs away like a mad dragon. The stress flows out from the exhaled smoke. I strain to make out what she's saying, but her mumbles are incomprehensible. I wonder what she went through. Doesn't matter. Tonight will be the last night she'll ever feel stressed, so she better enjoy her last toke.

I tremble in disbelief that I got so close. With my fresh pair of driving gloves, I pull out the Glock. I had already put electric tape around the handle, the trigger, and the hammer. I know this from some crime movies and TV shows I watched. Seems logical. I inhale deeply a few times, my grip tightening around the Glock, and then I stand, raising the gun and aiming it towards Ms. Moffat, who does not know what's about to hit her. Suddenly, she breaks down in tears. It never occurred to me the devil would cry. I can feel my heart thumping in my chest as my hand trembles in fear. I pull back and drop behind a parked Mercedes. What the hell is wrong with me? Who am I, and why did I travel this dark path? I can't be here. I shouldn't be here. I need to go. Now!

I get up to make my escape and there she is, standing in front of me. Ms. Moffat has a look of concern. I quickly hide the Glock behind me as I stare into her worried eyes. My mouth quivers, trying to get some words out, but my speech falls apart. She wonders what I'm doing and attempts to peek at what's behind me. "What are you hiding back there?" She asked, voice worried.

I look behind me, playing stupid, and shrug my shoulders, then I answer, "It's not what you think, Ms. Moffat." Shit, I called her by her grade school name.

"I haven't been called 'Ms. Moffat' in years. Do we know each other?"

I wanted to tell her we do, but I didn't. "No." I said, shaking my head.

She nods and slowly walks backwards, keeps her eyes on me. "Well, I'll be heading home now."

"Sure," I said, "Have a good night."

"Yeah, you too." She jets to her car, probably thinking I'll chase her. I remain where I am, not even looking at her. She struggles to get her keys out, drops them and cusses under her breath. She looks back at me, noticing I'm still standing there looking away from her direction. After a moment, she snatches her keys, quickly opens the car door and cheeses out, leaving a smoke screen behind. Her adrenaline must be erratic because mine surely is. I shove the Glock behind my pants and run out the opposite side from where she drove off.

XVI

I'm still shaken by the experience. The thoughts make me cringe so much that I can't even unpack them. I can't sleep. The hotel room is pitch black, yet I can see the entire event unfold like I'm in a movie theater. I even overthink scenarios that will most likely never occur, such as shooting her and getting caught by the police. My body quivers as if it happened. A potential regret.

And then comes a knocking at my door. My blood rushes faster than when I was at the parking garage. It's 2 AM. I don't want to answer as I bury myself in the thin, white, clean sheets, pretending I can't hear. "It's Robyn."

My adrenaline suddenly ceases. Heartbeat slowing down. I immediately swing the sheets off and answer the door. There she is in tight jeans and a crop top. Her makeup is minimal and my God, she's gorgeous. I smile uncontrollably, like a child seeing his first crush. I go through the files of pickup lines in my brain and land on: "Did you find my wallet?"

Obviously, I'm not clever.

She giggles. "No, um, I was wondering. Do you think you can get us some booze?"

"Uh, how old are you?" I ask, confused about her age. She easily looks like she's in her twenties.

"Sixteen." She muttered, her words barely audible, as if she was trying to hide the fact she's underage.

My face turns pale. I'm in "frightened turtle" mode. This girl is about to get someone in trouble, and it will not be me. "Sorry, I can't. I have to sleep." Before she responds, I swing the door shut.

XVII

The Glock can't come with me to New York, so the only way left is to return it... only to find out there is a strict NO RETURN POLICY because, of course, there is. If only I knew, maybe I would've thought twice about buying the gun. Passion just didn't allow me to think clearly. So, what am I supposed to do with the gun? The clerk gave me a step-by-step breakdown of how to dismantle the gun and I did it. I take some pieces, put them in a plastic bag and dump them separately. I drop the bullets in the sewer because I didn't know better. Again, movies and TV taught me most of the ways.

I just want it away from me.

XIII

I finally land at JFK. I can kiss the ground of the cold, damp cement again. Oh, how much I miss New York. The family got together for the first time in three years. The twin cousins, Michael and Stephanie, play with Baily by chasing each other around the living room. My uncle Joseph calls out to them sternly, threatening that if they don't behave, they won't get to open the presents laying under the tree. I help my mother bring out a load of oven cooked sirloin steak with onions and gravy in the mix to the table. My aunt through marriage, Hala, has her eyes glued to the steak.

"Relax, it's not going anywhere," Joseph said.

"Oh, why do you have to call me out like that?" Hala replies.

"I'm calling you out? You're hawking the food."

"Yeah, you're probably going to eat four or five."

Suddenly, a picture frame falls. My cousin Michael jumps away from it and tries to blame Baily, who sits there panting with his goofy tongue out. Stephanie keeps quiet and walks away.

The bell rings. It's David and his thin wife Yael with their chunky four-year-old Lenny. I gave David a hug, welcoming him, and greeted his wife. She couldn't be more obvious with all the dark makeup. All she needs is a pentagram around her neck and she can be a descendent of Satan. She's a good sport, though. Their son, Lenny, runs off to play with the cousins and Baily. David warns him to behave himself, but Lenny is a little rebel. He talks back to his dad, which I find hilarious.

We sit at the dining room table, nearly done with dinner. I settle into my chair at the end of the table, feeling the wall against my back, while David takes the seat beside me. My mother, Uncle Joseph, Aunt Hala, and Yael gathered together in the living room, the smell of wine in the air as they discussed current events and politics. Of course, Uncle Joseph has to sound like he's lecturing as everyone, including Aunt Haley, and everyone rolls their eyes.

David finishes his last bite of the steak, lightly belches. He pulls out his phone to show me his Instagram page, a picture of a gorgeous blonde woman holding hands with a tall woman with a pixie hairstyle.

"Who is that?" I ask.

"You can't tell?" David said, expecting me to know for some reason.

"Am I supposed to?"

"Look closer."

I take David's phone and observe the image up close. Still confused. "I really don't know."

"It's Christina O'Neil. From St. Anselm's. You remember Christina, right?"

"Wow, she looks…" I hold back and look towards the group who's still talking about nonsense. "She looks good."

"You mean the blonde?"

"Yeah."

"That's not Christina." David said. Then he points to the tall woman with the pixie cut. "That's Christina."

"Holy shit." I am indeed shocked. "She changed!"

"Wild shit, no?"

I decide to talk about Florida. "You won't believe who I saw."

"Who?"

"Ms. Moffat." I said as I chew on a piece of asparagus from my plate.

David looks confused. His eyes squint. "Was she on vacation?" He wondered.

"No, she's a professor at Miami University."

"That wasn't her." David said. "I know who you're talking about, too. It's not her."

I remain silent, shocked to hear this. I lean forward to hear better. "What do you mean, that wasn't her? She looked exactly like–"

"Nope. That was another Moffat. Ms. Moffat from St. Anselm is a high school teacher at New Brunswick. I thought I told you after I found her LinkedIn."

I stare, still confused and shocked.

"Look, I'll show you." David browses through LinkedIn and shows me the profile of a woman with the same name and the same occupation. It's the one with the pearly white teeth. My hands tremble as I take the phone, observing her picture. She looks nothing like how I remember. Then David continues, "I probably should've mentioned the plastic surgery she had over the years. She's smoking, no?"

His voice fades as I continue staring at the photo of this... pretty woman. The deeper I observe, the more of a resemblance I can see. I hear my uncle's voice, announcing to the kids to open the presents. Their excitement, along with Baily barking, isn't getting my eyes off the screen.

"Tony?" David tries to get my attention. "Are you okay?"

ENVY
PARANOIA IN TRANSLATION

I

John Gills was already twenty videos deep, swallowing the red pill hard. A podcast John immersed himself in, *Unveiled and Unfiltered Truths*, hosted by a group of young adults and a former kickboxer, discussed controversial topics, the current one being 'Why do women cheat?' It was videos like these that got John thinking about why Lisa, the love of his life of five years, cheated on him in the last two years of their relationship. He replayed every moment, every conversation, searching for the signs he might have missed. Had he done something wrong? Were there hidden red flags he had overlooked? Could a careless word have driven her away?

His mind was fixated on one troubling thought. The person in question, Lisa always assured him, was nothing more than a friend. John couldn't shake the irritating suspicion eating him alive. Perhaps it was someone from her past, an ex-lover she had reconnected with? The more he listened to the podcast, the determined voices of the young hosts, the more his mind spiraled into a vortex of doubt and paranoia as he hunted for an answer. *She was never yours. It was just your turn.*

No matter how many videos he watched, he'll never find out the truth of why Lisa cheated.

These videos taught John what hypergamy was. *Women only want men with a big bank.* A quote he couldn't stop repeating to himself. There has always been a debate about this, with John believing that the man's job title matters more. The fact he was a teacher was good enough. *Women are attracted to what they hear, while men are what they see.* As an English teacher, this was a breeze. He still did his research and practiced his vernacular to entice women. And like that, it got him with Venera Novák, a Croatian supermodel who immigrated to America to start a new life.

Venera stayed with her uncle, Ivo, who told her to learn English, then get a part-time job as she pursued her dreams to be on Vogue or Victoria's Secret or whatever predatory agency would take her. Just not porn, he begged. Her uncle knew how beautiful she was. He went out of his way and helped her find work as a waitress in a family-owned Croatian restaurant, Mariner's Table, in Astoria, Queens. Her charismatic cousin, Damir, was in charge. As long as the family is behind her, she is comfortable.

Meanwhile, Venera studied English second-language at Kingsborough Community College. Her instructor was the enlightened John Gills, or Mr. Gills, as his students would call him. In the classroom, there were only twelve desks, creating a more personal atmosphere. The group of students was incredibly diverse, with people from different races and ages. The youngest was seventeen from Belarus, while the oldest was forty-three from Nigeria. Despite everyone's differences, they all had one thing in common. They didn't speak a lick of English and were willing to learn. Before class began, students would observe each other in the classroom, wondering what to say or how to greet one another. A young woman from Chile complimented the jewelry belonging to an older Turkish woman by gesturing at them and attempting to say "beautiful." She returns the compliment with a smile and a nod.

John prepared the class by calling out attendance and butchering their foreign names. Not on purpose. He genuinely tried his best. Students would attempt to correct him as he tried to repeat the names with as much respect as possible. Then, into the classroom, walked a vision of elegance and attraction: Venera Novák, her tall frame moving with a grace that commanded attention. With each step, her auburn hair swayed in soft waves, capturing the sunlight. John couldn't help but notice her striking cheekbones, perfectly shaped and elevated, giving her face a sophisticated and almost mystical allure. Her vibrant energy, confident stride, and friendly smile left a lasting impression on everyone in the room.

Especially John.

In her, John saw a resemblance to a young Elizabeth Hurley, not just in her poised stature and attractive figure but in the magnetic charisma that seemed to surround her. Growing up, he always had a crush on Elizabeth Hurley after watching *Bedazzled* in 2003. His heart skipped beat after beat as he slurred his words, attempting to pronounce her name. "V-V-Ven-Era." John says, tongue slipping out. "Ven-era? Venera."

"*Da*." she said with a smile as she took her seat.

During their days of class, the young boy in John felt like he was having a high school crush as he watched Venera improved her English. After the tenth and final week of class, he wanted to offer Verena free lessons, but he didn't want to come off too strong or creepy since she was his student. She was only five years younger than him, but his integrity as a teacher would still be diminished. But it's not like he's tenure material. This was a part-time gig John got after no luck getting his master's degree in English literature from NYU. Bills and student loans were stacking and needed to be paid someday.

Maybe one day he'll be a bestselling author. Until then, he celebrates his small wins, publishing short stories about the complexities of modern relationships in decent magazines. He prays that one day someone important reads it and turns it into a film, just like what happened to one of his colleagues. All it took was one short story about dealing with personal demons published in a low level magazine and a month later got picked up for a movie deal. John would lie to himself and say he wasn't hurt nor jealous by this after working his ass off building his craft. But it took one, just one short story from someone who's not even an English major to get the ultimate reward. He would also lie to himself if he said he was happy for him. The fuck his colleague knows about literature?

Nothing at all!

John felt disrespected, even though no harm was done. At times, he even dreamed about his own personal success, yet it was overshadowed by his being the underdog.

While waiting in line for pizza at the cafeteria, John's mind was filled with the characters and plot of a story he was eager to write. A story about a teacher falling in love with a student. Or vice versa. But not in a creepy way. Again, he insists he is not in fact a creep. Instead, this story would be something romantic, soothing. Something that would get women to fall in love with the story and cater to their fantasies.

At the end of the day, that's what they are.

Just fantasies.

The story would play out in his head and kept his focus on the premise. A soon-to-be successful man getting with a woman to make his colleagues jealous of him. Or even make his ex-girlfriend jealous. Imagine the sensation of being with someone more beautiful than Lisa, their physical appeal captivating every onlooker.

That would drive her nuts.

But catching his eye, waiting in line ahead of him, was the better version of Elizabeth Hurley herself. Venera scrolled through Facebook on her phone, reading statuses and laughing at memes. All John did was stare at the back of her wavy hair, thinking of a way to say something. He took a peek at what she was doing on Facebook. Until she looked back with a double take and a bright smile. "Mr. Gills!" Verena said with her strong accent, rolling her tongue as she spoke. "It's good to see you!"

"Same here, Verena!" John said with a smile. "Your English is amazing!"

"*Hvala!* I mean, how do you say? Thank you?" Venera said with her radiant smile.

"Yes, it's 'thank you.'" John said.

"I still need help. My English, still hard."

"Oh, don't worry, you speak better than most of my friends born here."

Verena chuckles loudly with a snort. "Come on, Mr. Gills."

"You can call me John." John said.

"Okay. John." She said with a nod.

"Maybe I can help you improve your English on the side."

Verena gave a look of surprise. "Are you sure?" She says. "You can do that?"

"Of course. Private tutoring."

"Oh, *divno!*"

As they sat together in the cozy corner of the cafeteria, the chatter of other students and faculty fill the room, John found himself increasingly lost in Venera's presence. The soft glow of the overhead lights cast a warm hue on her face. It brought out her features and making her seem all the more captivating. He reached for his slice of pizza, his mind racing for something to say, something that would sound casual yet meaningful. "So, Venera," he began, his voice slightly unsteady, "this pizza is really... um, it's quite..." He paused, searching for the right word, but all that came out was, "cheesy, I guess?"

Venera looked up, a hint of amusement in her eyes. "*Da!*" Verena said with her mouth full. "It's delicious, yes? Flavor, so much." She makes an okay gesture.

John nodded, relieved at her response, but still feeling awkward. "Yeah, flavors," he echoed, then rushed to add another topic. "And, uh, the weather today was something, right? I mean, it was sunny, then rainy, and then... um, sunny again?" His attempt at small talk felt clumsy in his own ears.

Venera's gentle smile didn't waver, but John couldn't shake off the feeling that he was fumbling with every word.

So much for being an English teacher.

Trying to regain his composure, he took a sip of his drink, hoping it would steady his nerves. "I also wanted to, uh, ask about... your day. How was it at the... restaurant, and um, your modeling stuff?" The words came out in a rush, a jumble of half-formed inquiries that made him wince internally. He mentally chastised himself for not being more eloquent, more put-together in front of her.

Remember, women like confidence. They want a man who takes charge.

He remembers the quote from one of the young hosts of *Unveiled and Unfiltered Truths*, as he watches Venera devouring the pizza. "I'd love to, uh, maybe, show you my favorite pizzeria. One day." John says.

"Okay!" Verena said after swallowing her food. After, she wipes her mouth with a napkin. "That nice."

And so he did. John and Verena had pizza together at his favorite pizzeria, Luca's Brick Oven in Park Slope. They shared their stories outside of the class. She described the bittersweet feeling of leaving everything behind in Croatia to chase her dreams in the modeling industry. John expressed his desire to make a difference by teaching and mentoring young minds. However, he did add he wanted Croatia to win the World Cup. This made Verena smile, no matter how bullshit it sounded. But it was the thought that counted for her. She even liked his presence and her English-speaking skills improved as they continued to see each other.

After John left Kingsborough, he got hired to teach seniors Advanced English Literature at a private high school in Astoria called St. Gabriel Preparatory. He and Venera celebrated with a more romantic dinner in Midtown, Manhattan and officially kissed for the first time. This was the moment John knew she was the one. She was so passionate about him and his improvement. John felt the same way about her when she would get some modeling gigs here and there. The pay was okay, but she moved on up to be a manager at her cousin's restaurant. Life got better when they moved in together, renting a two-bedroom home in first floor of a private house for two grand a month. Being close to their workplaces, John and Venera found the house on Steinway Street, near the Mariner's Table and many Mediterranean restaurants. Nothing is more convenient than that.

Two and a half years later, Venera got a surprise visit.

II

Bogomir Zlato, AKA Bogo, arrived in New York City to visit his longtime friend Venera. He landed in JFK where he was picked up by an Uber driver to take him to an Airbnb at the Financial District on Gold St, a cozy studio that cost no more than five hundred a night. His win with Dogecoin allowed him to have enough money to pay for the expensive price. It made him a few million dollars thanks to Elon Musk and his vocal support, but mainly thanks to selling his Bitcoin, that also went up in price. That poverty life he had in Croatia decimated overnight.

Once he had settled into the studio and casually tossed his luggage onto the queen bed, he immediately reached for his phone and called Venera. *"Zdravo, lijepa."* Bogo said with a smile.

Venera, on the other line, is happy to hear from him. Mainly, she was quite surprised that he arrived because of his lack of funds from the time she left Croatia. A year ago, they exchanged messages on Facebook, sharing memes and nostalgic childhood photos. Sometimes John would see, but he had no interest in seeing a picture of her with another man, despite them just being friends.

In fact, John questioned the relationship between Venera and her friend Bogo. He wondered if they ever dated, but she would deny it quickly. Her response was, "Oh, no, never. He's just a friend." Wouldn't be the first time John heard that. It brought some painful memories he had with Lisa. Then found out Lisa had her mouth full of her friend's dick.

Women never have guy friends. Only rebounds and side dicks. John remembered as Venera expressed her friendship with Bogo.

Venera even let John in the picture and introduced Bogo to him over FaceTime. Of course, John remained cordial just for Venera. This was a unique experience for him, since he never had the opportunity to be introduced to any of her friends.

Or is this a new tactic that women are doing these days? *Introduce their man with their side piece. A way to assert dominance and humiliate the other party's masculinity. A woman will always play innocent when introducing their 'friend' to their partner. Don't fall for it, guys.* He continued the conversation with Bogo, who had a very heavy accent and could barely understand English without Venera translating for him. There were a couple of laughs and praises from Bogo who admires high school teachers. "Tough job to teach young boys." Bogo said.

"I couldn't agree more." John said as he thought about how quickly Bogo got rich with his crypto luck. It left John dumbfounded. Baffled even. He had a feeling crypto was going to hit big, but kept making excuses to himself that it wouldn't be worth it. And here it is in full picture. Bogo became a crypto millionaire. A simple follow-your-gut moment.

As Venera spoke to Bogo in Croatian, her phone screen displayed his face glowing with amusement. *"Bogo, stvarno izgledaš sjajno! Teško je povjerovati kako si se promijenio,*" she exclaimed, her tone one of genuine surprise and happiness.

Bogo responded with a hearty chuckle, his Croatian words lost on John but clearly indicative of his pleasure at the compliment. John shifted slightly, feeling like an outsider in this exchange of old friends sharing a language and memories he wasn't a part of. Curiosity finally got the better of him. "What did you say to him?" John asked, trying to keep his voice casual.

Venera turned to John, still smiling. "Oh, I was just telling Bogo how different he looks now. You know, from our childhood days in Croatia," she explained, her eyes dancing with memories.

"And how is that?" John prodded gently, though a small knot of discomfort was forming in his stomach.

"Bogo wasn't always like this," Venera continued, oblivious to John's growing discomfort. "Back home, he was very fat, and also he didn't care about his looks. Life was tough for him. But now it's like he's a new person! It's amazing, no?"

John nodded, his smile not reaching his eyes. "Money changes people," he remarked, a subtle edge to his voice.

Venera squeezed his hand, mistaking his tension for concern. "It's not just money, John. It's happiness, you know? No stress. It's good to see him happy and successful." The unsettling feeling caused by her innocent compliments to Bogo lingered in John's head, refusing to go away.

As the conversation on the screen continued, John's smile remained, but his heart was heavy, laden with thoughts that cast a long shadow over the cozy evening. The quotes of the young hosts of *Unveiled and Unfiltered Truth* were littered in John's mind. *A woman will leave their man for the next best thing always. It's in their nature.*

John wasn't having it even though Venera was beside him in bed before they slept. There was a strange feeling rising in the air. It was not comfortable. After Venera blew a kiss goodbye to Bogo and hung up, it left John thinking. Is Venera not the one after all?

III

The seniors finally behaved themselves in class today, allowing John to scroll covertly through Venera's Facebook posts. He scrolls endlessly on her page from cringe worthy statuses to liking left-wing politics on human rights. She even had a previous argument with a stranger on abortion rights on a page belonging to a far-right politician. She doesn't take things well, but that's not concerning John at all, as he continues to scroll obsessively. He then stumbled upon a 2019 post showcasing her on the cover of a prominent Croatian magazine MareDalmata, modeling in a pink bikini showing off her tan body, embodying the brand's vibrant coastal essence. *"Vrata me"* captioned above the picture. John clicks [see translation] "take me back."

John reads through the comments and sees the most recent one is from two weeks prior to Bogomir Zlato. *"Jedva čekam da te konačno opet vidim!"* [see translation] "I can't wait to finally see you again!"

John clicks on the profile of Bogomir Zlato. His profile picture shows a very handsome man, well dressed in an expensive suit, standing next to a Ferrari. He has thousands of friends and gets compliments on all of his pictures, along with many likes and love reactions. All the comments are in Croatian, including one from Verena. *"Moj zgodni prijatelj!"* [see translation] "My handsome friend!" John continues to scroll through Bogo's Facebook page and saw his pictures. It's the typical red-pilled ideology all in one profile. Another picture is of Bogo shirtless, showing his very fit physique performing a Maui Thai kick against a hanging sandbag; then other pictures of him showcasing his travels abroad standing in front of vast landscapes. John sees Bogo as a man in great shape, handsome, rich, and with a lot of freedom. What more does a man want?

He gets interrupted by a student raises his hand. "Mr. Gills," the student calls out, "I don't understand the last question."

"What is it you don't understand, Billy?" John says, eyes still on his phone.

"I feel Othello should've seen it coming from Iago from the beginning, no?"

"How so?"

"Iago looks obviously cunning in the play. I'm actually mad someone like Othello would fall for Iago's tricks so easily."

Another student adds on, "Othello is also very aggressive."

Then another student said, "Which makes him stupid like the royalty."

"I don't think all royalty is stupid. Othello is just stubborn, I think." Billy said.

John takes one last look at Bogo's profile, then sets his phone down to teach the class for the remaining ten minutes that's left before the bell. "Let's reread Act Four, Scene One, when Othello confronts Desdemona." All the students pull out their copies of *Othello* and turn to the page collectively.

***

In the teacher's lounge, John sat alone in the back, almost hiding in the shadows. He found a moment of solitude to reflect on the play. He barely ate his favorite turkey sandwich, which he promises himself he'll stop so he can lose his gut. His eyes were locked onto his phone screen, scrolling through Venera's Facebook page. Each status, each like, each photo, felt like pieces of a puzzle he was desperately trying to solve.

Her online interactions, especially with Bogo, distressed him, feeding the ever-growing suspicion in his mind.

Around him, the usual of the lounge. Teachers discussed lesson plans, and their own plans to get drinks after school. It faded into a distant hum as John's world had narrowed down to the digital window into Venera's life. Every comment from Bogo, playful and innocent as it might seem to anyone else, was a red flag to John. His thoughts spiraled back to Lisa, to the pain and betrayal he felt, to the vows he made to never be that naïve again and that vulnerable again. "Once bitten, twice shy," he thought bitterly. But with Venera, everything felt more intense, the stakes higher. She wasn't just anyone; she was the epitome of what he had always desired, yet seemingly unattainable. It was the way she listened, really listened, when he spoke. The way her laughter seemed to light up the room and how she shared her dreams and fears with such openness. She offered a companionship he hadn't known he was longing for, a connection that felt both exhilarating and terrifying. Yet, he couldn't shake off the fear that it was all too good to be true.

The shadow of Lisa's betrayal loomed large, tainting even the purest moments he shared with Venera. He found himself scrutinizing her words, her actions, searching for signs of deceit, even as he despised himself for doing so. The question that haunted him, keeping him awake at night, was whether he could truly let go of his past and trust again. Could he accept the love and companionship Venera offered without the constant fear of it being ripped away? As John sat there, wrestling with his thoughts, he realized that this struggle within him was about more than just his relationship with Venera. It was about whether he could find a way to heal, to believe in the possibility of a love that doesn't end in betrayal. These thoughts continued to swirl in his mind, a silent storm that showed no signs of stopping.

The bell rang, signaling the end of the break, but John barely noticed. His thoughts were interrupted only when a fellow science teacher,

Calvin, approached him, a friendly smile on his face. "Hey John, you're zoning out, man. Everything okay?" Calvin asked.

John locked his phone, offering a forced smile. "Yeah, just lesson plans," he lied, tucking away his phone.

Calvin raised an eyebrow but didn't press further. "I hear you, John. If you saw the amount of red ink I used grading papers, I'd paint the town."

John laughed, but it was hollow, his mind still entangled in the web of his insecurities. As he walked back to his class, John's mind raced. He needed to keep a closer eye on Venera, to understand what was happening before it was too late. The idea of surveillance crossed his mind. Just a glance at her messages, her calls, something to put him at ease. He calls Venera, "Hey babe, are you busy?"

Venera, happy to hear from him, "No, John. Everything okay?"

"Could you come by the school? I want to talk to you about something."

"Sure. Let me tell Damir and I'll see you there."

The class that followed was a blur. John's eyes would occasionally flicker to the clock, counting down the minutes until he could see Venera. He needed to see her face, to hear her voice. Anything to reassure him that his fears were just that.

Fears.

After class, John lingered in the hallway, his gaze following the dispersing students, yet his mind was elsewhere. The corridors of the school, once a place of academic pursuit and professional satisfaction, now felt like a maze trapping him in his own thoughts. He couldn't shake off the image of Venera laughing at something Bogo said, an image he had conjured up in his mind, replaying it like a broken record. In an attempt to see Venera, he took a slight detour on his way to the cafeteria. As he walked, he rehearsed a casual greeting to himself, something that wouldn't make his concerns obvious. *Just a normal conversation, nothing to show what's really going on.*

Upon entering the cafeteria, he scanned the room under the pretense of looking for a seat. His eyes finally settled on Venera, sitting alone at a table, her attention on drinking tea. John felt a momentary relief seeing her there, alone. But that relief quickly turned into a familiar sting of jealousy as he imagined Bogo sitting there, sharing that space with her. He approached her table, his heart pounding in his chest. "Hey Venera," he greeted her with a kiss, while trying to keep his voice steady.

Venera's face lit up with a smile. "Hey, John."

John lingered over his words with unusual care, each question to Venera subtly probing, layered with an unspoken agenda. "So, how was your day?" he inquired, feigning casual interest.

Venera, her tone light and unsuspecting, replied, "It was good, busy as usual at the restaurant. And yours?" She said, then sips her tea.

"Same old. Just grading papers, preparing lectures. The usual." John paused briefly before continuing, "Are you planning anything special for the weekend?"

A hint of curiosity tinged her smile. "Oh, nothing much. Maybe catch up on some rest. Why?"

John's casual demeanor barely concealed his insistent tone. "Just curious. You're not meeting someone, are you? Like, maybe Bogo?"

Venera's expression flickered with surprise. "Bogo? No, I haven't made any plans with him. Why would you think that?"

He leaned in slightly, his urgency thinly veiled. "Just wondering. You two seem to get along well."

Her smile dithered, a hint of concern creeping into her eyes, noticing how John's hands were gripped tightly together, the knuckles turning a shade paler from the pressure. "John, is everything alright? You seem a bit... tense."

"Me? Tense?" John quickly attempted to dispel her concern, but his voice betrayed him. "No, not at all. I'm just interested in what's going with your life, that's all."

Her tentative smile, now shadowed with unease. "I understand. I just wasn't expecting you to ask about Bogo."

John nodded, his expression strained. "Right. It's just that you two seem... close. So, no weekend plans with Bogo, right?"

Venera's discomfort grew more pronounced. "No. Why are you asking about him so much?"

He attempted to sound nonchalant, but his voice was laced with insistence. "No. I guess I'm just trying to understand your friends better."

Venera reached out, touching his hand gently. "John, don't worry about Bogo. We're just friends. You mean a lot to me."

His gaze softened momentarily at her touch. "I know. Maybe I'm being overly cautious. Sorry if I came off too strong."

She gave his hand a reassuring squeeze. "It's okay. Let's just focus on us. Okay? There's nothing to worry about."

John managed a smile, but his eyes remained clouded, his thoughts an unresolved current of doubt and fear. Then those young hosts from the podcast creep up on his thoughts. *If you think your woman is cheating on you, don't confront her about it. She'll just give you sweet talk and reassurance, but it's all part of the game. Don't believe a word of it.*

John, meanwhile, analyzed her responses, searching for any hint of deceit, any sign that she was hiding something. But all he found was her usual sincerity, which only served to confuse him more. *Is she really that good at hiding it, or am I losing my mind?* He wondered silently.

As they parted ways, with Venera heading back to work and John to his next class, the seeds of doubt planted in his mind continued to grow. He felt caught in a web of his own making, unable to escape the paranoia that was slowly consuming him.

That evening, alone in his apartment waiting for Venera to arrive, John replayed the day's interactions in his head. The more he thought about Venera and Bogo, the more convinced he became that there was something going on. He needed to find out the truth, no matter what it took. It led him to make a decision that would take him down a path of no return.

IV

In the dim glow of his computer screen, John's nights blurred into a relentless pursuit of validation for his suspicions. The red pill forum AlphaSphere was a rabbit hole, each post dragging him deeper into a world that mirrored his darkest thoughts.

> The Unvarnished Truth About Modern Relationships: What Society Won't Tell You
>
> Hypergamy Unmasked: Understanding Female Nature in the 21st Century
>
> From Beta to Alpha: Reclaiming Your Strength in a Decadent Era
>
> Navigating the Minefield: How to Spot and Avoid Female Manipulation
>
> The Illusion of Equality: A Realist's Guide to Power Dynamics in Dating
>
> Cultural Conditioning: How Men Have Been Programmed to Fail

As John read through the posts and threads, he couldn't help but feel a chill down his spine as he encountered countless cautionary tales of betrayal. He would read them, one after another, his eyes reflecting the cold light of the screen, not noticing hours slipping late into the night.

John's side of the bedroom, once meticulously kept, had succumbed to neglect. Stacks of ungraded papers lay forgotten on the computer desk. The air was stale, thick with the scent of unwashed laundry and the tang of desperation. He would sit there, surrounded by the debris of his unraveling life, his fingers occasionally drumming a restless rhythm on the table. This side contrasted with the clean and organized of Venera's. No evidence of clothes or makeup scattered.

His exploration of Venera's social media was both systematic and frantic. He scrutinized every photo, every comment, building scenarios in his mind where every smile, every friendly exchange, was a clue to a betrayal. He would zoom in on pictures, searching the backgrounds, the faces, for Bogo or any unknown male figure that could be perceived as a threat.

One evening after an abysmal day of lecturing, John sat on the couch of their living room, laptop opened, lost in thought. Venera's voice broke through the silence, brimming with the day's tales. "Hey, guess who I ran into today?" she asked, her tone light and conversational.

John responded without looking up, his voice tinged with disinterest. "Who?"

"Bogo," Venera said, a smile in her voice. "He was at the café near my work."

At the mention of Bogo's name, John's demeanor shifted subtly. His eyes, which had been fixed on the screen, narrowed ever so slightly, a flicker of something unreadable passing through them. He nodded, maintaining a facade of indifference, but the air around him seemed to grow heavier, charged with an unspoken tension.

Later, in the kitchen, the atmosphere thickened further. Venera stood by the stove, stirring a pot, while John sat at the table, surrounded by ungraded papers. The sound of Venera's laughter, light and carefree, punctuated the room as she glanced at a message on her phone.

John's voice, cold and sharp, cut through the warmth. "Something funny?"

Venera turned, still smiling. "Oh, just a meme Bogo sent." She continued laughing as she stares at her phone.

John isn't amused. Instead, he nodded stiffly, his eyes following her every movement. The once-comfortable spaces of their home were now tinged with an undercurrent of doubt and watchfulness, originating from John's unspoken but increasingly apparent suspicions.

Each interaction, each shared moment that used to be filled with ease, was now clouded by the growing chasm between them. John's scrutiny of Venera's every action, every word, intensified, the invisible threads of trust slowly unraveling. Venera, initially oblivious to the change, soon began to sense the shift in John's attitude, her own confusion and concern mirroring the growing disconnect.

As days passed, the signs of John's internal turmoil became more clear. His passionate lectures at school were now disjointed, his thoughts often wandering into a distant, troubled realm. In the faculty lounge, where casual banter once flowed, his contributions were now forced, his attempts at normalcy increasingly unconvincing.

As the days melded into weeks, the once warm and loving interactions between John and Venera grew strained, the air between them heavy with unspoken words and growing unease.

Then one evening, as they sat in the living room, watching Venera's favorite movie, *Amélie*, she reached out, placing her hand over John's. "John, is everything okay? I noticed you're distant," she asked, voice laced with worry.

John withdrew his hand subtly, avoiding her gaze. "I'm fine," he replied, his voice betraying a hint of irritation.

Venera's brow furrowed in worry. "You know you can talk to me, right? Whatever it is, we can work it out together."

John let out a sigh, his eyes fixed on some distant point. "There's nothing to talk about, Venera. I'm just tired, that's all." His tone was dismissive, shutting down further conversation.

Venera bit her lip, the hurt almost noticeable in her eyes. She moved closer, attempting to bridge the emotional gap with a soft touch. "John, I just want to help..."

But John stood up abruptly, creating physical and emotional space between them. "I need some air," he muttered as he left the room and leaving Venera alone with her growing concerns.

John stood outside of their building contemplating about his relationship. In the privacy of his mind, he justified his behavior as caution, a shield against potential heartache. *Keep your guard up. Protect yourself from heartbreak. Don't be vulnerable.* He reminded himself of these thoughts, a defense mechanism honed from the scars left by Lisa's betrayal. Yet deep down, a part of him recognized the self-destructive path he was treading, the silent sabotage of the one relationship that had brought him happiness. He needed to resolve this and it must be done before it's too late.

More issues occurred when he barely cuddled with Venera. The continued tormenting thoughts of her and Bogo gave him vivid nightmares. He would wake up sweating and seeing Venera not home. But of course, she's working, and he overslept, believing he's supposed to be in class lecturing. Turned out to be Saturday. This time, Venera didn't wake him up when usually she does before heading out to work. *Whatever was once normal in a relationship suddenly changes. Such as not doing the normal routine behavior. It means she's thinking about someone else. Be careful, kings.*

Sitting in the chaotic side of the bedroom, John felt a surge of reckless determination. The walls of the apartment seemed to press closer, suffocating him, the silence broken only by the relentless ticking of the clock. Filled with a volatile combination of anger, hurt, and an insatiable yearning for the truth, he leaped off the couch.

He found himself outside, the cool afternoon air doing little to clear the fog in his head. Driven by loud thoughts from the young hosts of *Unveiled and Unfiltered Truths*, he made his way to Mariner's Table, where Venera worked, each step heavy with unspoken accusations.

As he waited in the shadows, watching the restaurant's entrance, his heart was a drumbeat of conflicting emotions. The sight of Venera, emerging from the warm light of the restaurant into the shade outside, was both soothing and maddening. "Venera, we need to talk," he said, emerging from the shadows, his voice unsteady with his pent-up emotions.

Venera was surprised by his unexpected arrival and the intensity in his gaze, which made her feel uneasy. "John, what's wrong?" she asked, her voice filled with worry.

John stood there, torn between the desire to confront her and the fear of what he might discover. "You didn't wake me up before you left." John said.

"Because it was Saturday. You don't have work." Venera replied, voice irritated.

"But you usually let me know you're heading to work before you leave."

"John, you came here to tell me this?"

"Yes. I did. Are you thinking about someone else?"

Venera, taken aback by the question, wore a troubled expression and avoided answering. "What the fuck is wrong with you?" She turns and heads back to the restaurant.

When a woman is confronted and she acts aggressively, she is obviously hiding something. Do not cave. Yet, John was torn by this idea as he gazes at his love, noticing this is the first time he heard her voice filled with anger. John's voice, once pleading, turned accusatory, each word sharpened by a blend of fear and hurt. "Don't play games with me, Venera!" John's shout pierced the air, catching the attention of concerned customers. "I've seen how Bogo commented on your pics."

Venera's patience crumbled under the burden of his baseless accusations. She marches back to John. "Stop being insecure!" Her voice rose in frustration, echoing off the silent buildings around them.

John's face reddened, his emotions teetering on the edge of anger. "Maybe I am! Maybe I can't just stand by and let this happen again. Never again! Not by Lisa, not by anyone!"

Venera took a step back, her heart racing. She realized then that this wasn't just about Bogo. It's much worse. It was about every fear, every insecurity John harbored. "You're letting your past poison us, John. I'm not Lisa!"

The words hung heavily between them. John's eyes searched hers, torn between his love for her and the ghosts of his past.

Suddenly, Venera's face softened, a brief moment of clarity cutting through the wild emotions. "You're acting just like a friend I had back home. She let her jealousy ruin our friendship. And now, you're doing the same. Nothing different. I can't live like this."

The comparison struck a chord in John. For the first time, John saw a reflection of himself — the realization that his own jealousy and paranoia could lead him down a similar path of isolation and regret. This thought, which made him realize the harsh reality of his actions and the possible outcomes, left him feeling disturbed.

An awkward silence fell over them. Venera's words resonated in John's thoughts. He looked at her deeply and saw not just the woman he loved, but also the pain he was causing. Without another word, John turned and walked away, leaving Venera only to watch him go. The realization that she might have just lost him to his own unfounded fears was a much bitter pill to swallow.

V

Sitting by the harbor, Venera and Ivana felt a gentle breeze carrying the salty scent of the Adriatic Sea, as it whispered secrets to the cobblestone streets of Rovinj. They shared dreams painted in vibrant strokes. The runways in Paris, flashing cameras, and dazzling gowns. Ivana, with her laughter echoing against the sea walls, always dreamed out loud, while Venera's aspirations flickered quietly in her bright eyes.

Their days were filled with leisurely strolls along the narrow lanes, with its charmingly painted buildings and lively open-air markets, where the smell of seafood and baked goods lingered in the air. With each confident step and captivating story, Ivana effortlessly assumed the role of a natural leader, painting vivid pictures of distant lands and her dreams of becoming a famous model.

In the evenings, they would sit on the pebbled beach, watching the sunset paint the sky in shades of orange and pink. Ivana would talk animatedly about the future, gesturing to the horizon as if she could reach out and touch her dreams. Venera listened, her thoughts drifting to her own desires, a gentle longing etched in her gaze.

The night sky was peppered with stars as the girls made their way back through the quiet streets. Ivana's voice, filled with excitement for the future, was the melody of their walk, while Venera's silent steps wrote the harmony. Their friendship was a dance of differences. Ivana, bold and outspoken, and Venera, thoughtful and observant. Together, they were a perfect blend of dream and drive, each believing that their shared vision of a glamorous life beyond Rovinj was just a matter of time.

***

In the corridors of their school, Ivana's arm was always linked with Venera's. The day Venera whispered her decision to enter the Zagreb competition, a regional beauty pageant, Ivana's smile wavered, just for a heartbeat, before she exclaimed her excitement, "That's amazing, Venera! You're going to shine!" In the depths of her eyes, a brewing storm revealed an unspoken rivalry.

School days were a mix of mundane lessons and whispered plans between classes. Ivana often shared her elaborate ideas for their future careers, her words painting a world of fame and luxury. Venera's contributions were softer, yet filled with a quiet determination that complemented Ivana's fiery ambition.

The beauty pageant was the talk of the school, and as Venera's participation became known, she found herself the center of attention, a place she had never sought. Ivana, ever the supportive friend, was always at her side, her congratulations a bit too loud, her smile a bit too wide.

As the pageant drew closer, their afternoons were spent in preparation. Ivana helped Venera choose her outfits and practice her walk, each session an echo of their childhood dreams. They stood in front of the full-length mirror in Venera's room, the array of clothes spread out on the bed. Venera held up a sleek, black dress against herself, turning to Ivana for her opinion. "How about this one?" Venera asked, her voice hopeful.

Ivana scrutinized the dress, her lips pursed. "It's nice, but it's not the best choice for you," she replied, her tone carrying a hint of something Venera couldn't quite place. "Try the red one. It might highlight your features better."

Venera changed into the red dress, her movements slightly hesitant. She turned to face Ivana again, seeking reassurance.

Ivana nodded this time. "Yes, much better. But remember to stand straight, Venera. Your posture is everything. Right now, you're very sloppy. What's wrong? Do you have a hunchback?"

As Venera practiced her walk back and forth across the room, Ivana's instructions grew more pointed. "You need to be more graceful, Venera. And watch your stride, it's too wide. Do you not want to impress the judges? It looks like you don't."

Venera paused, a frown creasing her forehead. "I feel like I'm doing it right," she said, a note of defensiveness creeping into her voice.

Ivana's response was quick, her words sharp. "You see, that's your problem. It's always feel, feel, feel. The judges don't care how you 'feel' they care about your appearance. If you want to succeed, you need to do it perfectly. You can't afford to be just right." She said.

Venera felt the sting of Ivana's words as she bit her lip. She resumed her walk, each step now weighted with self-doubt. The room, once filled with the excitement of shared dreams, felt colder.

As Ivana continued her critique, Venera couldn't shake off the feeling that something had shifted between them. The support she once felt from Ivana now seemed mixed with criticism, as if each compliment had to be counterbalanced with a disparaging remark.

The night before the pageant, under the soft glow of Venera's bedroom lamp, the girls sat together, a sea of fabrics and cosmetics around them. Ivana's voice had a nervous edge, her fingers fidgeting with a ribbon. "You're going to be amazing," she said. But there was something else going on, something like a distant thunder, a warning of the storm that was brewing in their friendship.

The night of the Zagreb competition, the air backstage buzzed with nervous energy. Ivana's grip on Venera's hand was tight. Her "Good luck" felt there was a hidden tension. Venera, draped in a gown that glittered like the Adriatic at sunset, felt a flutter of nerves. Ivana was there, offering last-minute touches to Venera's hair, her movements precise but hurried. "You're going to dazzle them," Ivana said, forcing a smile that didn't quite reach her eyes.

As Venera stepped onto the runway, the bright lights and the gaze of the audience felt like a wave she was riding. Ivana watched from the wings, her hands clasped tightly, her smile faltering with each stride Venera took. The applause that followed Venera's walk was a melody that Ivana had longed to hear for herself.

When the announcement came, declaring Venera the winner, the room erupted in cheers. Venera's heart soared with a joy so pure it was almost painful. Ivana was by her side in an instant, her embrace warm but brief. "You did it, Venera," she whispered, but the words were heavy, carrying unfulfilled dreams and a friendship tilting into the shadows.

As they left the venue into the night, Ivana walked a step behind Venera, lost in her own world. The congratulations from friends and family were a blur to Venera, who noticed the growing silence from Ivana, a silence that spoke louder than any words of envy. It became concerning, but Venera didn't address it as she was afraid of coming off as accusatory. She kept things quiet between them before she took the flight to America in hopes of changing her life.

***

Much later, after settling in her tiny New York City apartment, Venera scrolled through Ivana's life unfolding on social media. The images showed Ivana draped in elegance, the star of local Croatian shows. Venera saw pictures of Ivana at events and parties, always the center of attention, yet there was a consistency in her expressions, a certain persistence in proving her happiness.

Venera often paused at photos of Ivana on the familiar streets of Rovinj, her pose confident yet her eyes searching. It was as if with each click of the camera, Ivana was trying to capture something more, something that remained elusive even in the flash of success. She was no Venera. In fact, there were times Venera would notice a mirror effect of certain poses and expression from Ivana to her own modeling pictures. It was eerie, to say the least.

Among the comments and likes, Venera noticed the occasional reply from Ivana, sometimes wistful, sometimes tinged with an unspoken question – what if?

On a photo of Venera at a New York landmark, Ivana commented, "Looks amazing. Makes me wonder what it would've been like if I'd joined you there."

Then another responding to a post about Venera's latest modeling shoot, Ivana wrote, "Stunning as always. Do you ever think about what our lives would be like if we'd taken different turns?"

It was in these messages that Venera felt the distance between them growing. A chasm widened by paths taken and choices made. Venera would sometimes type out a message to Ivana, words filled with memories and a hope to bridge the gap. But each time her finger hovered over the "send" button, she would delete the message, leaving their conversations in the realm of silent thoughts and untraveled roads.

Things weren't the same despite the efforts from Ivana when she visited New York City for a week. They had a brief reunion in a café in SoHo. Ivana's anecdotes of local fame were punctuated with veiled barbs, "Of course, it's not New York, but we can't all leap into the unknown." Venera, sipping her coffee, felt Ivana's words, a silent dance around the envy that simmered beneath. It wasn't comfortable, but she didn't express it. Yet, as Ivana spoke of her life in Croatia, her achievements, and the people she had met, there was an undercurrent of comparison in her tone, a measuring of lives that no longer aligned as they once had.

Venera listened, her responses careful, offering congratulations and nods at the right moments. Yet, her mind wandered to the streets of Rovinj, to the days when their dreams were shared, not silently contested. She noticed Ivana's glances, sharp and calculating, as if trying to uncover any flaws, whatever they may be.

The conversation shifted to memories, to the days of laughter and shared plans. In these moments, their connection flickered back to life, a reminder of a friendship that had once been about more than envy and ambition. But these moments were fleeting, like snapshots from a different time, overshadowed by the reality of the paths they had chosen.

As they parted ways, their goodbye was filled with lingering hugs and bittersweet promises to stay connected, aware of the uncertainty that loomed. Venera watched Ivana walk away, her steps confident yet somehow hesitant, a mirror of the complexity that now defined their friendship.

It was a relief.

Venera noticed a reflection of John's subtle possessiveness in Ivana's thinly veiled envy, becoming aware of the unsaid insecurities that lingered in his compliments and his persistent questions about her day. It was a realization that unsettled her, the parallels too poignant, casting shadows on the walls of her heart.

The way John spoke, which used to bring comfort and encouragement, now resonated differently in Venera's thoughts. His casual inquiries about her whereabouts, the people she met, took on a new meaning. The sound of unspoken doubts and the silent counting of time away from him filled her ears. Each time John mentioned Bogo, his voice held a note of suspicion, a subtle probing that Venera could no longer ignore. It was a tone she had heard before, in Ivana's voice, when speaking of others' successes, a tone that masked envy as concern.

These realizations brought a sense of clarity, but also a sense of loss. The John she had known, the one she had turned to for guidance and support, now seemed like a stranger, his motivations clouded by the same envy that had changed her friendship with Ivana.

At times, Venera would stand at the edge of the Hudson, gazing at the water as it reflected the city lights. In those quiet moments, Venera would think of her family, of Ivana, and of the young girl who once sat by the Adriatic Sea, dreaming of a life filled with glamor and spotlight. She pondered the innocence of those dreams, untainted by the complexities of reality.

Venera felt a renewed sense of purpose as she turned away from the waterfront and the city's pulse embraced her once again. The lessons learned from her journey had given her a clearer vision of what she wanted her future to be. A future where her dreams were not just about success, but about finding a balance between her ambitions and her true self. Stepping forward, her steps more assured than ever, Venera embraced the city as both her challenge and her sanctuary.

VI

In the living room of the house, the city lights outside cast a soft dance of shadows across the room. John sat rigidly on the edge of his couch. His eyes fixated on a photo on his phone he has yet to delete. It's a snapshot of him and Lisa, caught in a carefree laugh, a ghost of a happier past. Lisa's pale face contrasts with Venera's. In fact, Lisa varies many differences from the thick glasses to her messy brunette hair and thinner lips. John's gaze remained unflinching on the image, as if trying to decode a message hidden in her smile.

Memories flooded his mind, transporting him back to a time when laughter filled their days. He remembered Lisa's her carefree spirit that seemed to fill the gap in his heart. His memories of her played like an old film. Scenes of them cooking together in Lisa's cramped kitchen, their playful banter, and the quiet evenings spent drinking wine while writing random flash fiction together.

The memories, once warm and comforting, began to cool like a fog settling over a landscape. John's mind replayed the subtle shifts. The late nights Lisa began spending "with colleagues," the increasing distance in her eyes, the sudden jumpiness every time her phone buzzed. As he recalled the memories, he could feel his unease growing like a knot in his stomach.

The night of Lisa's confession unfolded in his mind with painful clarity. The way she hesitated at the door, her eyes averted, her hands wringing the stitch of her shirt. And then, her voice, trembling and broken, shattering their world with the confession of her affair. When she admitted to only one affair, John found out much more than that.

One evening, haunted by lingering doubts and the thought of Lisa sleeping with another man, John decided to look through Lisa's phone while she was asleep. Gently, he taps the phone with her fingertips, unlocking it, a feeling of betrayal knotting in his stomach. There was a never-ending stream of notifications and messages. The truth made itself known, without mercy. Tinder conversations and flirty texts, arranged like a mosaic of deceit. Each message was a painful revelation, confirming a year-long string of affairs with people who believed Lisa to be single and seeking short-term fun. John sat there, the phone heavy in his hands, as the reality of Lisa's betrayal sank in, reshaping his world irreversibly.

John hadn't been the same since.

In the aftermath, his once orderly life had spiraled. The apartment at the time felt too big, too quiet. He found himself wandering through the rooms, tracing the ghosts of their life together. It was during one of these aimless nights that he stumbled upon the forum AlphaSphere. A damaged world full of damaged men that resonated his disillusionment and anger. The posts and comments resonated with his sense of betrayal, wrapping him in a cocoon of vindication but also warping his perspective on trust and love.

Now, with John's relationship with Venera disintegrating, his apartment felt like a capsule, sealed off from the world. The photo of him and Lisa now deleted, as if getting rid of the memory could erase it from history. John's thoughts drifted to Venera, thinking about her laughter, her beauty and innocence. As he visualized her face, he couldn't help but feel Bogo's presence overshadowing their relationship.

As the night deepened, John lay in bed, staring at the ceiling. The path ahead was murky, the ghosts of his past still holding him in their grip. A part of him yearned to break free, to trust again, but the scars Lisa left were deep, and the fear of repeating history was a constant shadow.

Sleep eventually came, but it was fitful, filled with dreams of lost love and whispered doubts.

VII

New York hummed with its usual morning fervor as Bogo navigated the crowded streets, a comfortable smile playing on his lips. His steps led him to a corner local café, Kozy Kafé, where the aroma of freshly brewed coffee wafted through the air. He exchanged pleasantries with the barista and settled at a table outside and set two coffee cups. As he watched people passing by, lost in their own worlds, he mused over the city's ceaseless dance of anonymity and intimacy.

Just as he took his first sip of coffee, Venera appeared, her brisk steps slowing as she approached the café. "I'm so sorry I'm late," she apologized in Croatian with a warm smile, taking the seat opposite Bogo. "The subway was a nightmare this morning." She took her coffee cup that was waiting for her and sipped.

Following this, their conversation felt like a warm embrace, interlacing laughter and memories. Around them, the café buzzed with the gentle hum of conversations and the clinking of coffee cups, a serene backdrop to their intimate dialogue. Bogo entertained Venera with a funny childhood story, and her laughter filled the air. "Remember the time we tried to sneak into the old Marinković estate, convinced it was haunted?" he began, a glint in his eye as he pondered the fond memory. "We were so scared, but so curious. And just when we thought we heard a ghost, it turned out to be old Mr. Marinković's cat!"

Venera chuckled, recalling the thrill and their shared mischievous adventures rich with nostalgia. In these moments, she found a piece of home, a connection to her past that was untainted by the complexities of her life in New York. "I was terrified, but you were always the brave one," she said, shaking her head in amusement. "I still think about the summer festival where you joined the dance competition. What a night!"

"Oh God, who was it again that dared me? Was it Ivana?"

"I believe so. We were with so many friends that night. But I was surprised by your moves. Your feet were flying all over."

Bogo burst into laughter at the memory, his eyes lighting up. "Had a lot to drink for sure. I also think I invented new dance steps," he chuckled.

"If only you won. We would have gone crazy!"

"But I did win, Venera. I won the heart of the people."

They shared more laughter, bridging the years and miles that had separated them. Each memory they unearthed was a reminder of the carefree days of their youth in Croatia. Then, a pensive shadow crossed Venera's face, a subtle shift that Bogo noticed even as he leisurely sipped his coffee. "You seem full of energy." Bogo teased.

Venera observes the park where people are enjoying themselves, then faces Bogo. "It's probably nothing."

"Well, don't be so mysterious."

"It's... my boyfriend."

"John? That lovely man?"

Venera's lips curled into a teasing smile. "Is he your type?" she quipped, her eyes twinkling with playful mischief.

"Oh, totally." Bogo laughed, then sipped his coffee. "No, but seriously. What's going on?"

Venera hesitated, her fingers tracing the rim of her coffee cup. "He thinks you're going to take me away from him," she finally admitted.

"Only for a few moments." Bogo chuckled lightly, a sound that usually brought a genuine smile to Venera's face, but today it was a forced one, her eyes betraying the underlying worry.

"I'm serious, Bogo. He thinks you came here to woo me."

"Do you want me to talk to him?"

"No, I don't think that would resolve anything. Might make him more paranoid. Maybe he'll think I'm setting him up."

"It might be his insecurities. You know, you have this unique beauty that stands out, even here in the States."

"Oh, stop it, Bogo." She playfully dabs Bogo's arm.

From across the street, John's eyes were fixed on them, hidden from view. Each laugh, each gesture between Venera and Bogo, was a live wire to his insecurities. He saw Venera's hand innocently dab Bogo's arm, but to John, it was a signal, a confirmation of his darkest fears.

***

The evening at the apartment unfolded like a slow burning forest. Venera, sensing John's growing anger, braced herself. The air was thick with tension, an electric charge that preludes the inevitable outburst.

"Why do you always have to be around Bogo? What's going on between you two?" John's voice was strained, a controlled veneer over boiling emotions.

Venera's response was a blend of exasperation and disbelief. "John, what's wrong with you? I told you Bogo is just a friend, nothing more."

But John was like a dam breaking, his words flooding the room with accusations and doubt. "It's not just 'nothing,' Venera. I've seen the way you two are together. You think I can just ignore that?"

Venera's patience frayed under the onslaught, her voice rising in defense. "You need to stop letting your past control you, John."

"I'm not!" John retorted.

"Yes, you are! Stop thinking every woman is sneaky! How can you live like this!?"

John, still suspicious, calmed his demeanor and simply walked away. Venera watched him go, but her expression was uneasy. The blood in her body began to rush as she suspected something more was off with John.

VIII

The night was quiet in the house, the only sound being the occasional hum of the city that drifted in through the slightly ajar window. John sat in the dim glow of the computer screen, his usual evening ritual of browsing academic articles that he will use to lecture his class. His eyes, usually tired from grading papers, were wide and alert as he read an article on the evolution of *Othello*. Then it was replaced by a more insidious habit. He had monitored Venera's email, convincing himself it was necessary to ease his growing suspicions.

First, he took a peek outside of the bedroom, glancing at Venera cooking in the kitchen as she talks to her relatives overseas through FaceTime.

The coast is clear to John, and he begins scrolling through her inbox. One particular email caught his eye, its subject line: "Invitation to 'Luminous Expressions' at The Elysian Gallery." John remembers The Elysian Gallery was renowned in the city's art scene, a place where the elite mingled under the guise of artistic appreciation. As he clicked on the email, John's pulse raced, feeling increasingly anxious with each word.

The message was from Bogo, written in his characteristically charming style. "Pomislio sam na tebe kad sam primio ovaj poziv," Bogo had written. "Vaše cijenjenje umjetnosti i ljepote čini vas savršenim društvom za ovaj događaj. Nadam se da ćete mi se pridružiti na večeri u 'The Elysian'."

John copied and pasted the message on to Google translator. From Croatian to English, the message is translated as:

"I thought of you when I received this invitation. Your appreciation for art and beauty makes you the perfect companion for this event. I hope you'll join me for an evening at The Elysian."

Dread consumed John when he discovered the email had gone unanswered for a week, and he anxiously sifted through Venera's inbox for a response. He wondered if they had spoken about it in person, a possibility that only fueled his paranoia even further.

Dinner was a quiet affair, with John's mind miles away, lost in the maze of his suspicions. He tried to calm himself as Venera served his favorite meal. Ćevapi, a small, grilled minced meat sausages, made of pork and beef, seasoned with simple yet flavorful spices served with ajvar, a savory roasted red pepper and eggplant relish, which adds a rich, smoky flavor to the dish. As he chews on his food, he couldn't help but watched

Venera across the table enjoying her food like their previous conversation didn't happen. *She is definitely hiding something*, John thought.

They had just finished dinner, and the clinking of dishes being cleared away into the sink provided the backdrop for John's bottled-up anxiety and suspicion to erupt. "Are you going to an art gallery with Bogo?" he blurted out, his voice filled with accusation.

Venera, caught off guard, turned off the sink and looked at John, her eyes widening in surprise. "Yes, he invited me to a gallery opening. It's this weekend. But how did you know about it?" Her voice was a mixture of confusion and concern. *She will make plans without you. Once this stage is set, you know she's up to no good.*

John, realizing his mistake of speaking too soon, scrambled for an explanation. "I... overheard you talking about it," he lied, avoiding her gaze.

"Where? How?" Venera wondered.

John hesitant then caved. "Okay, I saw your emails."

Blown away by this surprise, Venera realized her privacy had been compromised. "You are a piece of shit."

That stung John in the heart. The compassion and love she once had for John has now faded into the abyss. He can't seem to latch on any longer. His mouth quivers with an attempt to say something.

"And I was going to let you know, by the way. But forget it. I don't even want to be near you. You're too much." Venera walks off to the bedroom, slams the door shut, leaving John lost in his own maddening world.

That night, as John lay on the couch, the shadows of the room seemed to echo the darkness of his thoughts. The image of Venera and Bogo at the gallery haunted him, a vivid picture painted by his jealousy and fear. Something had to be done. He must go to the gallery, somehow make his way in, and confront the situation head-on, and unveil the truth as he saw it.

XI

The night of the gallery opening, the evening sky cast hues of deepening blues and purples, creating an ominous atmosphere as John stood in the bedroom. His dreadful and determined heart raced as he prepared himself for what was to come. In his hands, he held a printed copy of the invitation of the gallery. John dressed meticulously. He chose his attire carefully. A crisp, dark shirt paired with a tailored jacket. This choice for an appearance was his attempt to somehow fit in at the gallery. As he looked at his reflection in the mirror, a myriad of emotions flickered across his face. Doubt, fear, anger. Each took its turn as he contemplated the evening ahead. He practiced what he would say, how he would present his accusations, and how he would demand the truth. Every run-through of his confrontation felt like adding fuel to his determination.

John's mind replayed the discovery of the email, the words burning bright in his memory. Each time, they reinforced his conviction that he was right, that his suspicions were justified. But underneath the layers of certainty, there was a tremor of uncertainty. *What if I'm wrong?* He said to himself. Then he remembered what the young hosts of *Unveiled and Unfiltered Truths* said. *She will make you doubt, gaslight you because they could. They know they're pretty so they can manipulate you into believing you're the crazy one and not them.*

Crossing to the point of no return, John took a deep breath and grabbed his keys, and stepped out of the house into the night. The drive to the Elysian Gallery was a blur and twenty minutes away. His fingers gripped the steering wheel with such intensity that his hands seemed to fuse with it. The streets were busy with the usual night-time traffic.

As he neared the gallery, his heart pounded louder in his chest. The Elysian Gallery stood before him, its facade illuminated by soft, inviting lights. But to John, it looked like a fortress, guarding the secrets he was planning to unearth.

Parking his car, John took a moment to collect himself. He watched as elegantly dressed guests made their way into the gallery, passing their invitations to the large security team, with conversations a distant echo in his ears. He knew Venera and Bogo would be among them, unaware of what's coming.

Bracing himself, John got out of the car and headed towards the gallery. With each step, his fortitude hardened.

This was it.

The moment of truth.

Tonight, everything would change.

John hands over the invitation to the gigantic bouncer.

"Enjoy your night." The bouncer said as he hands back the invitation.

John entered the Elysian Gallery, pushing the doors open and immersing himself in the warm ambiance of the interior. He looked around the crowd, searching for the two people who had unknowingly changed the course of his life. Further down, he saw Venera and Bogo, their heads tilted in laughter. Venera captivates all who lay eyes upon her in her timeless elegance, dressed in a sparkling red mermaid gown.

With every single step, the fiery sensation in John's chest intensified, adding fuel to his determination. He moved with a purposeful stride, his gaze fixed, cutting a determined path through the crowd. The ambient chatter and clinking of glasses faded into the background, drowned out by the pounding of his heart. As he drew closer, their laughter continued, each peal stoking the flames of his suspicion.

"Venera!" John announced upon reaching them, his voice steely and cold, slicing through their laughter like a blade. "We need to talk!"

Venera's expression shifted from amusement to alarm, her eyes widening in confusion. "J-John, what's going on? Why are you—"

Her words were cut short as John turned to Bogo, his gaze sharp and accusing. "You!" he spat out. "I know everything!"

Surprised by the sudden hostility, Bogo raised his hands in an attempt to calm the escalating situation, turning to Venera for translation.

But John's anger had reached its boiling point. "Don't play stupid! You understand what I'm saying."

Voices around them hushed as the confrontation escalated. Bogo stepped forward, hands still raised. Just as he's about to say something, Venera stepped in, trying to ease the situation. "Babe, you got it all wrong. Bogo is not what you—"

"Shut the fuck up! I know what I need to know." John retorted.

Bogo, once again, with his voice calm and collective to maintain some sort of peace. "John, I am—"

In a split second, the tension exploded into action. John, propelled by a surge of fury, shoved Bogo with a force that surprised even himself. Bogo's foot caught on the corner of a sculpture stand. Time seemed to crawl as he fell backward, his head connecting with the sharp edge of a metallic installation.

A collective gasp rippled through the crowd. Venera screamed, rushing to Bogo's side. She cradled his head in her lap, blood staining her trembling hands as she called his name. "Bogo!" But he was still, his eyes closed. A growing pool of blood stained the white marble floor.

John stood frozen, shock washing over him in icy waves. The gallery spun around him, the faces of the scared onlookers blurred and distorted.

An older, distinguished gentleman pushed through the crowd, his face etched with panic. He dropped to his knees beside Bogo, his voice breaking the stunned silence. "Bogo, my dear?" The gentleman said with an English accent.

The words echoed in John's ears, each syllable a hammer blow to his perception of the truth he had so firmly believed. Confusion, regret, and horror mingled in his gaze as he looked at the man beside Bogo, his world unraveling.

The man looked up at John with fury in his eyes. "What did you do? What did you do to my husband?!"

"H-husband?" John said, confused. Then he comes to a realization that shook him to a core as flashing red and blue lights spilled inside the gallery.

In a state of shock, Venera briefly glanced at John before diverting her eyes to the floor.

X

The interrogation room was a stark, unforgiving space, its bare walls and harsh fluorescent lighting creating an atmosphere of cold reality. The room felt both claustrophobic and infinitely vast. John sat at a metal table, his hands clasped tightly in front of him. He had a rigid posture, with dull eyes fixed on a point beyond the room. Shadows played across his face, deepening the lines of stress and worry that seemed to have etched themselves permanently into his features. Every so often, a muscle in his jaw twitched, the only hint of the nervous energy that coursed through him. He appeared as a man engulfed by the gravity of his actions, weighed down by a mixture of regret, fear, and a profound sense of disbelief at how his life had unraveled in the past 24 hours.

Detective Harris entered the room, her expression stern yet not unkind. She sat across from John, her eyes scanning his face, seeking to understand the man before her. "Mr. Gills," she began, her voice measured, "can you tell me what happened last night?"

John's gaze remained fixed on the table, his voice barely a whisper. "It was an accident. I didn't mean for any of this to happen."

Detective Harris nodded slowly, noting his demeanor. "I understand this is difficult, but I need you to walk me through the events. Why did you confront Mr. Zlato and Ms. Novák at the gallery?"

John lifted his eyes, meeting the detective's gaze. His eyes were pools of trouble, reflecting a storm of regret and confusion. "I thought... I believed... I don't know. Thought there was something going on between them. I was convinced they were... together behind my back."

"And what led you to believe that, Mr. Gills?" Detective Harris asked, her pen poised over her notepad.

John's fingers twisted together, the knuckles whitening. "The little things, the way they were with each other. Feelings."

Detective Harris leaned forward slightly, her voice softening. "But were these feelings based on evidence, or were they assumptions, Mr. Gills?"

John's mouth opened, but no words came out. He looked like a man drowning in his own thoughts, struggling to separate reality from the narrative that had consumed him. The certainty of last night now eroded by the harsh light of reality.

Detective Harris continued, gently but firmly unraveling the layers of John's actions. "Did Mr. Zlato say or do anything to threaten you or Ms. Novák?"

"No, he... I think he tried to calm me down." John's admission was a choked whisper, the realization of his misinterpretation dawning on him like a cruel sunrise.

The detective sighed softly, closing her notepad. "Mr. Gills, I know this is hard, but understanding your mindset is crucial. This isn't just about what happened, but why it happened."

John looked up, his face full of pain and realization. The detective's words resonated in the room, emphasizing the seriousness of what had happened. The truth, now untangled from his madness, lay bare and undeniable.

As Detective Harris stood to leave, John's voice halted her. "I swear, I never meant to hurt anyone," he said, the words heavy with a sorrow.

The detective paused at the door, offering a nod of acknowledgment. She understood. It wasn't the first time she had heard someone say this.

The door closed with a soft click, leaving John alone in the room, a man enveloped by the consequences of his actions. The silence was oppressive, a void where once there was the chaos of his unfounded fears. Now, there was only the stark reality of what he had done, a reality from which there was no escape.

****

In the days following the tragedy, Venera found solace in the comforting presence of her family, their arms wrapped tightly around her. Her uncle Ivo offered quiet strength and wisdom. Her cousin Damir, with whom she worked at the restaurant, provided support and some normalcy amid the chaos. They openly discussed Bogo and John, but also empathized with her sadness, her confusion, and her moments of reflection.

As she managed the restaurant, Venera's interactions with patrons and staff were tinged with a new perspective. Her dream of modeling, once a driving force, took a backseat as she found purpose and fulfillment in her role at the restaurant, a testament to her resilience and adaptability. In the heart of Astoria, Venera stood behind the counter of the Croatian restaurant, her eyes alight with a blend of pride and determination. Each day, as she interacted with customers, sharing stories of her homeland through the dishes she served, a profound sense of fulfillment coursed through her.

She found joy in the little things – the way patrons' faces show delighted reactions upon tasting authentic Croatian flavors from Ćevapi to Crni Rižot or Black Risotto, the conversations that sparked over shared plates, the warmth of the community that gathered within these walls. Every satisfied customer was a tribute to her heritage, a piece of Croatia brought to life in a foreign land.

Managing the restaurant had also carved out a new version of Venera. She's more confident, adept, and resilient. She had grown in spirit. The challenges of the role had honed her leadership abilities and her capacity to innovate and adapt. The restaurant's success was a reflection of her journey, a testament to her hard work and passion. Her cousins are proud of her accomplishments and what she has provided for the restaurant.

In this little corner of Astoria, Venera had created a home away from home, not just for herself but for all who sought a taste of Croatia. It was a realization of a dream she hadn't known she carried – to share her culture and heritage with the world. By doing so, she discovered purpose and pride, connecting with her roots on a personal and communal level.

After a day's work, Venera strolled towards the East River. The night had draped the city in a cloak of tranquility, and as she reached the riverbank, the distant Manhattan skyline greeted her. Its lights, a constellation against the night sky, sparkled with a quiet promise. By the water, she paused, allowing the rhythm of the city to meld with her thoughts. The challenges, the heartaches, and the triumphs of her journey in this new land. She noticed before her the city lights shimmered and reflected on the river, creating a path of illumination through the darkness.

GREED
JACK OF DIAMONDS

I

Jack Hoffman was only sixteen when he made his first bet. It started in the back room of Wolfgang's Den, a pub his Uncle Wolfgang Braun owned. The air was thick with the scent of alcohol and cigarette smoke – a smell that Jack had grown accustomed to during his summer visits. He would help out by cleaning, but it was the Texas Hold 'em games that captivated him. These games, reserved for a select group of regulars, were like a private club. Jack would often sneak peeks at the players, their faces illuminated by the faint glow of the pendant lamp, as colorful chips clinked and crashed in the pot's center.

"Bet," Rudy grunted, a bearded man, his voice husky from years of smoke, "two hundred." With a casual flick, he sent chips spiraling into the pot.

"I call," retorted Marvin, a shorter, stumpy man with a surprisingly high voice. "Can't make life any easier, eh, Rudy?"

"Gotta keep things interesting, know what I mean?" Rudy replied with a grin.

The River revealed a Queen of Hearts. "All in," announced Rudy.

"Call!" Marvin showed a full house, tens over queens, but was quickly outdone by Rudy's four queens. "Quads." Rudy said.

Marvin, cursing under his breath, jumped out of his seat in a huff, his cards fluttering to the floor.

The rest of the players hardly responded, showing how common these outbursts were. Jack watched, fascinated by the dynamics at play.

Rudy, catching Jack's eye from the green-baize table, beckoned him over with a gesture that was both commanding and friendly. "Fetch me a beer from Wolfgang, kid. Here's for the trouble." He handed Jack a five-dollar chip, its red surface glinting under the dim lights.

Jack made his way through the smoky haze to the bar, where his uncle Wolfgang was polishing glasses. "One beer for Rudy," he said, pocketing the chip. Wolfgang raised an eyebrow but said nothing, sliding an open bottle across the counter.

Returning to the table, Jack handed the beer to Rudy, who flicked him a black chip. "That's twenty dollars for you, kid," Rudy said, a hint of a smirk playing on his lips.

The men at the table were shuffling and rearranging their chips, the rhythm of the game unbroken. Rudy gestured to the now-empty chair next to him, the one recently vacated by Marvin in a fit of frustration. "Why don't you sit down, kid? See if you've got more than just luck."

Jack hesitated, but before he could decline, Elijah Steinberg, exuding a refined air, gestured to the seat beside him. Dressed impeccably in a tailored suit that spoke of understated elegance, his well-groomed beard shaped into a precise point, Elijah radiated an aura of cultured confidence. He wore a vintage watch that caught the light with its subtle gleam, moving with deliberate grace. "It's okay, Jack," he said, his voice smooth and relaxed, each word measured and intentional. "Come sit here. I'll show you the ways."

Jack hesitated for a moment, then mustered up his courage and sat down beside Elijah, his curiosity fascinated. The cards were swiftly dealt by Rudy to five other players and Jack. He held a Jack of Diamonds and a Four of Clubs. His heart raced under the watchful eyes of the players.

The flop came – a Seven of Diamonds, a Three of Spades, and an Eight of Diamonds. Jack's mind raced with the possibilities. Elijah's low, calm voice provided a subtle guide. "Think about the hands, the odds. Do you understand?"

Jack gives a nod and faces the community board that's on the table.

The turn brought another diamond, a Two, heightening the tension at the table. Jack felt the flush a possibility, but his inexperience weighed heavily on him.

Rudy, with a smirk, makes a bet. "Let's see what the kid is made of," he said, half-mocking, half-curious.

Elijah's hand on Jack's shoulder was reassuring. "Trust what you see, and play your game, Jack."

Another nod. Jack takes the chips he got from servicing Rudy and tosses them.

Elijah gives a nod. "You're all-in, which means you can only collect whatever matches your bet equal to the amount of players." He takes the two chips that belonged to Jack, a total of twenty-five dollars times the five players who happily call. More like donating to Jack if he wins.

Rudy flips the River... a Five of Diamonds.

Murmurs circled the table. Jack, with a deep breath, barely hides his nervous excitement. Elijah can see through him, but nonetheless smiles about it like a mentor to his protégé.

The reveals began. Rudy, with a confident smirk, showed a three of a kind with pocket eights. But the mood shifted when Jack, under Elijah's nod, turned his cards over – a Jack-high flush.

A few chuckles erupted around the table, and Rudy's smirk faded into a begrudging nod of respect. Elijah's voice was warm. "Well played. Risky hand to begin with, but well played."

Jack's hands trembled slightly as he collected his modest winnings, feeling a rush of confidence and excitement. He had stepped into a risky venture and emerged victorious, with Elijah's guidance illuminating the path. It was a small win, but it marked the beginning of a much larger journey for Jack, one that extended far beyond the green felt of the poker table.

II

Jack sat in his small, cramped office, surrounded by a mountain of paperwork – invoices, rent reminders, and debt notices that seemed to multiply with each passing day. The table was cluttered with scratch-off tickets, and a few had fallen onto the floor. The fixture light cast long shadows across his face, accentuating the worry lines that had become almost permanent. He rubbed his temples, the weight of the world seemingly pressing down on his shoulders. The lively sounds of laughter and conversation from Wolfgang's Den filtered through the walls, a bittersweet reminder of what he was fighting to keep alive.

Then a beep came from his laptop.

A notification that a VPN is online. A perfect opportunity to continue his game on AceQuest Poker, an online gambling website that provides various games like Texas Hold 'em, Omaha, and Seven-Card-Stud. Of course, Jack picks his favorite, Texas Hold 'em as he has bad luck in the other two games. With each click, his hopes rose and fell, the virtual world echoing the all-too-real thrills and despairs of gambling. As the final hand played out, a sinking feeling gripped him; his digital opponent went all-in, and Jack, instantly following suit, believing his hand, a Six of Spades and a Seven of Clubs, was good enough. But he saw his virtual fortune slip away with a losing hand. His virtual opponent won with an Ace high. Not even a pair, but a high card. One of the most embarrassing ways to lose.

It was more frustrating.

In a moment, he snapped the laptop shut, a harsh click cutting through the room's silence. With a heavy sigh, Jack stood up, smoothing out the creases in his shirt – a futile attempt to bring order to the chaos that was threatening to engulf him. He rubbed his weary eyes, the loss a stinging reminder of the risky dance of luck and skill. He took one last look at the disarray on his desk before stepping out into the pub.

The warm glow of the hanging lights, the clinking of glasses, the buzz of stories being exchanged all painted a picture of cheer and company. Jack forced a smile as he moved through the space, a practiced mask of confidence and ease. He paused to exchange pleasantries with a group of regulars huddled near the dartboard. "Ay yo, Jack!" called out a burly man with a friendly grin. "You gonna join us for a game or what?"

Jack chuckled, shaking his head. "I'd love to, Mike, but you know I'd just embarrass you."

Mike's fiancée, Sarah, chimed in with a little laugh. "He's been practicing this time."

"Yeah, man," Mike said, following a chuckle.

Jack offered a smile. "Maybe next time. You guys enjoy your evening."

As Jack walked away, their laughter and chatter fading behind him, Jack couldn't help but feel a pang of longing for the simplicity of their enjoyment. But behind his eyes, there was a distant, almost haunted look – the mark of a man grappling with unseen demons, his mind a world away from the carefree banter of the pub's patrons. As he navigated the familiar territory of the pub he had grown to love, every pat on the back from a patron, every nod of respect, felt like a small victory against the tide of anxiety that was never far from his mind. He reached the bar, leaning casually against it, his eyes briefly meeting those of Adam, the bartender, and a longtime friend. There was an unspoken understanding in Adam's gaze, one that had become all too familiar.

"You're doing that thing again," Adam said quietly, polishing a glass with a worn cloth.

"What thing?" Jack replied, feigning ignorance, though he knew exactly what Adam meant.

"That thing with your crooked smile. Something's up."

Jack let out a small, weary sigh. "It's just the usual, Adam. Business concerns. You know how it is."

Adam set the glass down, leaning in. "It's this place, isn't it?"

Jack offered a reassuring nod, a practiced gesture. "I've got this under control. Really."

Adam's eyes revealed his worry as he looked at him. "This place is important to all of us. Tell me what's going on?"

"Money." Jack said nonchalantly.

"You have money." Adam reassured him.

"I need more."

"Jack, we're in debt, and you refuse to pay. How much more do you need?"

"Whatever it takes."

"What does that mean, 'whatever it takes'?" Adam trying to understand the situation. "Jack, do you even care about this bar?"

Jack forced a smile. "Of course, Adam. Don't want to taint my uncle's name." But as he turned away, his expression faltered. How much longer could he keep up this facade, he wondered, before everything came crashing down?

Turning away, Jack let his gaze drift over the patrons – his patrons. Wolfgang's Den was a legacy, a piece of his Uncle Wolfgang that he clung to, a reminder of a time when life was simpler and the future seemed bright. As he mingled and smiled, he felt the pressure of expectation settling more firmly on his shoulders.

After the Den quieted down, Jack found himself alone at the bar, his attention absorbed by his phone. He was scrolling through FanDuel, fixated on a parlay bet that was teetering between a promising win and a disheartening loss. He would dart his eyes back and forth from the TV and his phone. It was a critical NBA playoff game, game six to be exact, between the Golden State Warriors and the Boston Celtics. The fate of his ambitious parlay bet hinged on this game. Jack had put his faith, and a $3,500 moneyline on the Celtics pulling off a win. The odds had been favorable, the stats and player performances aligning with his prediction.

Jack's focus was interrupted when a group of loyal patrons since Wolfgang's time converse loudly. Tom, a local theater enthusiast, called out to him. "Hey Jack, you still remember the Halloween party Wolfgang threw? When he dressed up as Elvis?", asked with a laugh.

Jack looked up, a fleeting smile crossing his face. "Of course. How could anyone forget?"

Tom turned to the group and continued the conversation about Wolfgang. "He sang 'Heartbreak Hotel' like he was the King himself."

Jack's eyes briefly lighting up with the memory before returning to the phone screen.

"He also played poker like a king, too," Linda, the flower shop owner from across the street, added. "He was so entertaining to watch."

The warmth of the conversation was overshadowed by the cold glow of the screen, the imminent loss looming over him. Jack half-listened, his anxiety growing as the last game of his parlay inched towards a conclusion. His eyes followed the real-time updates, the scores fluctuating with every play.

The drama of the game unfolds – Curry's three-pointers, Thompson's defensive maneuvers, Tatum's aggressive drives. In the last nail-biting minutes, the scores were too close for comfort. Jack's heart pounded in his chest as he watched the seconds tick down. The Celtics were trailing by just a few points, the possibility of a comeback keeping hope alive. But as the final buzzer sounded, that hope evaporated. The Warriors clinched the victory, their jubilation stark against the backdrop of Jack's sinking heart. The FanDuel app on his phone screen coldly confirmed his loss. His bold bet, driven by a desire for a quick financial fix, was ruined.

"FUCK!" Jack slams his fist on the table, overwhelmed by the defeat. The patrons turned to Jack with concern, but didn't want to bother him. Jack let out a quiet sigh of frustration and set the phone aside. The Warriors' victory was being celebrated somewhere, but here, in the Den, only the sting of defeat. Jack's disappointment was obvious. He tried to mask it to regain his composure, but the patrons at Wolfgang's Den were more perceptive than he gave them credit for.

"Tough night, Jack?" Linda said, her eyes soft with concern.

Jack forced a smile. "Just one of those nights, Linda." He began vaguely wiping down the bar, trying to appear busy.

Tom, with his easygoing demeanor, chimed in. "We've all been there, buddy."

Jack returns a nod.

Tom wanted to cheer Jack up with a story. "Hey! Remember when your uncle Wolfgang bet on the Giants against the Patriots? What was it, the 2008 Super Bowl?"

Jack couldn't help but smile at the memory. "Yeah, I thought it was over when Randy Moss got that touchdown."

"Damn, Wolfgang was a risky better," Harold, a retired teacher and a regular for decades, added from across the bar. "I thought he was always careful with his bets."

The words resonated with Jack more than he expected. He looked around at the faces of the regulars – people who had been part of the Den's story for years, who had seen the highs and lows. He thought about the poker games as he saw some pictures hanging on the walls with regulars and players. "Actually, I've been thinking about bringing back a bit of that old Wolfgang spirit," Jack said, a new idea forming. "How about a poker tournament? Right here, in memory of Wolfgang. It would be his sixty-fifth birthday. I want to do something special for it."

The suggestion sparked interest among the regulars. "A poker tournament? Hell yeah!" Tom exclaimed with enthusiasm. "It's been ages since we had a proper game here."

"Wolfgang's poker nights were legendary," Maria, another regular, added with a nostalgic smile.

As they discussed the idea, Jack felt a flicker of hope. A poker tournament could be the perfect tribute to his uncle, a chance to bring back the glory days of the Den, and perhaps ease his financial woes. Then the regulars dispersed, leaving Jack with his thoughts. He knew the risks involved, but the tournament felt like a gamble worth taking – to honor his uncle's memory with the possibilities to turn his fortunes around and definitely add some funds to his pockets.

***

In his office, Jack sat surrounded by lists and plans for the upcoming tournament. The event was shaping up to be larger than anything the Den had seen in years. He could almost hear the buzz of excitement, the clinking of chips, the murmur of conversations. A lively atmosphere that could potentially pull him out of his financial abyss and bring in some extra cash. As Jack was finalizing the list of invitees, Adam walked in, his eyebrows raised in skepticism. "You're running a poker tournament?" he remarked, leaning against the door frame.

Jack looked up, a practiced smile on his face. "That's right, my friend," he replied, but his tone lacked conviction.

Adam crossed his arms, his gaze steady on Jack. "Quit bullshitting, Jack. This isn't just about honoring Wolfgang. You're trying to collect."

Jack's smile faltered, and he looked away. "What? I can't do a poker night, Adam? It's my uncle's birthday and I want to make an event out of it."

Adam sighed, moving closer. "Okay, if you say so. But I'll host the event, keep things running smoothly. So I can keep an eye on you, not because I agree with what you're doing."

Jack nodded in response.

As Adam was about to leave, he paused, turning back to face Jack. "Who are you planning to invite?" he asked, a note of concern in his voice.

Jack started listing names, most of them regulars and old friends of Wolfgang. As he spoke, he watched Adam's reactions, each name met with a nod or a simple hum of acknowledgment. "Oh, and Elijah," Jack added, almost as an afterthought.

Adam's expression shifted, his concern becoming more pronounced. "Elijah? Why?"

Jack leaned back in his chair, his gaze steady. "Elijah was one of Wolfgang's closest friends. He's a part of this place's history. Besides, we could use the stakes he brings to the table."

Adam let out a slow breath. "Just remember what you're getting into, Jack. This isn't just a friendly game among pals. With Elijah in the mix, it's a whole different ball game."

Jack nodded with apprehension in his eyes. "I know what I'm doing, Adam. But if I don't invite him, then it would be disrespectful, not just for the Den, but for my uncle's honor."

Adam gave him a long, searching look, then finally nodded. "Alright, Jack." As he left the office, Jack sat alone, thinking about the upcoming event. Inviting Elijah was indeed a risk, but Jack felt it was one he needed to take. High stakes could mean high rewards, and right now, Jack was playing for more than just money.

III

Wolfgang's fiftieth birthday at the Den was a night of high-spirited celebration. The pub buzzed with energy, filled with friends, family, and a chorus of well-wishers. Amidst it all was Wolfgang, the heart of the revelry, his laughter booming like a melody that everyone knew by heart.

"Ah, Wolfgang, fifty years young!" Elijah called out with a chuckle as he clinked his glass against Wolfgang's. "This is not only a celebration for the big fifty, but also a celebration of a major closing at the Upper East Side. Two penthouses sold!"

Wolfgang grinned, raising his glass. "You're always overshadowing me. But that's why I like you." He turned to the gathering crowd. "This man here is deadly with cards in his hands. He will drain your life savings."

Elijah interrupted, feigning resentment. "Now, now, Wolfgang, let's not give away all our secrets."

"Should I tell everyone bluffing tells?"

"I mean, I'll just adjust." Elijah chuckled with a dab on Wolfgang's shoulder.

Wolfgang's gaze met young Jack's, and he beckoned his nephew closer. "Come here, Jack. Learn from the masters, eh?"

Young Jack shyly approached, and Wolfgang put an arm around him. With a warm smile, he shared a piece of wisdom that Jack would carry with him for years to come. "Remember, Jack, life's a bit like poker. It's not just about playing the good hands, but also playing the bad ones well. And Elijah is a master at it."

"That's why I do well in real estate." Elijah bragged.

"A hell of a salesman you are. Better than when I was doing it." Wolfgang said.

"Our partnership was still timeless."

"The good ol' days, thanks to you."

Elijah, though rarely, shies away from the compliment. Humbled only because it's from his friend Wolfgang. The night went on, filled with stories, laughter, and Wolfgang's larger-than-life presence. It was a celebration of life, friendship, and the simple joys that made everything worthwhile.

***

Jack sat in his office, surrounded by the silence of the empty pub, reminiscing about his simple times as a young man. Wolfgang's words echoed in his mind, but they carried a different weight now. Where Wolfgang had seen poker as a dance of minds and a symbol of camaraderie, Jack couldn't help but view it through the lens of his desperate need for money.

As he planned the tournament, there was a nagging awareness of the divergence between his intentions and what his uncle stood for. Wolfgang had cherished the joy and unity such events brought. Jack, on the other hand, saw it as a means to an end – a necessary gamble to ease his suffocating debts. He felt a twinge of guilt at the thought of exploiting the regulars' loyalty and the legacy of the Den for personal gain. Yet, the pressing urgency of his financial situation left him feeling justified, if not entirely comfortable, with his decision.

Jack spent some time in his office before finally standing up, feeling determined yet conflicted. He had in his hands a large, elegantly designed flyer, the result of his earlier planning. The flyer was bold and eye-catching, with "In Honor of Wolfgang" in large, stylish letters at the top, as well as the details of the tournament.

He made his way to the front of the pub, where the morning light was just beginning to filter through the windows, casting a soft glow on the interior of Wolfgang's Den. Jack paused for a moment, looking around the space that held so many memories, now poised to host an event that felt like a crossroads in his life.

Jack carefully placed the flyer on the inside of the glass at the front of the bar, positioning it so it was visible to everyone who walked in. A call to the community that had grown around the pub. As he stepped back to look at the flyer, Jack felt a mixture of pride and apprehension. This tournament would be a fitting tribute to his uncle, a way to bring back the spirit of the old days. At the same time, Jack can earn some quick cash. He wondered how much he could benefit without his patrons realizing it.

IV

The sun in the morning filled Wolfgang's Den with a comforting light, indicating the beginning of a day filled with both excitement and unease. Inside the pub, Adam effortlessly orchestrated the setup for the poker tournament, creating a buzzing atmosphere. "More tables over there, and let's make sure the bar is fully stocked," Adam directed the staff, his voice calm. Despite his concerns about the tournament and what it represented for Jack, he couldn't deny the thrill of hosting such an event.

Jack, meanwhile, hovered nearby, his mind a tumult of thoughts and calculations. Every now and then, he offered a suggestion or nodded in agreement to Adam's decisions, but his gaze often drifted, thinking about the possible winnings.

As the afternoon gave way to evening, guests began to arrive. The Den gradually filled with the sounds of greetings and laughter, a reunion of old friends and loyal patrons. Each arrival seemed to bring a piece of history, a fragment of the joyous past Wolfgang had cultivated within these walls.

First came Mrs. Clara Henderson, the owner of a local organic foods shop, a woman in her fifties with a sharp wit and a surprising passion for poker. Her arrival came with a basket of fresh organic fruits as a gift for the Den.

Behind her, Joe "The Mechanic" Mancini, a burly man with hands calloused from years of labor, entered with his usual husky voice.

Recognized for his talent in bluffing, he was a permanent fixture at the poker tables in the Den, seamlessly blending into the ambience alongside the aged wood of the bar.

Then there were Emily and David Park, a middle-aged couple who had their first date at the Den years ago. David, a quiet accountant, and Emily, a vibrant school teacher, found common ground over poker and had been regulars ever since.

Lingering near the entrance was young Kevin, a recent college graduate and an aspiring poker player. He is also a big fan of the World Series of Poker and hopes to join one day.

Each guest, from the familiar faces to the less frequent visitors, brought with them stories and memories, resonances of the vibrant community Wolfgang had nurtured. Greetings and laughter filled the Den, creating an atmosphere of a long-awaited reunion among old friends and dedicated regulars, as they shared their unique stories that seemed to be ingrained within the walls of the establishment.

Stepping in with his trademark sophistication, Elijah's mere presence became the center of attention. Adam extended his hand respectfully, aware of the man's formidable reputation as a poker player. "Glad you could make it, Elijah," Adam said warmly.

Elijah nodded, his eyes scanning the room. "Wouldn't miss it for the world." Elijah said, his voice remaining smooth and relaxed.

Jack, observing from a distance, experienced an indescribable feeling as he watched Elijah interact with the guests. He recognized that inviting him was a risk, but he couldn't help but take it.

As the night progressed, the air in Wolfgang's Den became thick with nostalgia. Gathered around tables laden with drinks, groups of regulars exchanged stories about Wolfgang, each tale underscoring the man's remarkable character.

Adam found himself among a circle of old-timers, their faces alight with memories. "I remember one night there was a terrible blizzard,"

Tom began, a hint of amusement in his eyes. "Something cut the power and we couldn't get it working. It was so dark, we thought the game was over. But I'll never forget when Wolfgang hauled out candles, turning it into the most memorable poker night ever. He said, 'A little darkness can't dim the spirit of this place.' We played by candlelight. The entire bar lit up like some old-time saloon. I couldn't help but laugh."

Sandra added, her voice warm with affection, "I heard about that. Sounded like a good time. But I don't know if you remember when he caught that hustler trying to cheat? I swear, I thought Wolfgang was going to beat the shit out of him. I know I would've. Even thinking about it boils me. But no. He took him to the side, gave that man a drink and had a conversation. By the end of it, the guy was practically in tears, apologizing. For some reason, Wolfgang always saw the good in people and believes they can be better."

Nods of agreement rippled through the group. His ability to read people, to connect and impart lessons, not just in poker but in life, was legendary within the walls of the Den.

Jack joined them, listening more than contributing, each story a reminder of the legacy he was trying to uphold. "He had a way of knowing when to take a risk," Jack finally said, his voice tinged with a mixture of admiration and something darker. "I guess that's what tonight is about – taking a risk."

Before the tournament commenced, Jack stood up, silencing the murmurs in the bar as all eyes focused on him. He took a moment, gathering his thoughts, then began with a voice that resonated with emotion and respect.

"Today, we're here to celebrate what would have been my Uncle Wolfgang's sixty-fifth birthday." Jack's gaze drifted across the room, meeting the eyes of those who had known and respected his uncle. "He wasn't just the man who ran the bar; he was a cornerstone of our community. This tournament is a tribute to him, to the legacy he's left in each of us." He paused, allowing his words to resonate. "In the spirit of Wolfgang's love for poker and competition, we've put together a significant prize for tonight. Thanks to your enthusiasm and the buy-back option, our total pot has reached an impressive $20,000."

Excitement rippled through the crowd at the mention of the amount.

"The breakdown is as follows. Our winner tonight will walk away with 50% of the pot, that's $10,000. Second place will earn themselves $6,000. And third taking $4,000."

Members of the crowd looked at each other, drinks in hand, excited to play as they heard the prizes.

Jack continues, "Let's play this game in a way that would make Wolfgang proud. With integrity, skill, and a little bit of that luck, he always seemed to have in his pocket. Best of luck to all of you!" Jack stepped down, filling the room with purposeful anticipation, as he paid homage to his uncle's memory.

***

The Den was alive and full of energy. Jack, his skills honed over years of practice and observation, took his place at one of the tables. His expression displayed focused determination. Around him, the atmosphere had a variety of characters trying their luck at the tables. Laughter and cheers would occasionally break out, only to be replaced by hushed anticipation as the next hand was dealt.

The games were intense. Every decision at the table was a mini-drama, from the tight-lipped newbie making a bold all-in, to the seasoned regular deftly bluffing their way through a weak hand. But for Jack, he played with a calculated precision, his uncle's advice echoing in his mind with each hand he played. The thrill of the game revived a long-lost feeling of exhilaration. At the same time, he thinks about all the money he could win. However, as the night progressed, so did the tension.

An argument broke out at a table, disrupting the cool atmosphere of the room. Two players, their faces flushed with agitation, stood up, their chairs scraping loudly against the floor. The argument was over a contentious hand – one player, a burly man with a gruff voice, held a flush, while the other, a wiry, quick-talking young man, had a straight. The argument had nothing to do with their hands, but with the bitterness that seeped into their words.

"Gotta teach these young ones some respect!" the burly man bellowed, his disbelief mixing with anger.

"Dude, go fuck yourself!" retorted the young man, his tone defensive and sharp.

"What did you say, boy?" The burly man threatened.

"You heard me, old man."

The argument quickly escalated, drawing the attention of the entire room. Voices were raised and gestures became more animated as other players and onlookers gathered around, murmurs and whispers filling the air.

Adam, ever the mediator, swiftly intervened. Cutting through the rising tension, he approached the table, his voice firm yet calm. "Hey, hey! Let's keep it friendly, gentlemen," he said, placing a hand on the burly man's shoulder in a gesture of peace. "I'll kick the both of you out and none of you will have a chance to win some money."

Adam's calm authority acted as a soothing balm, gradually extinguishing the fiery tempers. The room, sensing the resolution, began to buzz with life once again, the recent outburst fading into just another memory in an otherwise peaceful night.

Jack watched the scene unfold with relief, grateful for Adam's help. He caught his eye and nodded in silent thanks. Adam, ever the vigilant guardian of the Den's peace, returned the gesture with a subtle nod, his eyes never straying far from the pulse of the room.

Throughout the evening, Elijah moved through the tables, his presence almost spectral. He played effortlessly, his wins accumulating as the night wore on. Every so often, his eyes would meet Jack's, an unspoken acknowledgment passing between them. Jack couldn't shake off the feeling of rivalry, which was accompanied by a reluctant admiration.

Midnight approached. The field had narrowed down to the final table. Eight players remained, including Jack and Elijah. The crowd around the table had grown, spectators drawn in by the high stakes and the skill of the remaining players. Jack looked around at his competitors – a mix of seasoned players and determined underdogs.

Adam stood nearby, watching Jack with a keen eye. He had seen many poker games in his time at the Den, but none quite like this. This game was more than just a competition. It was a culmination of history, personal struggles, and the unspoken battles each player brought to the table.

V

Aside from Jack, with his inner conflicts, and Elijah, the embodiment of cool, calculated skill, were four seasoned players, each a regular with a deep connection to the pub. There was Tom, the theatrical director, known for his flair and unpredictable style; Frank, the retired mechanic, whose methodical and patient approach often outlasted flashier players; Sandra, the high school teacher, whose analytical mind made her a challenging opponent; and finally, Lester, a local business owner in his early sixties, and an aggressive player with the ability to read people. Completing the table were the newcomers. Kevin, the young, eager enthusiast, and Clarence, the older player whose calm exterior masked a sharp, strategic thinking.

The room had completely changed its appearance, now resembling an exciting arena, with a ring of spectators comprising eliminated players, regular patrons, and friends of the Den. Their murmurs and whispers created a background hum, a soundtrack to the high-stakes drama unfolding. The air was electric with expectation, each spectator keenly aware of the blend of history, personal ambition, and raw emotion that this tournament represented.

Oscar, a retired dealer from Atlantic City who frequented the Den every other weekend, shuffled and dealt the first hand of the final table with expertise. As the cards were slid across the table, the players could sense destiny's playful nature being dealt on the smooth felt surface. Jack glanced at his hand: a Jack of Diamonds and a King of Clubs. A promising start.

The betting started cautiously, with players gauging each other's reactions. Lester, known for his aggressive play, was quick to raise the stakes, his eyes flicking around the table with a confident glimmer. His betting was bold, almost reckless, suggesting a strong hand.

Jack weighed his options, the memory of Wolfgang's words on risk and reward echoing in his mind. He decided to call, matching Lester's bet. The air was thick with tension as the other players folded one by one, leaving Jack and Lester to face off.

The flop was revealed: a Jack of Spades, a Seven of Hearts, and a Four of Diamonds. Jack's heart skipped a beat – he had hit a pair of Jacks. The odds were tilting in his favor, but Lester pushed a colorful mix of chips into the pot's center. "Three hundred," he announced firmly.

Jack pondered Lester's move. With the Seven on the flop, a possible three-of-a-kind loomed in his mind if Lester held pocket sevens. He studied Lester carefully, searching for a tell. That's when he caught it – a quick, almost slight flick of Lester's eye before it darted back to the table. With assertiveness, Jack made his decision. "Call," he said calmly, pushing an equal amount of chips forward to match Lester's bet.

The turn brought a Two of Hearts. Another strong bet by Lester, "A thousand," he said, tossing the chips.

But Jack can't let go of the Jack of Diamonds as he never lost with it in his hand. He makes the call by simply tossing the matching chips.

Now, the river completed the board with another Jack – the Jack of Hearts. Lester pushes all of his chips, "All-in," his demeanor exuding certainty.

The room held its breath. The spectators leaning in to catch every nuance of the showdown.

Jack, with a mixture of apprehension and hope, knows Lester's play is always aggressive. This could be a way to intimidate Jack and fold.

But no.

He called the bet. The moment of truth had arrived. Lester, with a slight smirk, revealed his hand – pocket Aces hitting an Ace high two-pair.

Jack let out a small chuckle as he confidently flipped his cards, revealing his three of a kind – Jacks. A murmur rippled through the crowd. Jack had taken the hand, his luck holding against Lester's aggressive play.

Lester leaned back, a rueful smile on his face as he accepted his defeat. "Fucking Jack of Diamonds," he conceded, standing up to leave the table amidst a round of applause.

As the chips were pushed towards Jack, he allowed himself a brief moment of relief. But the victory was fleeting – there were still more hands to play, more decisions to be made. The game was just beginning, and the stakes were only getting higher.

As the game progressed, each turn of a card seemed to ratchet the tension higher at the final table. The once casual chatter had dwindled to an occasional murmur, replaced by the sharp snap of cards against the felt and the clinking of chips. One by one, players were eliminated, their sighs of resignation and the soft shuffling of their departure punctuating the air. The chips, now stacked in a towering, glittering heap in the center of the table, caught the dim overhead lights, casting long shadows across the players' focused faces. The scent of anticipation was almost palpable, mixed with the faint aroma of spilled beer and the distant echo of laughter from other parts of the bar. Each remaining player's eyes flickered with a mixture of determination and unspoken hopes, their hands subtly trembling as they placed their bets.

The game eventually narrowed to four players: Jack, Elijah, Sandra, and the young upstart Kevin. With each hand, the tension grew stronger. Jack and Elijah, both skilled and seasoned, played with a careful mix of aggression and restraint, their eyes occasionally meeting across the table in a silent acknowledgment of each other's prowess.

A pivotal hand unfolded with Sandra and Kevin going head-to-head, while Jack and Elijah, having folded earlier, watched from the sidelines. Sandra, with her analytical mind, was a picture of concentration, while Kevin, fueled by youthful enthusiasm and a streak of good fortune, matched her bet for bet.

The rest of the room seemed to hold its breath as Kevin and Sandra revealed their cards. The community board laid out the Ten of Hearts, Jack of Spades, Queen of Diamonds, Three of Clubs, and a King of Hearts. Kevin, with a confident flourish, flipped over his hand to reveal a Queen of Hearts and a Queen of Clubs, a three-of-a-kind. But it was Sandra who triumphed as she revealed an Ace of Hearts and an Ace of Spades, completing an ace-high straight.

The room burst into applause, acknowledging the exceptional level of play they had just witnessed.

As the clapping continued, Jack and Elijah shared a brief, intense look. There was an unspoken understanding, a recognition of the inevitable showdown that was drawing closer. Elijah, ever the gentleman, offered a gentle clap for Sandra, his expression one of mild amusement and respect.

With Kevin's elimination, only three players remained: Jack, Elijah, and Sandra. There was a noticeable shift in the dynamics at the table. Each player was acutely aware of the stakes now – not just the chips on the table, but the prestige of being the last standing in a tournament. But really, it's the first place prize money of $10,000. Actually, $14,000 since some players bought back in. Kevin being one of them.

No wonder he was so angry and didn't say a word as he left.

Jack glanced at the remaining chips in front of him, then at his opponents. Sandra was a tough opponent, her play style methodical and calculated. However, Elijah remained a mystery - skilled at making daring moves and using unexpected strategies. In previous rounds, he had made bold, daring moves that defied conventional poker wisdom – like the time he went all-in on what seemed a weak hand, only to reveal a masterful bluff. He was also known for his unorthodox strategies, such as switching from an aggressive to a passive playing style mid-game, throwing off his opponents' ability to read him. Jack knew the toughest part of the game was yet to come.

Oscar the dealer shuffled the deck, the cards whispering against each other as the next hand was prepared. As the room fell silent, the echoing sound served as a reminder of the game's delicate balance, hinging on every move and decision.

The final table had transformed into an arena of sharp minds and steady nerves. As the crucial hand unfolded, Sandra and Elijah engaged in a one-on-one, their light-hearted banter masking the high stakes of their play. Elijah leaned back, a playful glint in his eye. "The math genius, Ms. Sandra Pike," he remarked. "How did I ever get so lucky to face you heads-up?"

Sandra chuckled, a hint of warmth in her voice. She adjusted her glasses, a blush of humility crossing her face. "Oh Elijah, I'm the lucky one to be here with you."

"Don't be so modest," Elijah replied, his smile genuine and disarming.

Across the table, Jack, out of this round, watched intently, his eyes flicking between the seasoned players. Each gesture, each casual exchange, was a piece of the strategic puzzle unfolding before him.

The tension was almost tangible as the dealer fanned out the flop: Queen of Diamonds, Queen of Spades, and a Ten of Clubs. Sandra, holding a strong hand with pocket Tens. She tried to read Elijah, waiting for his move.

Elijah appeared relaxed but attentive. His gaze fixed on Sandra with an almost playful curiosity. "Check," he said smoothly, a slight smile playing on his lips.

Sandra paused for a moment, assessing the situation. Carefully weighing the odds, she confidently pushed a considerable amount of chips into the center of the table. The chips clinked as they landed, a sound that echoed the growing suspense in the room. "Six hundred," she said.

Elijah watched the chips settle, his expression contemplative yet unfazed. After a brief moment, as if weighing his options, he casually nodded and matched Sandra's bet, sliding his chips forward with a calm, deliberate motion. "I call." Elijah replied.

Oscar revealed the turn – a Two of Clubs. Again, Elijah, with an air of nonchalance, glanced at Sandra. "Check," he said, passing the action back to her.

Sandra, feeling a growing confidence, placed another bet, larger this time. "Twelve hundred." She said as her eyes never left Elijah, searching for any tell. The chips sailed across the table, a bold declaration of her conviction in her hand.

Elijah, pausing slightly longer this time, continued his calm demeanor and called the bet, his movements measured and unhurried. "I'll call you." He said.

Oscar revealed the river card – an Eight of Hearts. Elijah, maintaining his composed posture, turned once more to Sandra, giving her the lead. "Check," he stated, his voice even.

Sandra, convinced of her advantage, didn't hesitate. She pushed all her remaining chips into the pot, going all-in with determination. Her eyes locked on Elijah, challenging him to respond. "All in, Elijah."

Elijah regarded the amassed chips, then Sandra, and finally glanced briefly at Jack. He took a moment, as if savoring the climax of their contest, before calmly calling, his action sealing the fate of the hand. "I call. Let's see what you got."

With a steady hand, Sandra flipped her cards to reveal her full house – Tens over Queens. She looked at Elijah keenly, a subtle smile of triumph on her lips.

The crowd leaned in, awaiting Elijah's response. He remained calm, almost serene, as he revealed his hand – pocket Queens giving him a four of a kind. A winning hand from the flop. A stunned silence fell over the room, broken only by a few gasps of disbelief.

Sandra sat motionless, her smile fading into an expression of utter shock. She was left speechless when she realized that Elijah's quiet strategy had outmatched her analytical skills.

Elijah offered Sandra a sympathetic nod, an acknowledgment of the close battle they had just fought. Sandra, still processing the turn of events, slowly stood up from the table, her exit marked by a quiet respect from the onlookers. She walked away without a word, the impact of the hand leaving her momentarily speechless. "At least she won something." Elijah said, shrugging his shoulders.

With Sandra's departure, the final showdown was set – Jack and Elijah remained, each prepared for a confrontation that had been brewing throughout the night. Nervous energy coursed through Jack's veins as he squared off against Elijah, his mentor, in a battle that held profound implications beyond the chips on the table.

Oscar, recognizing the intensity of the moment and the need for a brief interval, announced a short break. "We'll take a brief pause before the final head-to-head," he said, his voice cutting through the charged atmosphere.

Jack, however, was restless, his mind racing with strategies and what was at stake. "No, no. Let's just keep going," he insisted, eager to maintain the momentum and confront the challenge that Elijah posed.

Adam, the voice of reason, stepped in. "Jack, we need to reset. It's how we've always done it. Plus, everyone could use a breather, get some drinks." Adam's firm but friendly gaze caused Jack's initial resistance to waver. He knew Adam was right; this brief interlude was part of the tradition of the Den's tournaments, a moment to regroup and prepare for the final battle.

Around them, the crowd began to disperse, some heading to the bar, others discussing the night's events in hushed, excited tones. The break was as much for the spectators as it was for the players. A chance to speculate, to catch their breath, and to prepare for the climax of what had become an unforgettable night.

Elijah used the opportunity to stand and stretch, his demeanor relaxed, but his eyes betraying the sharp focus of a seasoned player. He gave Jack a nod, an unspoken acknowledgment of the respect and rivalry between them.

Jack watched as the chips were being redistributed evenly, a symbolic reset before the last duel. This pause, though brief, was a moment to reflect on how far he had come, from a young boy watching his uncle's games to standing at the brink of victory – or defeat in the most significant game of his life.

VI

As the crowd diminished, Jack began to feel a familiar restlessness. His palms were sweaty, his breathing shallow. Around him, the clinking of glasses and the murmur of conversations felt distant, muffled by the louder clamor of his own compulsive thoughts. Jack's eyes darted towards the cash register, a silent but intense battle raging within him. The urge to grab some cash, to rush out for scratch-offs, was overwhelming. It was a craving for the instant rush, the immediate gratification he felt with each scratch of the card, each revelation of a potential win. His heart raced, and he could almost feel the texture of the tickets under his fingers. Jack's foot tapped rapidly on the floor. He felt trapped in a cycle, a relentless tug-of-war between the fleeting euphoria of a win and the crushing despair of loss. The patience to continue the poker game was fading.

With effort, he tore his gaze away from the bar, trying to steady his shaking hands. Jack's internal struggle reached a crescendo, the compulsion overwhelming his better judgment. With a glance around the room, ensuring no one was paying him particular attention, he edged toward the cash register. His motions were almost automatic, fueled by the ingrained urge that had haunted him for a while.

Engrossed in serving a group of customers at the bar, Adam briefly observed what Jack was doing. Concern etched his face as he realized what was unfolding. "Jack, no," he called out, his voice laced with worry, but the noise of the crowd swallowed his words.

Jack's hand trembled as he opened the register, the clink of the drawer sounding unnaturally loud in his ears. He grabbed a wad of cash, the paper bills cold and impersonal in his grasp. Without a word, he headed for the door, his pace quickening as he crossed the threshold of Wolfgang's Den. The cool night air hit him, but it did little to dissipate the burning impulse within.

Across the street, the lights of the deli glowed invitingly. Jack made his way there, each step feeling heavier than the last. He knew this was a betrayal of everything the tournament stood for, of Wolfgang's memory, and yet he couldn't resist the siren call of the scratch-offs.

As he entered the deli, the familiar sight of the lottery tickets behind the counter offered a twisted sense of comfort. He approached, exchanging the cash for a stack of scratch-offs, the transaction a ritual that had become all too familiar. Jack's obsession with scratching lottery tickets had him lost in a never-ending pursuit of riches.

The door chimed, heralding Elijah's entrance. His eyes quickly found Jack hunched over and absorbed in his fruitless endeavor. A look of disappointment crossed Elijah's face as he witnessed the extent of Jack's addiction. As he approaches the counter, Elijah opted for a simple purchase – sunflower seeds. Turning to Jack with his purchase in hand, Elijah greeted him politely. "Evening, Jack." His voice was gentle.

Jack responded briefly, barely glancing up from his tickets. "Elijah," he acknowledged, his tone laced with bitterness.

Elijah notices Jack's frustration as he tosses out the losing tickets. "This is not healthy, Jack. Wolfgang would be so disappointed."

Jack stopped his scratching. Elijah's words, hitting a nerve. "What do you want from me? You're the one who introduced me to poker. This started because of you."

Elijah's gaze was steady, understanding, yet firm. "Poker, yes. But not this, Jack. Not the path you're on. Blaming the game, or me, won't help you face your problems."

Jack's eyes, filled with a turbulent mix of emotions, met Elijah's. "What will? Huh? Tell me. I'm fucked if I lose. You know that?" He said, a defensive edge to his voice.

"That's your problem, not mine. You should've learned when to walk away."

"If only my uncle wasn't so busy before he passed, he would've got me away from you. You're the devil in my life, and I can't shake you off."

Elijah steps closer to Jack, now more personal. "Trust me, if I was the devil, you wouldn't have the Den." Elijah left the deli, leaving Jack to contemplate what he meant by that. He stared at himself and the aftermath of his scratching with all the losing tickets piled on top of each other, over the counter and on the ground.

Jack's return to Wolfgang's Den filled the night air with a charged sense of excitement. The crowd, though smaller now, following Jack's every move.

Bathed in soft, ambient light, the final table beckoned like a theatrical stage, ready for the tournament's climactic conclusion. The chips were neatly stacked. The cards lay pristine and untouched, waiting to decide the fate of the final players.

Elijah sat calmly at the table, his demeanor serene but alert. There was a knowing look in his eyes as he watched Jack approach. It was the look of a mentor recognizing the turning point in his protégé's journey. Or the rivalry between them. Around them, the spectators buzzed with hushed conversations, creating a symphony of murmurs that filled the room. Their eyes darted between the two players.

As Jack took his seat opposite Elijah, Oscar the dealer gave a nod, acknowledging the readiness of the players. A hush fell over the crowd, a collective breath held in anticipation.

Jack's gaze met Elijah's across the table, a silent exchange of respect and understanding passing between them. The lessons of the past, the trials of the present, and the uncertainties of the future all converged at this moment.

The dealer shuffled the deck, the sound crisp in the quiet room. "Ladies and gentlemen," he announced, "the final battle begins."

The cards were dealt with a rhythmic precision that resonated through the silent Den. Jack and Elijah, the final two gladiators in the stadium, picked up their hands, their expressions unreadable masks honed by hours of play. The moment carried a tangible weight, a culmination of every decision, bluff, and calculated risk taken throughout the night.

Jack glanced at his cards, feeling a surge of adrenaline. He can almost taste the money at this point.

Elijah showed great composure as he carefully examined his cards. His years of experience in reading both cards and opponents were now focused on this final encounter.

Jack observed his hand — a Jack of Diamonds and an Ace of Spades. Another lucky promising start, one that resonated with the personal symbolism he had attached to the Jack of Diamonds. The card had been a silent ally in many games. Fueled by a mixture of excitement and the significance he placed on the card, Jack raised the stakes and bets pre-flop. "I bet a thousand." He said as he tossed the chips in the center of the table.

Elijah, across the table, regarded Jack with a thoughtful gaze. There was a moment of contemplation, a weighing of possibilities, before he made his decision. With a calm yet decisive motion, Elijah folded his hand, tossing the cards face down to Oscar. He effectively sidestepped the confrontation that Jack had sought.

This unexpected move by Elijah sent a flicker of frustration through Jack. Internally, he had been hoping for a call, to capitalize on the perceived good fortune of his hand. Elijah's fold, however, was a clear indication of his ability to see through Jack's enthusiasm. A reminder of the depth of experience and skill Elijah brought to the table.

Jack tried to mask his irritation, collecting the few chips that now represented a hollow victory. It was a win, but not the kind he had hoped for. The lack of engagement, the absence of a challenge in this hand, felt like a missed opportunity to test his luck and his skill against his mentor.

As the cards were gathered and the next hand set up, Jack took a brief pause to sharpen his focus. He understood that the final showdown demanded not just his usual blend of skill and strategy, but an elevation of his game to its highest level. It was about reading his opponent more acutely, anticipating moves before they unfolded, and finding the perfect balance between aggression and caution. In these decisive moments, every nuance mattered – the slightest twitch, the briefest hesitation, the most subtle of tells. Jack prepared himself, ready to use all his poker skills to outplay his last opponent.

The room itself seemed to pulse with the rhythm of the game, every spectator drawn into the intricate game unfolding before them. They watched, mesmerized, as Jack and Elijah traded victories and defeats, each hand a mini-drama that captivated and enthralled.

In one corner, a group of regulars leaned forward with every turn of a card, their faces a mirror of the tension at the table. Gasps, murmurs, and occasional cheers punctuated the air, reflecting the collective investment of the crowd in each play. Jack's bold move left the onlookers in awe, their admiration swept through the crowd like a soft breeze. Then, as Elijah countered with his own masterful play, the room would erupt in low, appreciative murmurs, acknowledging the skill of the seasoned veteran.

With each hand, the spectators rode a roller coaster of emotions, living and breathing each moment with the players. It was as if the entire room was playing the game, feeling the highs of triumph and the lows of setback right alongside Jack and Elijah. The atmosphere was electric, charged with an intensity that made every onlooker feel a part of something extraordinary.

It was almost 3:00 a.m., yet the energy in the room showed no signs of waning. The Den, usually quiet at this hour, was alive with the tension and excitement of the tournament.

As the hands were played, the dynamic between Jack and Elijah shifted subtly. It was no longer just a game between mentor and protégé; it had evolved into a clash between two equals, each with their own strengths and weaknesses, each learning from the other.

However, as the clock ticks at Wolfgang's Den, once a hive of tension and excitement, now bore the signs of a prolonged battle. The once lively spectators had dwindled, with some dozing off in their seats, their earlier enthusiasm waning in the face of the late hour. In a corner, Adam, usually the ever-vigilant observer, had succumbed to slumber, a testament to the night's extraordinary length. His presence, a comforting constant throughout the tournament, now took the form of soft snores that occasionally punctuated the quiet room.

Jack and Elijah, though wearied by the long hours of play, remained locked in their contest. The increasing blinds added pressure, yet several hands had passed with little progress, each player cautiously navigating the high stakes and their own fatigue.

Elijah, the stoic and seasoned player, showed signs of weariness. His movements were slower, but his eyes still held the sharp focus of a player committed to the game. In a rare moment of concession to the night's toll, he leaned towards Jack, offering a proposal. "Jack, let's split the winnings. It's been a long night for everyone."

Jack, with fatigue seeping into his bones, considered Elijah's offer. Yet, the fire of determination, kindled by his recent realizations and desire to truly overcome his challenges, still burned within him. "No," he replied, his voice filled with determination. "We're going to play out until one of us wins."

Elijah, upon hearing Jack's refusal, shifted slightly in his seat, a flash of annoyance crossing his normally composed features. He had played countless games, but this night was turning into an endurance test that even he hadn't anticipated. "Very well," Elijah said, his voice betraying a hint of weariness mixed with frustration. The proposal to split the winnings had been a rare olive branch from the veteran player, an acknowledgment of the night's extraordinary length and their shared fatigue.

The cards were dealt again, and the game continued, its pace slower now, weighed down by the late hour and the accumulated tension. Each hand that passed seemed to draw more energy from the players, their movements becoming more labored, their decisions taking longer. Adam, in the background, remained oblivious to the unfolding drama, his gentle snores a counterpoint to the quiet shuffling of cards and the soft murmur of the few remaining spectators.

The night at Wolfgang's Den had transformed into a battle not just of skill, but of sheer willpower. Elijah, for all his experience and stoicism, was showing signs of human limitation, his patience tested by the relentless passage of time and Jack's unwavering resolve.

Jack, meanwhile, seemed driven by a deeper motivation. Each hand he played was a step away from his past, a defiance of his own weaknesses.

The tension in Wolfgang's Den had peaked as Jack, taking a deep breath to steady his nerves, went all-in with his chips. "Fuck it."

Elijah, observing Jack's determined gesture, mirrored him. He called the bet, the finality of the decision hanging heavy in the air. As they laid their cards open for the decisive showdown, the room held its collective breath.

Jack revealed his hand first – the Jack of Diamonds and Queen of Diamonds. The significance of the Jack of Diamonds was not lost in the room. Murmurs rippled through the spectators, echoing Jack's belief in the card's lucky charm.

Elijah's reaction was subtle, a slight tightening of his eyes betraying his acknowledgment of the card's symbolism for Jack. As he revealed his own hand – Ace of Clubs and King of Spades. Despite his experienced composure, there was a flicker of concern, a rare hint that he considered the possibility of Jack's storied luck turning the game.

Oscar began to reveal the community cards. The flop came: Three of Spades, Nine of Hearts, and Six of Diamonds. It was uneventful for both hands, prolonging the suspense. The room remained still, every spectator engrossed in the unfolding drama.

Then came the turn – the Jack of Clubs. A collective gasp filled the room. Jack's hand improved, hitting a pair. His eyes lit up, excited. He couldn't help but glance at the Jack of Diamonds, his lucky charm, as if in silent gratitude.

Elijah, watching the turn card with a stoic expression, maintained his composure. He understood the game wasn't over. The last card is yet to be revealed.

The tension was almost tangible as Oscar slowly revealed the river — the Ace of Spades. In an instant, the atmosphere shifted. Elijah had the winning hand with a pair of Aces.

The room erupted in a chorus of surprised exclamations. Jack sat frozen, his momentary triumph shattered by the turn of a card. His face crestfallen, the high of potential victory replaced by the stark reality of defeat.

Elijah showed no signs of gloating. He accepted his win with a quiet nod, a gesture of respect to the game and to his opponent. His win was dignified, a reflection of his experience and understanding of poker's unpredictable nature. And of course, sheer luck.

Jack, still processing the outcome, looked at the table, the cards, and the chips that were no longer his. The loss felt like a culmination of his battles, both at the poker table and within himself.

VII

The morning following the tournament, Wolfgang's Den was in a state of unusual silence. Remnants of the previous night's drama lingered in the air, a silent testament to the events that had unfolded. Jack sat with Adam at the bar, the weight of his loss compounded by the stark reality of the pub's financial troubles. Even with the second place winnings of $6,000 and the nearly $8,000 from the patrons buying beer nonstop, it wasn't enough to pay off the tens of thousands of debt.

"We're in deeper than I thought," Jack confessed, his voice heavy with the burden of debt and the responsibility of the Den. "I don't see how we can keep the doors open much longer."

Adam, leaning on the bar, his expression a full of concern. "I thought you had the money. Are you hoarding it?"

Jack shook his head in shame. "I don't. All gone to either FanDuel or AceQuest."

"And scratch-offs." Adam reassured then took a deep breath. "It's been a tough ride, Jack. Maybe it's time to consider other options. We can't keep fighting a losing battle."

A phone call interrupted the conversation. Jack answered to find Elijah on the other line, his voice calm and reassuring. "How are you, Jack?"

Although Jack doesn't want to admit that he's not doing well, he still gives him a response. "Could be better." Jack said. "I can't stop thinking about last night."

"Actually, I wanted to bring that up. I've been thinking about the tournament and about the Den. I'd like to meet and discuss a possibility that might benefit us both." Elijah said.

Jack shared a glance with Adam. "Who is it?" Adam asked.

Later that day, Jack and Elijah sat across from each other in the now-empty pub. Elijah laid out his proposal with straightforward sincerity. "I want to buy Wolfgang's Den," he began. "Not to change it, but to preserve what it stands for. I believe in its legacy, and I think this is what Wolfgang would've wanted. No disrespect to you, of course."

Jack, taken aback by the offer, listened as Elijah continued. "I'm offering $500,000 for the Den. This amount will cover your debts and leave enough for a fresh start. Whatever happened at the deli, I don't ever want to see you go through again."

There was a moment of hesitation from Jack as the offer filled the space between them. The Den, steeped in so many memories and dreams, was more than just a business to him. It was a legacy, a connection to his uncle Wolfgang. The thought of selling it, even to someone like Elijah, who understood its value, was jarring. "Elijah, I'm not sure," Jack stammered. "This place has been a part of me for so long. I can't just let it go."

Elijah's nod was steeped in empathy. "I understand, Jack, but consider the Den's future and yours. This offer is an opportunity to preserve and start afresh. Opportunities like this are rare."

Jack's gaze flickered, torn between attachment and practicality. "This place is a part of me, a part of my history. Selling it would mean... it feels like I'm admitting defeat." His voice trailed off, hinting at the deeper struggle within.

With a slight forward lean, Elijah's tone balanced firmness and understanding. "Opposite. Letting go doesn't mean defeat. It means having the courage to make a change. And as for your personal battles, consider this a step towards confronting them."

Jack rubbed his forehead, the decision pressing heavily on him. "But what if I regret it? What if I'm just running away from my problems instead of facing them?"

"At first, you might feel that way. It's a big step. But it's about giving yourself a fighting chance at something better." Elijah replied, his voice tinged with conviction.

Jack's eyes met Elijah's, a storm of emotions swirling within. "This is a lot to process. I need some time to think."

With a gentle smile, Elijah conveyed his understanding. "Of course, take your time. Just remember, some doors don't stay open forever."

Their conversation gradually wound down, leaving Jack immersed in a sea of thoughts, the prospect of selling the Den a path filled with both fear and potential freedom.

After their initial meeting, the days passed in a blur for Jack. The decision to sell Wolfgang's Den was not made without careful consideration. It took a little more than a week before he sat across from Elijah, each accompanied by their lawyers, in a small conference room in Elijah's real estate brokerage to finalize the sale. The atmosphere was professional, yet there was an undercurrent of emotion, especially from Jack's end.

The lawyers laid out the agreement, a document that symbolized the end of one era and the beginning of another. Hopefully, that is. Jack's hand hesitated momentarily over the paper. This legal transaction represented a surrender of a segment of his life, an abandonment of dreams, and still a move towards resolving his burdens. The instant he signed the agreement, he could feel an overwhelming sense of conviction settling in. The Den, which had been a beacon in his life, was now Elijah's. Elijah reminded him of the agreed sum of $500,000, a figure that held the promise of erasing his debts and granting him a fresh start. But no amount could measure the emotional cost of this decision.

With the documents signed and the formalities concluded, Elijah gently placed a hand on Jack's shoulder. "Don't worry, Jack. I promise to take care of the Den as your uncle wanted."

The keys to Wolfgang's Den were then handed over to Elijah, the metal glinting under the room's lights. Jack watched the exchange, a clamor of emotions inside him. He kept reminding himself that this was the closure of a significant chapter in his life.

VIII

In the vibrant and lively atmosphere of the Atlantic City casino, Jack found himself lost in thought as the sights and sounds of the busy crowd filled his senses. He sat at the poker table, cards and chips in front of him, but his focus was elsewhere, drifting through the highs and lows that had brought him to this point. As he drifted off into his own world, he was startled by the sight of three familiar faces approaching – regulars from the Den.

"Jack! Never thought we'd find you here," exclaimed Tom, the local theater director, his voice tinged with the same dramatic flair he brought when he was at the tournament.

Frank, the retired mechanic, and Sandra, the high school math teacher, joined in with warm greetings.

Jack, snapping out of his daze, greeted them with a semblance of his old energy. "I didn't expect to see you guys here. What brings you to A.C?"

Tom leaned back, his theatrical nature never far from the surface. "Ah, Jack, just having a little escape, you know?"

Sandra, more pragmatic, added with a soft chuckle, "I needed a break from the endless pile of papers to grade. That's all."

Frank, with his easy-going demeanor, chimed in, "I was in the mood for slots till I stumbled upon you here, Jack."

With a quick flicker, Jack's eyes scanned the group. "It's always good to see familiar faces. How's everyone back at the Den?"

Tom's expression softened. "The Den's holding up. Elijah's doing a fine job keeping its spirit alive. It's different without you, but it's still got that warm, familiar feel."

"We all miss you, Jack. You should stop by whenever you can," Sandra said.

"Sure, I'm not gone forever." Jack offered a faint smile, a reflective glint in his eyes.

The dealer began dealing the cards. Jack focused on the game, along with the regulars also peek at their respective hands. Jack's introspective mood was set against the familiar banter and rhythms of poker during the game. He was here, yet part of him remained in the Den. As Jack surveyed his hand – the Jack of Diamonds and a Seven of Clubs – a flicker of his old instincts stirred within him.

The contemplative silence at the table was suddenly broken by an impulsive move from one of the players. With a reckless bravado, he pushed all his chips to the center. "All-in," he declared, a boldness in his voice that echoed through the casino's din.

Jack's eyes momentarily fixed on his own stack. It was modest compared to the towering pile now at stake in the center of the table. Yet, as he calculated his chips, a cautious instinct, a subtle echo of the knowledge gained from the tournament, guided his decision-making. He rolled the Jack of Diamonds between his fingers, considering the gamble. But after a moment's hesitation, he laid his cards down, folding his hand. "I'm out," he murmured, more to himself than to the others.

Another player called the all-in, and the tension at the table escalated. But Jack, feeling a sudden need to distance himself from the outcome, excused himself and walked over to the bar. He wasn't going for a drink. He was stepping away from what might have been – from seeing whether the Jack of Diamonds would have brought him the victory he once would have desperately sought.

Leaning against the bar, the NBA game playing on the television above caught Jack's attention, diverting his gaze from the poker table. For once, Jack wasn't there to place bets or predict outcomes of the basketball game. He was simply a spectator, caught up in the raw excitement of the sport. Hell, he didn't even know who was playing unless he saw it on FanDuel. It was a recap of the NBA Finals – Golden State Warriors versus Boston Celtics.

As he stood there, the distant sound of cheers and groans from the table reached him, signaling the conclusion of the hand. Jack didn't turn to look. He didn't need to know the outcome, nor cared. Instead, he continued watching how The Warriors won the championship.

LUST
DESPERATE ENCOUNTER

I

The thoughts of naked women run rampant in young James Rossi's mind. It's ten in the morning on a Friday. The chilling air breezes through the cracks of the windowsill. Another bitter day in January that doesn't seem to show mercy to the people of Brooklyn. The asshole Greek landlord still hasn't fixed the busted radiator yet.

Nothing new.

James covers his sick self on the couch with a wool blanket he had since he was ten. It's been a while since he had a fever this bad. Aggressively, he blows his nose into Kleenex tissues and piles them on the ceramic table next to his second cup of Lipton green tea. A third cup will be on the way as soon as the pot whistles. He knew he shouldn't have slept over at his cousin's place, who refused to believe he had a cold. Instead, he could've stayed home alone and binged watched porn. But *Resident Evil 4* just came out, and it was the one day he could play. They played for hours, and nightmares fueled their brains as they adventured through the horrific village.

The last time James took off from Zander Catholic High School was during sophomore year, after an unfair fight with the captain of the baseball team. Unfair not because of the athleticism of the baseball captain, but because James, ever since he was a freshman, had been on the varsity wrestling team and didn't give that tall bully a chance to lay a finger on him. The odds were naturally in his favor. Not to mention that James has an undefeated record till now. Even then, this gave James the utmost respect among his peers. The teachers were definitely disappointed after the fight, especially his computer science mentor, who helped pave the way to DeVry University.

Disciplinary action left James the only one suspended. There was protest by a few of his peers, which included his wrestling teammates, his coach, and his mother, who took a rare day off from work to argue with the dean about the matter. This is what happens when the baseball captain's father is a huge contributor to the high school, donating hundreds of thousands that resulted in major renovations. But did James care? No. All he cared about was going on the computer to satisfy his depraved cravings.

As James' mom leaves through the front door, she gives him directions on when to take the cold medications just as he coughs out a lung and spits out a block of brown, gooey phlegm onto a napkin. He finishes his fourth cup of green tea, then empties what's left in his stomach by 12:28 PM. It's definitely a rough morning, but James feels a little better after he popped a white tablet of 600mg Ibuprofen that the pharmacy a block away provides under the table for the family. Mainly used for James' dad's migraines, since he's always dealing with loud subway cars constantly passing by.

It's quiet, and to make things cozier, James turns off the lights, allowing only the muted, cloudy daylight to seep through the window onto the navy carpet. Despite his sickness, he finds peace in this serenity. There's no constant ringing of bells, no teachers reprimanding unruly students. He doesn't miss the principal's monotone announcements about uninteresting school events or the ceaseless chatter and collisions in the crowded hallways. The absence of childish pranks like spit-balling, the relief of not enduring the unpleasant odors of an unwashed classmate. Just the thoughts of beautiful naked women fucking each other with large strap-on dildos.

This was peace.

Feels like some days when the school was closed for a Catholic holiday when he had the house to himself because his parents were still at work for several hours. He sits at the corner of the couch staring at the black mirror of the twenty-seven-inch Sony Trinitron/WEGA CRT TV, seeing his sinister doppelgänger staring back at him right before NY1 News appears. Thirty-eight degrees Fahrenheit is the first thing to catch James' eye. Meanwhile, the news wraps up a story about published pictures of Prince Harry dressing up as a Nazi.

In other news, the anchorman, Pat Kiernan, discusses an unfortunate case about a missing local blonde woman after going on a blind date. It's been two weeks since the time of the event. Then, most importantly, the weather. It's going to rain throughout the day, leaving the rest of the week in freezing temperatures. Not something James nor anyone in New York is looking forward to. But that's what makes New Yorkers tough. At least, that's a reason they give to each other to deal with the weather.

James grew bored of the news, and no other channels on Time Warner showed anything more interesting. It was just game shows, daytime talk shows, recycled cult classics from the 80s and 90s, and Video-on-Demand movies. An advertisement announces *Saw* will be streamed next month On Demand. A movie James remembers sneaking into at Alpine Cinema with his classmates before crashing a Halloween party. He remembers bumping into more Jigsaws in the city than any other costume. He swore the next morning he jumped out of bed after hearing, "Wanna play a game?"

As he scrolls through the channels, he notices Pay-Per-View movies with a price tag of $2.99. Where did the time go when the cable box was a thing showing only eighty-five channels, three of them being free Pay-Per-View movies? A time he discovered his love, or better yet, obsession with B-horror movies like *Deep Blue Sea* and *House on Haunted Hill.* But one specific channel got his full attention.

Spice Networks, or as his classmates would call it, the Spice Channel. A channel of free adult entertainment displaying the delightful sexual experiences of stunning women. It was the last channel on the cable box. Channel 85. Some people had it on channel 80, others would joke around and say channel 69. Without a doubt, it might be true.

At the ripe age of thirteen, having just finished *Sleepy Hollow* for the fiftieth time, James realized he had passed his bedtime. It was a weekend and his parents were out with friends, leaving him under the lackadaisical watch of his overweight uncle, who was currently snoozing on the lazy boy. Flipping through channels in search of something captivating, James found no cartoons to his liking. Distracted momentarily by a roach scurrying under the TV stand near the PlayStation, he settled on a random channel.

Upon their late return, James' parents disrupted the quiet of the evening. His father, with a heavy hand, delivered a sharp smack to the back of James's head, accompanied by loud reprimands. "Don't ever watch that channel!" he bellowed, startling the dozing uncle into a sudden snort. Amidst the chaos, James' mother scolded her brother for his negligence. Rubbing his sore head, James caught a fleeting glimpse of the fast-moving images on the TV. Right before his dad snatched the remote, James saw reflecting before his very eyes in his oversized spectacles two perfectly shaped naked women showing off their smooth tan skin, one blonde, one brunette, making out and scissoring. Then his father switched the channel that's showing a commercial from Circuit City advertising a sale on the new Compaq computer and printer.

Within those few years, James' curiosity bested him, and he had been on a softcore porn extravaganza every Saturday morning instead of watching *Pokémon* on Kids' WB or his favorite show, *Spider-Man Unlimited,* on Fox Kids right after. It got so bad that he would miss out on conversations with his friends who would discuss the last episodes with each other. His friends thought something was wrong, even asked him from time to time if someone died. James was unusually quiet when most of the time he gave his input on what villains would appear in the next season of *Spider-Man*. At least he didn't have to suffer from the cliffhanger in the last episode. Instead, he would look for an excuse to head home to watch The Spice Channel.

No one knew his depraved secret.

It was the taboo nature of The Spice Channel that got him glued to the screen. It was forbidden to watch. His entire surroundings weren't in his peripheral view. There were a few occasions he almost got caught by his mom, but that didn't stop him. His ears sharpened, he poised his thumb above the remote's back button, ready to switch channels instantly. At moments of sound, his eyes would dart back and forth from the living room door and back to the TV screen.

Then finally, after James graduated junior high, his dad reluctantly installed the internet. Just another bill added on top of the ridiculous rent, along with Time Warner and the phone line. One hot and humid summer day, James had a whole eight hours to himself. Once his mother departed for work, the initial action he took was to search for porn on Google.

Instantly, a ton of results would pop over the horrible Verizon broadband. In fact, any other "normal" search would take much longer. But search for porn and it took milliseconds. James got a closer look at women's vaginas for the first time. The Spice Channel only showed tits and ass, but never explicitly showed penetration.

But hardcore porn is different. Way different.

It was much more graphic. The sex was rougher than the softcore "love making." This changed James' perception of the objectification of women. He didn't care nor understood what it was like for women to be objectified. All he wanted was to satisfy his own callous curiosity and perverted pleasure. It was easy too. After clicking the first hyperlink, the front page would show a seductive woman with a warning sign stating "if you're not 18 years of age, you must exit." But did thirteen-year-old James listened?

Absolutely not.

Three hours passed by so quickly after his first search. He's already seen a hundred genres and searches deep and yet can't get enough until he struck with one niche. A typical guy favorite: lesbian porn. The internet only offered ten to thirty-second clips. That's how much time James would last anyway once he touched himself. An innocent young mind, corrupted by the very thing humans do naturally. But this was only the beginning of an obsession yet to take over anything a kid would normally do. Like video games and watching cartoons.

This time, he didn't go on a virtual trip to the objectified fantasy land. Nearly desensitized after turning eighteen last month, he realizes he's graduating soon, and he's graduating as a virgin. He now craves for the pleasure like those he watches like a voyeuristic madman. Only because he cannot get it up anymore. One of his most terrifying moments was realizing that nothing was turning him on anymore. He even repeated some of the old clips he used to watch and still, no hard-on. There needed to be a way to meet a woman in person. An older woman at that. Experienced and someone who can show him the tricks of the trade. But how and where?

One day, at the high school cafeteria eating cheap pizza, a loud, overweight friend of his caught his older brother using Craigslist to advertise himself to get laid. It was outlandish to think, not only can one sell old unwanted products like dressers and TVs for a cheap price, but one can also sell their bodies for the sake of fornication. But James didn't believe it, nor even thought about it because he worried he might get caught. Maybe a relative of his who might use it will find him. James was curious and wanted to explore, but in secret. Hopefully, he can fulfill his fantasy fast.

II

Craigslist, a classifieds and forums website, offers everything from job listings to second-hand items like cellphones and car parts. It's where James' parents were misled about broker's fees when they found their current home. The site also hosts lively discussions on topics ranging from celebrities to religion, and sports to life's end. Among its categories, "Casual Encounters" caught James' eye. Clicking the hyperlink, he was led to an extensive list of options: m for men, w for women, t for transgender. There's something that appeals to everyone.

James clicks on the w4m hyperlink, which shows ads of women posting themselves looking for sex. To James, this is too good to be true. Women actually looking for sex and literally advertising themselves. Not every ad had a pic, but those that did would show just tits, ass, and a stretched vagina. Rarely a face. This didn't intrigue James because the women who showed their face looked like the grotesque enemies, the Gorgers, from *The Suffering*.

Of course, no men would really approach these women in real life, leaving them to be sexually frustrated enough to humiliate themselves online, showing their desperation. Finally, a post got James' attention. There was a pretty face, blonde, mature yet had a youthful look:

I broke up with my boyfriend not too long ago, looking for excitement. 45.
"5'5" no diseases, no drugs, just simply looking for a good time before moving back to California. Help me create good memories in this cold city."

James realized he didn't want to use his actual email address. Instead, he attempts to create a new AOL email. Staring at the screen, wondering what he'll create. How can he make it not sound fake and generic? Think, think, he says to himself. What was his wrestling nickname? The Bear.

No.

He can't use that or people will know. Use another predator. Lion. Okay, Lion. Now a surname-like word to attach to it. Maybe use a Zodiac. Capricorn. Still close to home. Use the one that comes before. Sagittarius. Use the first syllable. Sag. LionSag. Now add some numbers to it. Birthdays seem to be popular. December twenty-sixth. But again, trying to stay away from anything personal. Sagittarius goes from November twenty-first to December twentieth. Again, trying to avoid anything personal, he uses November and avoids the twenty-six. He uses the thirtieth. LionSag1130@aol.com.

Perfect!

James replied to the ad:

"Heyy! I saw your ad on Craigslist and I'm interested. I'm 5'7" also no disease and no drugs, stocky and built like a tank also looking for a good time. I'm in Bensonhurst. Where are you located?"

It's been two hours without a reply and James already responded to nearly thirty ads using his fake email address. He blows his nose in the bathroom, spits out the remaining phlegm, stares at himself in the mirror with droopy eyes then stands up straight, thinking it will help fight the sickness. He then coughs out a lung. Finally, he hears, "YOU'VE GOT MAIL!" from the AOL voice.

James drops to his chair, hands trembling, opens the email, mis-clicks and hits the X, closing the email. Then suddenly, the computer system slows down. AOL freezes. It's overshadowed by a white fade. The fan of the desktop winds up, causing it to overheat. What else could go wrong?

James asks himself as he presses his thumb on the red button tower, holds it for a few seconds, like taking a pillow and suffocating your victim.

Black screen.

After rebooting Windows 97 and getting back online, James returns to AOL to read his new email. "WELCOME!" The AOL voice said. "YOU'VE GOT MAIL!" It's the reply from Craigslist with an email address. PrintsessaVolk1218@msn.com:

RE: I broke up with my boyfriend not too long ago, looking for excitement. 45.

"Hi! Nice to meet you :)

I'm in Hell's Kitchen and hosting.

Do you have any pics?"

Pics? James didn't think he'd get this far. He reaches for his Motorola RAZR, opening it reveals a cracked screen from dropping it so many times while playing flag football with his friends. There's always that one friend who takes the game way too far.

He takes a few pictures in the bathroom mirror, but none seems right. Awkward angles, dim lighting, blurs from slight movements – even when the pose is perfect, there are smudges on the mirror or distractions like a spider lurking in the background. After nearly sneezing his phone out of his hand, he pauses to breathe deeply, coughing slightly. He freshens up – cleansing his face, fixing his hair, brushing his teeth – striving for a rejuvenated look. Dressed in a flannel button-down, he captures several more photos from different angles. The red of his shirt stands out vividly against the bathroom's blue tiles, and finally, he nods in satisfaction.

He replies with a pic:

"My pic is attached.

I can be there."

That's hoping he'll feel better soon and hoping she actually likes how he looks. While James browsed upcoming video games online, his mom popped in to check on him, carrying chicken soup and a two-liter bottle of Canada Dry ginger ale. Pausing at the doorway, she noticed his new attire and well-groomed appearance.

"What's going on?" she asked with a hint of curiosity. "Got a date or something?"

Feeling a bit self-conscious, James shrugged. "Just wanted a change. Felt uncomfortable."

"That's odd," she mused, her hand already on his forehead, feeling the heat. "You're burning up, like the stove's on high," she teased. "No going out this weekend."

"I'm fine, really," James protested, his words interrupted by a cough. He wiped his hand on a tissue, trying to downplay his condition.

His mom chuckled, shaking her head. "Stubborn as always. But you're staying in, no arguments. This," she said, setting up a small table with the soup and ginger ale, "is the best cold remedy."

James sniffled appreciatively. "Thanks, Mom."

She smiled, tapping his forehead with a kiss from her fingertips, as if casting a healing spell. Duty called her back to the receptionist's desk at the doctor's office nearby, but for now, her motherly care was finished.

Left alone, James savored the soup, finding comfort with every taste. Finishing it in big gulps, he chased it down with ginger ale, feeling a momentary relief. Lying back, his eyes drifted shut.

YOU'VE GOT MAIL!

James rises like the Undertaker, interrupting his own funeral on SmackDown. He hops off the couch and heads towards the off-white IBM computer, nearly tripping on his way.

RE: RE: I broke up with my boyfriend not too long ago, looking for excitement. 45. [attached file]
"You're cute! OMG!

Here's a pic of me from last night bathing."

The attached file is a picture of a petite blonde, her hair in a bun, having a bubble bath. Her silky tan skin glows as her blue eyes shine brightly in the candlelit bathroom.

YOU'VE GOT MAIL!

RE: RE: I broke up with my boyfriend not too long ago, looking for excitement. 45.
"Show me your cock :)"

James's blood flows rapidly through his veins as he reads this. But nothing going down to the area he wants. There was a thrill but no spark yet. Even though nobody is home, he still looks around just to make sure and drops his pants and prepares the camera on the RAZR. He stares at the blondie's photo as he feels himself up. Trying to find the perfect angle, he shifts his body in an attempt to have his Johnson look harder and bigger than it is. As soon as he snaps the picture, his mom calls, leaving James frustrated. "Yeah, mom, what?!" James unwittingly gets aggressive, shuts his eyes and realizes.

"I'm sorry. Did I wake you?" His mom said, her voice with empathy. "I just wanted to know if you liked the soup."

James draws in a long breath and calmly answers. "It's amazing. Sorry, I'm... in a little pain."

"It's okay. Get some rest. I'll be home in a few hours with your dad." His mom said.

"No problem. See you soon."

"Feel better! Love you!" She hangs up.

As James shuts his phone, he stares at the pic of the blonde, then stares at himself half naked. He exhales sharply and coughs. He lifts his pants up and prepares the poorly made image of what's supposed to be a hard-on.

Barely, if anything.

III

It's been a few hours with no response. He wonders if the pic was the deal breaker. He hears brakes pulling to a stop and glances out the window where he sees a 2002 red Pontiac Aztek parking up front. His tall father, in his oil-stained engineer's uniform, steps out of the driver's side along with his mother from the passenger's. They grab the groceries from the trunk and head inside the house. His dad, tired from working on the train tracks, greets James and goes straight to the bedroom. This is the normal routine whether James is sick or not, his stoic dad just keeps it going. As much as James likes to be left alone, it's really because he can't stop thinking about naked women. Then his mother kisses his forehead, making him cringe.

YOU'VE GOT MAIL!

RE: RE: RE: I broke up with my boyfriend not too long ago, looking for excitement. 45.

"I noticed you are using AOL.

Do you have MSN messenger so we can chat?
It'll be faster."

Without hesitation, James downloads MSN messenger, creates another email using the same AOL email he created, and replied. After a few minutes, a pop up from MSN messenger shows: **PrintessaVolk1218** wants to chat. James wipes the sweat off his feverish head, and allows the chat to go through.

    PrintessaVolk1218:Hi!

    LionSag1130: Hey, sup

    PrintessaVolk1218:This is so much easier :D

    LionSag1130: i agree :)

    PrintessaVolk1218: How long have you lived in NY for?

    LionSag1130: my whole life. u

    PrintessaVolk1218: I was here for a while, but now I'm
leaving end of the week.

    LionSag1130: o cool. sorry about ur bf, i'll take care of
u b4 u leave

    PrintessaVolk1218: That's so sweet! I will definitely
prepare myself for you.

    LionSag1130: u better be prepared, u'll be screaming lol

James squeezes his eyes shut after he hits send. Instant regret. He mocks the line, "u'll be screaming." Couldn't be anymore charming, he says to himself. It's been almost ten minutes since he sent that and accepts defeat. It's obvious that's not what women want. Suddenly, **PrintessaVolk1218 is typing...** James pulls the chair closer and waits as he glares at her username.

PrintessaVolk1218: I'm excited! Are you free around 8:30 tonight?

LionSag1130: Yea wats ur address

James sends instantly. As he waits for a reply, he blows out some snot into a tissue and wipes off nervous sweat. She responds with a with a phone number and asks to be called to assure that the LionSag is actually him behind the computer.

In his small room, James squeezes himself in the corner away from his door, hoping no one can hear him. The ringing takes him to a voicemail. "We're sorry, but the number you have reached is un—" James hangs up. He exhales sharply, believing that he might've been played. Scammed. Too good to be true. A hot blonde woman advertising herself on the internet could be far from the truth. She can simply walk in the middle of Times Square, fully clothed and yell out she needs sex. Guaranteed men will line up and simp for her. She'll get a gangbang if she pleases and will turn men gay for entertainment... Thoughts like these ran rampant in his head. Then a ringing from his phone.

It's her!

James takes a deep breath and flips open the phone. After a few seconds of awkward silence, James breaks the ice. "H-hello?" He says in a low tone as he waits for another few seconds.

"Hey!" a raspy voice behind the line responds. "Is this the Lion Sag?"

"Y-yes," He said, heart racing. "My name is James."

"Aw, you're a cutie pie."

James smiles embarrassingly, but quickly becomes stoic again. "Thank you. Uh, what's your name?"

"They call me Peaches."

"Is it because... uh, you taste like peaches?" James cringes in his own words, but the response comes with laughter.

"You ARE a cutie." She responds. "You sound a little sick. Are you okay?"

James, realizing his voice does indeed sound scratchy, but clears his throat as he covers the speaker of his phone. "Yeah, sorry. I had something lodged in my throat."

"You know, I'm in need of something lodging in my throat." She says seductively.

James, nearly tripping over his tongue, "Oh, yeah? Well, we can arrange that."

"Mmm, I bet! Your cock looks big, daddy. How big is it?"

Turned on, James attempts to control his shaking by sitting on the edge of his bed. "I'm about, uh, you know, seven, eight inches." He says with a lack of confidence only because he never once measured himself and can only be compare it with a Red Bull can.

"Wow, daddy!" she said with excitement. "I don't think it can fit me. Looks like I really have some prepping to do."

"Yeah, for sure."

"So, we're confirmed for 8:30 tonight?" She said after a chuckle.

James looks at the time. It's 6:16 PM. "Yes. What's your address?"

"So, there's no building number since there is construction. Just come to West forty-eighth Street and tenth Avenue. Let me know when you're here, so I'll tell you exactly where to go and I'll buzz you up."

"Sure, sounds good."

"Great! I'll see you soon, daddy." She hangs up.

James stares at his phone, feeling less sick, yet more nervous. He exhales slowly as he makes his way back to the desktop, searches Hell's Kitchen through Google Maps. It'll take him at least an hour if the D train arrives on time.

His mom walks in his room and with more soup but notices James is dressed up in baggy jeans and a North Face jacket over his oversized long sleeve Green Day's *American Idiot* shirt. "Where do you think you're going?" His mom asked sternly.

"I have to go see a friend."

"Excuse me? No, you're not. You're very sick." She places the soup on the folded table.

"Mom, come on, I need to—" His mom cuts him off with her finger over her mouth. "But—" Again, his mom responds with the same gesture.

"I don't care. It's freezing out, and it's going to rain later. Look at you. Your eyes are puffed, your face is red. Do you want to get sick again?"

James looks around, trying to come up with a response. There is no logical answer to that.

"Now take off your jacket and have your soup." His mom walks out.

He looks at the clock hanging on the wall next to a poster of Beth Ostrosky in her blue bikini posing at the beach. It's 7:15 PM. One Hail Mary attempt to convince his mom, but the second he opened his mouth, her phone rings. There's an emergency with the next-door neighbor and they need her help. Saved by the bell, he says to himself. Still, his mom warns James not to leave, and rushes out the door.

After about fifteen minutes, his mom calls to tell him that she'll be taking the Italian lady living next door to the hospital because of a possible collapsed lung. As soon as he sees his mom drive off with the old lady, he pumps up nasal spray and grabs his house keys. Suddenly, his dad's deep voice comes from the kitchen. "Going somewhere?" His dad says as he watches *The King of Queens* on a thirteen-inch Panasonic CRT TV over the counter.

"Just... seeing a friend," James said.

After a moment, his dad still focused on the TV, sipping his soup. "Be home before ten."

"No problem." James said after an awkward pause. Then he heads out into the freezing night as his dad continues watching the show and slurps on some soup.

IV

The N train from the 18th Avenue stop came on time. James looks at his poorly written notes on where to transfer next. As the subway gets closer to his next stop, his heart pounds rapidly. He cannot believe this is actually happening. He felt the butterflies bubbling inside him. To soothe his nerves, he reaches into the inner pocket of his jacket and pulls out a sleek white iPod Mini, filling his ears with *Disco Inferno* by 50 Cent. As he jams to the music for the thousandth time since its release, he sends a text message to Peaches, "On the way!"

The subway stops at 36th Street Station where James has to transfer to the D train. He waits and looks around, trying to contain himself. He checks his phone for any missed calls from his mom. Then he realizes there is no service underground. As soon as he makes his way towards the stairs, cell phone in the air trying to get a bar or two, the D train arrives. Can't afford to miss this train just in case he has any texts from his mom or Peaches. He hops in the subway car where it passes Atlantic Avenue and then heads outside where he can see the view of Manhattan. A text notification from Peaches, "You have no idea how wet I got preparing myself ;)"

James can already feel the heat in his pants as he sends a text back, "Can't wait to see you! Halfway there!" A dry cough comes out, then a harsher one catches the phlegm between his teeth. He realizes there is nowhere to spit it out, searches his pockets but no extra napkins so he does what anyone would do in this situation... swallows it.

The 7th Avenue Station has a long stairway to heaven. As soon as he steps out of the station, the chilly wind blasts through his exposed face, almost hurting. Instantly, he sneezes and covers up with the collar of the jacket as he looks for the street signs. The green sign shows W 53rd Street. He heads south to W 48th Street and then makes a right to the long avenues heading to 10th Avenue. A long brutal winter walk to a dead block full of lofts and small condos. A few are under construction. With freezing, jittery fingers, he sends a poorly written text as he tries to jam the buttons properly, "I'm here!" Now, he waits. Hands in his pockets. No matter how much he tries to keep warm, his body keeps shaking. Either from anxiety, the cold air, or the impatience. The thought of his mom came briefly, knowing she'll be home late. Normally, James would argue about having his mom always catering to other people before herself, but he didn't mind at all for the first time.

James walks around aimlessly on the dead block, observes each building, and wonders how much a unit would be worth. The light fixtures give a warm vibe to the buildings. The brick layout gives a vintage look. Suddenly, his phone vibrates. His heart races as he pulls out the RAZR from his pocket, only to see that it's a warning that his phone is dying.

5%

Disappointed, but his stomach gurgles after noticing the time, 9:12 PM. He even checks the last time he sent the text, 8:29 PM. Knowing he wasn't late, he wondered if she received the text or not. He quickly shakes it off, knowing how ridiculous that sounds.

4%

Come on, he says to himself. He continues to walk around; this time walks one avenue up to 11th. It's getting colder, but he's numb to it now. Couldn't care less about the wind blowing by. After going further away from the block, he turns back to where he was originally told to meet up. He keeps checking his phone, thinking it's vibrating, but it's just him moving it around.

3%

His stomach kicks in from all that green tea. It's not what he thinks, it's his gut attempting to empty what's left of the soup he ate. Anxiety flares up as his stomach growls violently. Relax, he tells himself with a reminder that he can use the Peaches' bathroom. She just needs to invite him in so he can make a rush for it. He wants to send another text back, but he doesn't want to appear desperate. The indecisive decision, going through her contact, attempting a text, then backspacing, then texting again, but not sending it. Just preparing before lights out.

2%

Might as well leave. Go home and have better luck next time. Still got till June before graduating. He erases the text, reminding her he's here, and instead prepares a draft stating he's going to leave and they'll arrange another date. The cold air isn't making anything better, nor is his stomach. A dry cough here and there just to remind him he's still ill.

1%

It's 9:32 PM. He makes his way back down from 10th Avenue to 9th Avenue. Meanwhile, he grabs his phone with the draft text ready. Suddenly, a TEXT! Peaches responds. James stops in his tracks, reads the message. "Omg! I'm so sorry! Got caught up with things. I'm in the building with the construction barricades. If you didn't leave yet. I'm so sorry if you did :("

Without hesitation, James responded, "I'm still here! What's your apartment number?" He sends the text as he rushes back to 10th Avenue looking for the building in hopes his phone doesn't die.

"3E. Take the stairs. I'll buzz you in." She said in a text. Then his phone blacks out. Damn.

The one building Peaches is talking about is under construction with a brightly lit lobby. There are still cones and orange barricades on the street in front of the building. James pushes and pulls on the paned glass door, but it stays put. Suddenly, the buzzer goes off and James pushes it open and walks in. Now his heart is pumping faster than ever. He stands there, observes the bright lobby. There are paint buckets over a folded dusty tarp. There are canvases laid out on the linoleum tiles that were freshly placed not more than a week ago. The steel elevator doors still have blue tape over them with a yellow barricade blocking it. Across is the lobby desk, still in its wooden beams. James finds the staircase with a sign showing a stick figure walking down the stairs with a fire symbol behind it. **Staircase A: IN CASE OF EMERGENCY USE STAIRS.**

The freshly painted gray stairs, leading both upstairs and down to the cellar, echo under James' footsteps. He ascends, holding the banister for support, and blows warm air into his fists to fight the chill. Reaching the third floor, he gently pushes the bar on the door, grateful the alarm system hasn't been installed yet. The hallway, carpeted in forest green, stretches out before him. He glances briefly at the neighboring units, their doors indifferent sentinels, but it's unit 3E at the end of the hallway that draws his attention. A painting of roses marks the turn in the corridor, leading to the unit with blue masking tape and paint buckets by its door. James stands before the maroon door of unit 3E, nerves tangling within him. He takes a deep breath, steadies his shaky arm, and taps lightly on the door, then steps back and holds his breath, waiting.

No answer.

After a few dry coughs that James' attempt to cover in his elbow, he makes another attempt and knocks harder. Again, no answer. Confused, he notices a square black button under the brass peephole. With his thumb, he carefully jams it. DING! DONG! He steps back even further as he observes the door, shaking in his Timberland boots.

CLICK! The door unlocks and screeches open. James stares into the darkness of the unit, heart pounding harder than ever.

"James?" a raspy voice says.

"P-Peaches?" James' voice cracks. "It-it's, uh, it's me."

Emerging from the abyss, a beautiful blonde woman with a nicely tied hair bun. She stands there in her pink crop top and baby blue booty shorts. Her belly piercing glistens over her tan body, and her white teeth are straight to perfection. "I was so worried you wouldn't make it." She said as she giggles.

James, relieved, places his hand over his beating heart, laughing to himself. "Honestly, I'm surprised I made it myself."

"Would you like some tea? I just made some." Peaches gestures invitingly.

James nods, thinking about how he made it this far. "S-Sure. I, um, definitely need that. But first, um, may I use your bathroom?"

"Of course! *Mi casa es tu casa.*" Peaches walks in, allows James to follow, then shuts the door behind.

At the foyer, Peaches insists on helping James with his jacket and hangs it up on the wooden coat rack. "Please take off your shoes, too. I just cleaned the floor." She said as she points to the shoe rack that only holds lonely pink Nike sneakers.

"You know, for a girl, I'm surprised you don't have a bunch of shoes hanging around here." He said as he pulls off his Timberlands.

"That's because I have them in boxes." She said from the open kitchen as she pours tea into a mug. "I'm preparing to move out soon."

As he places the Timberlands on the shoe rack under the clean pink sneakers, he snaps his fingers and realizes, "Shoot! Do you have a charger for a RAZR?"

"Why? Did it die or something?" She asked.

"Right after you sent me that last text."

"Sorry, I still use Nokia." Peaches giggles.

An idea comes to mind using Peaches' phone to text his mom just in case she comes home early and does not find him. Then again, he fears hearing it from her and doesn't want any link of some stranger he met off the internet to his family. The trouble he'd face for that would be never-ending. Instead, he hopes his father will back him up as he did once when he snuck out of his house to hang with a couple of friends. Then his stomach growls. "Where's your bathroom?"

Peaches points to the end of the unit opposite from the entrance as she places the tea on the small coffee table in the living room. "I'll be waiting." She sits on the leather couch, crosses her silky legs with a smile. James' nerves jitters yet gives a slight smile as he heads to the bathroom. Right before he enters, "The fan switch is on the right side. Just in case," she said as he turns with a nod and shuts the door.

Instantly, James empties his bowls, causing explosions louder than a Michael Bay movie. He hopes the sound of the fan masks the destruction he's causing in the toilet, hoping Peaches doesn't hear or she might be turned off. Finally, after nearly ten minutes, relieved and washing his hands after completing the dirty deed, he blows out large amounts of gooey snot that stick to the porcelain sink. Not even the running water can grab the green slime and bring it down to the sinkhole. Using his index finger, James pushes the goo closer to the drain and allows the water to do the rest. He grabs the *Irish Spring* soap bar, rubs his hands thoroughly. The water runs down his hands, wiping away the suds, then wipes his face. He turns the steel knob, leaving the faucet to only drip.

Behind him is the burgundy towel he dives his hands right in, then buries his face. Nice and clean.

James shuts the bathroom door and makes his way to the living room, only to realize Peaches is not on the couch. Standing in place, he wonders where she could be. He notices his steaming tea sitting on the coffee table untouched. Suddenly, a grab on his right shoulder. He quickly jumps away, turns and sees Peaches with her hands in the air, meaning no harm. She has her mug in her other hand. "I was just getting myself some tea." James, relieved, holds his heart, chuckling to himself.

"You scared the hell out of me." James managed to stammer out

Peaches giggles as she returns to the couch, drags her fingers across his shoulders. "Are you going to join me?"

He pulls his collar, rubs the back of his head. They sit together on the couch. James gives her some space, but with her right leg, she reaches over James' left leg and rubs up and down. "Don't be shy, baby." She sips her tea and leans closer to him, then takes his shaking arm, throws it around her. "Much better." She said as James looks away. "Are you okay?"

James exhales some air. "I never met anyone off the internet."

"Oh, I understand. This is like my third time." Her fingers curl around his shirt. "Drink your tea. It'll calm you down."

He stares at the tea, reaches for it, but pulls back. "Honestly, it'll turn my stomach around."

"No, it won't. Come on, drink it with me." She said as she hands over his mug and holds up hers to him. The steam enters straight into his nose, unclogging the pipes. He stares into the olive-colored liquid with tea bag particles at the bottom of the porcelain mug. He peeks at hers that has a design of the blue, white, and red French flag and under it saying *...and good looking*, which he sneaks a smile over.

She holds up her mug. "Drink your tea."

His stomach growls. "I really can't." James places the mug back on the coffee table, leaving her disappointed. She jumps off of the couch and grabs the mug, and storms into the kitchen. He opens his mouth, "I'm sorry—"

"No, no. It's fine. If you don't want tea, then you don't want tea." Peaches lets the water from the faucet run down in the mugs.

"It's just that I have a long ride back and my phone is dead." James notices the time on the clock hanging above the foyer. It's 10:23 PM. He looks further down and notices his jacket and Timberlands are missing. "Uh, where is my jacket? And my shoes?" He asked with concern.

No response, but the water splashing around.

James pulls his collar. "Can... can I use your phone? I want to call my mom. Letting her know I'm okay."

Again, no response.

His heart beats faster. "You know, it's getting late. I think I should—"

Peaches shuts the sink off and heads back to the living room. "You should what?"

"Uh, I think I should get going. I have class tomorrow morning."

"Tomorrow is Saturday."

"Oh, right, um, it's a conference with the school principal."

"Yeah, no problem. Go ahead." Peaches said as she returns to the kitchen. "But where's my stuff?"

"What stuff?"

James laughs it off. "Okay, funny. I need my jacket and my shoes. Where are they?"

Peaches points to the racks, but nothing is there. Only the pink shoes.

"There is nothing there. Look, this isn't funny anymore. I need my stuff."

Peaches gives a stare.

CLICK! The front door opens. James slowly turns, noticing three much older men, at least in their forties, making their way inside. A silver bearded man, standing between the two other men, speaks to Peaches in an unknown language, only familiar because of a video game he used to play. Sounds Russian. She answers calmly and without any concern. It's clear she knows them. The silver bearded man throws his hands in the air in frustration and continues to speak, but it's now aggressive. An argument ensues between him and Peaches.

James, nervous, looks back and forth at the banter. "Who are you guys?"

The silver bearded man continues to argue with Peaches.

James continues, "You know, I think I should go." As James makes his way towards the entrance, attempting to squeeze past the men, a dark-haired man shoves him to the ground. James holds his sides, squeezing his face, attempting to mask the pain.

In his heavy accent, the silver bearded man speaks to James. "You're not going anywhere." Then he turns to Peaches and makes a gesture towards James.

She gives a nod and grabs the teapot from the kitchen, pouring tea in a clean mug. She brings it to James. "Drink this now."

James sits back against the wall. He pulls away from the mug.

Peaches turns to the silver bearded man. He rolls his eyes and nods to a bald man who pulls out a Glock from his jacket and aims it under James' chin. "Drink it, curly man." The bald man said in a deep, heavy accent as Peaches places the edge of the mug over James' thin lips. He gives a nod and takes a heavy sip... SNEEZES! Peaches jumps, surprised, splashing the steaming liquid over the bald man's face. He drops the Glock and screams in agony. The dark-haired man dashes to James, grabs his neck. James counters with a sweep to the man's right leg, then slides to his body, using his head against the man's chest. SLAM!

The silver-bearded man stands in front of the entrance with arms wide apart. James charges at the man, tackles him against the door. Then swings his arm with a fist into his gut, drops the man on his knees. From behind, the bald man pulls James by his shoulders, but he twists his body to face his attacker, then tosses his arm underneath where his elbow meets the bald man's crotch. Using his other arm, he grabs the bald man behind the neck and flips him over on his back, slams him against the shoe rack. The silver-bearded man reaches over to James, who swings his arms, one, two, cracking his cheekbones and knocking the man to the ground.

The three brutes agonize in pain as James catches his breath, coughs out a lung. He wheezes and holds his chest, then turns to Peaches, who stares back wide-eyed. "Stay back." She said as she extends her arms up front protecting her face.

"Where's my–" And just before he finishes, the dark-haired man grabs the Glock. James dashes out the entrance.

BANG! The bullet pierces through the molding.

James tosses his body against the door of Staircase B. He pulls on the handle and runs down the steps, nearly tripping. He reaches the first floor, but it's locked. He shoulders the push bar, but it won't budge. The sound of the staircase door opening echoes from the third floor, prompting him to swiftly make his way down to the basement as panic sets in.

Half the walls are finished with sheetrock, while the other half remain open frames. Staircase A is on the left side at the opposite end. Without hesitation, James charges for Staircase A, right before the red-faced bald man bashes through Staircase B with the dark-haired man running behind. James rushes up the stairs, makes it to the lobby and dashes to the glass door. It won't budge. Panicking, James searches the lobby, grabs a cement block next to the cones, and chucks it against the glass, shattering it. He makes a run for it, feet sliding against the glass, trips, slams his face to the ground. Rain pours down heavily as he turns to see two blurry figures approaching. Quickly, he rises with blood leaking from his torn socks, exposing his feet. In pain, he grits his teeth and treks his way towards 9th Avenue where people are roaming around the area.

"Help me!" He yells out. "I'm being chased!" A concerned vendor who is just about to leave with his food truck quickly makes his way to James.

"My friend, are you okay?" The vender lifts James up.

"There are men trying to kill me," James' voice quivers as he points behind him, guiding the vendor to look.

"Where, my friend?" The vendor looks with squinted eyes, trying to see through the torrential rain.

James looks behind him, then back to the vendor and weeps as he buries his face in his arms.

V

Just before midnight, James lies on a gurney, his feet bandaged, in the aftermath of the EMTs' swift escort. Two detectives, one struggling to stifle yawns, take his statement with apparent indifference. As his parents burst through the hospital doors, bypassing doctors and nurses, his mother envelops him in a tight, tearful embrace. "I'm sorry, Mom," James murmurs.

"Shh, you're safe now," she whispers, kissing his forehead, her tears mingling with his hair.

His father, a pillar of stoicism, exchanges a loaded glance with James, full of unasked questions, but relief softens his features. In the heavy silence that follows, his mother clings to him, clearly afraid of losing him. James's mind is filled with confusion and pain, accompanied by a light fever and a pounding headache. As his mother finally takes a seat, wiping away tears, James stares at the ceiling, haunted by the recent events and the haunting NY1 news report of the missing girl. Would he have shared the same fate? He wondered.

Breaking the tense quiet, his mother's voice is gentle. "When we get home, a hot shower and some tea will do you good."

The word tea made James cringe. This is the very first time he preferred being sick over tea. "No, thanks, mom," James said as he turns to her. "I'm just... going to head to bed. I'm tired."

His mom responds with a nod, understanding.

It feels like he hasn't been in his bedroom in years. It feels more comfortable than ever before. The sleep was deep, dreams were vivid, bringing James back to the dilapidated condo, reliving the moment as he makes his way to unit 3E, but with a twist. Stripping Peaches naked, kissing all over her body, her kissing all over his. As she reached further down to his crotch, the dream cloud pops after a loud BANG!

James jumps out of bed, gets in his wrestling stance, crouched down, arms open, ready to grapple. Another bang, with a loud engine blaring from the front porch. He looks outside and notices a sanitation truck with two workers in orange and yellow vests grabbing wrapped cardboards from the sidewalk and tossing them at the back of the truck. One worker pulls on the lever, causing the truck to roar and crunch down on the brown boards.

It's nearly 4:30 AM. James pulls out his fully charged RAZR from the outlet. With the blue-light blaring over James' face in the darkness, he skims through the text messages from Peaches. He exhales sharply, puts the phone back and opens the Dell laptop.

YOU'VE GOT MAIL!

James' heart pounds. He doesn't blink as he clicks on the purple mailbox icon with a letter sticking out. Four unread emails, all are replies to Craigslist ads occurring between 10:12 PM to 2:38 AM. Three of them have similar reply bodies, as if they're bots. Each of the three opened emails has different bot-sounding Yahoo email addresses. He deletes them, then opens the latest email that was sent at 2:38 AM.

RE: Off from work, looking for a man to please. 34. [attached file]
"Sup? I'm on vacation, but to be honest, I'm a TS looking to give head.
It'll be the best head you ever got. Interested?"

Attached is a pic that James doesn't open. He deletes the email, signs off and calls it a night. From the AOL voice:

GOODBYE!

NOTES

Crafting the *DEADLY SINS* required me to tackle a unique array of challenges, which diverged significantly from my usual writing projects. The creation of this book happened almost by chance. While researching for a character in a screenplay, I unexpectedly found myself comparing the mental disorders described in the DSM-V with Dante's Divine Comedy, which coincidentally was open on my web browser. This unique pairing sparked a creative concept: can I effectively connect mental disorders with Dante's sins?

This idea prompted me to conduct thorough research, finding a delicate balance between accurately and sensitively portraying mental health issues, all while keeping the storyline captivating. As someone who strongly supports mental health, it was extremely important for me to approach this subject with respect, using the concept of sin not as a way to pass judgment, but as a perspective to examine the causes and effects of these illnesses.

The creative process comprised carefully choosing disorders that matched each sin, although this was done after much thought and sometimes required rewriting. Certain initial ideas were discarded because they didn't fit well with the overall themes, or when they overwhelmed the intended storyline with darkness. The journey of crafting *DEADLY SINS* was as much about discovering the right balance as it was about storytelling.

One of my deepest hopes for *DEADLY SINS* is that it opens a window into the world of mental health, offering readers a more personal and empathetic understanding of what living with a mental illness can be like. I wanted to move beyond the stereotypes and judgments, to a place of genuine empathy and connection.

Even though my main objective is to enlighten my readers, I have also learned a great deal from this journey. Through delving into case studies and utilizing my background in forensic psychology and English, I experienced a growth in my knowledge of diverse mental disorders. Each time I learned something new, I would revise my drafts, consciously trying to infuse respect and authenticity into my portrayals.

The more I learned, the more I realized the importance of representing these conditions with care and sensitivity. My goal was never just to tell a story, but to hopefully change the way we see and interact with those who battle these invisible challenges every day.

I want to extend my heartfelt thanks to everyone who has journeyed through the pages of *DEADLY SINS*. If these stories have enlightened you, even just a little, about the complexities of mental health, then I've accomplished what I set out to do. Writing this book was tough. I hope I've been able to bring the characters experiences to life in a way that is both informative and moving.

Your engagement with this book means the world to me. Thank you for taking the time to understand, to feel, and to walk a mile in the shoes of these characters. It is my sincere hope that these stories resonate with you and contribute to a greater understanding and empathy towards mental health.

I would like to extend a special thank you to my editor, Brian Baker, for his invaluable contribution to *DEADLY SINS*. Brian's keen eye for detail, expert guidance, and unwavering dedication have been instrumental in shaping this book. His insightful comments and constructive critiques challenged me to refine my ideas and narratives, enhancing the depth and clarity of each story. I am immensely grateful for his expertise and support throughout this journey. You can find him on Fiverr @bbrianwallace.

For those of you who are curious about future projects or who seek a deeper dive into the stories of *DEADLY SINS*, I warmly invite you to visit my blog at markelayat.com. Here, I share not only writing tips and literary insights but also personal reflections on my journey as an author. It's a space where I explore the intersections of storytelling, mental health, and the many experiences that shape us.

I update the blog regularly, aiming to create a community where we can learn and grow together. Whether it's understanding the nuances behind each story in *DEADLY SINS* or getting a sneak peek into upcoming works, my blog is the hub for these conversations.

Thank you once again for your time and for joining me on this literary adventure. I look forward to continuing our journey together at markelayat.com.

www.ingramcontent.com/pod-product-compliance
Lightning Source LLC
Chambersburg PA
CBHW010742310726
48971CB00010B/2910